THE AWAKENING
OF MISS PRIM

Natalia Sanmartin Fenollera

D0584095

(ABACUS)

ABACUS

First published in Great Britain in 2014 by Abacus
This paperback edition published in 2015 by Abacus

3 5 7 9 10 8 6 4 2

A CIP catalogue record for this book
is available from the British Library.

ISBN 978-0-349-13951-7

Typeset in Garamond by M Rules
Printed and bound in Great Britain by
Clays Ltd, St Ives plc

Papers used by Abacus are from well-managed forests
and other responsible sources.

To my parents, Miguel and Cuca,
with love, gratitude and admiration

Contents

The Arrival

I   The Man in the Wingchair

II   It's Winter on the Russian Steppe

III Unravelling Skeins

Nursia

They think that they regret the past, when they are but longing after the future.

John Henry Newman

THE AWAKENING
OF MISS PRIM

The Arrival

*E*veryone in San Ireneo de Arnois remarked on Miss Prim's arrival. On the afternoon they saw her walking through the village she was just another job applicant on her way to an interview, but the inhabitants knew the place well enough to realize that a vacancy there was a rare and precious thing. Many still remembered what had happened a few years earlier when they were looking for a new primary school teacher: eight applicants had showed up, but only three had been given the opportunity to set out their talents. This did not reveal a lack of interest in education – educational standards in San Ireneo de Arnois were excellent – but rather the inhabitants' conviction that greater choice did not increase the likelihood of getting it right. The proprietor of the stationer's, a woman quite capable of devoting an entire afternoon to decorating a single sheet of paper, described the idea of spending longer than a morning selecting a teacher as extravagant. Everyone agreed. In that community, it was the families themselves, each according to their background, ambition and means, who were in charge of their children's intellectual development. School was considered supplementary – undesirable but necessary – though certainly many households relied on it. Many, but by no means all. So why devote so much time to it?

To visitors, San Ireneo de Arnois looked like a place that was firmly rooted in the past. Old stone houses with gardens full of roses stood proudly along a handful of streets that led to a bustling square full of small shops and businesses, buying and selling at the steady pace of a healthy heart. The outskirts of the village were dotted with tiny farms and workshops that supplied the local shops. It was a small community comprising an industrious group of farmers, craftsmen, shopkeepers and professionals, a retiring, select circle of academics and the sober brotherhood of monks who lived at the abbey of San Ireneo. Their interlocking lives formed an entire world. They were the cogs of a human engine that was proud of being self-sufficient through trade and the small-scale production of goods and services, and of its neighbourly courtesy. Those who said that it seemed to belong in the past were probably right. Yet only a few years earlier, there would have been no sign of the thriving, cheerful market that now greeted visitors.

What had happened between then and now? Had Miss

Prim, going to her interview, asked the proprietor of the stationer's, the latter would have replied that this mysterious prosperity was the result of a young man's tenacity and an old monk's wisdom. But as Miss Prim, hurrying to the house, did not notice the pretty shop, its owner was unable to reveal with pride that San Ireneo de Arnois was, in fact, a flourishing colony of exiles from the modern world seeking a simple, rural life.

Part 1

The Man in the Wingchair

1

At exactly the moment young Septimus was stretching awake after his nap, sliding his eleven-year-old feet into slippers made for those of a fourteen-year-old and crossing to his bedroom window, Miss Prim was passing through the rusty garden gate. The boy watched her with interest. At first glance, she didn't appear nervous or afraid in the least. Nor did she have the threatening air of the previous incumbent, who always looked as if he knew exactly what kind of book anyone daring to ask for a book was going to ask for.

'Perhaps we'll like her,' Septimus said to himself, rubbing his eyes with the heels of both hands. Then, moving away from the window, he quickly buttoned his jacket and went downstairs to open the door.

Miss Prim, just then making her way calmly along the

path between banks of blue hydrangeas, had begun her day convinced it was the one she'd been waiting for all her life. Over the years she'd dreamed about an opportunity such as this. She'd pictured it, she'd imagined it, she'd pondered every detail. And yet, that morning, as she came through the garden, Prudencia Prim had to acknowledge that she felt not the slightest quickening of the heart, nor even the faintest tremor of excitement that would indicate that the great day had arrived.

They would observe her with curiosity, she knew. People tended to look at her like that, she was well aware of it. Just as she knew that she was very different from the people who examined her in this hostile fashion. Few could admit to being the victim of a fatal historical error, she told herself proudly. Few people lived, as she did, with the constant feeling of having been born at the wrong time and in the wrong place. And fewer still realized, as she did, that all that was worth admiring, all that was beautiful and sublime, seemed to be vanishing with hardly a trace. The world, lamented Prudencia Prim, had lost its taste for beauty, harmony and balance. And few could see this truth; just as few could feel within themselves the resolve to make a stand.

It was this steely determination that had prompted Miss Prim, three days before she walked down the path lined with hydrangeas, to reply to a small ad printed in the newspaper.

Wanted: a feminine spirit quite undaunted by the world to work as a librarian for a gentleman and his books. Able to live with dogs and children. Preferably without work experience. Graduates and postgraduates need not apply.

Miss Prim only partly fitted this description. She was quite undaunted by the world, that was clear. As was her undoubted ability to work as a librarian for a gentleman and his books. But she had no experience of dealing with children or dogs, much less living with them. If she was honest, though, what most concerned her was the problem posed by 'graduates and postgraduates need not apply'.

Miss Prim considered herself a highly qualified woman. With degrees in international relations, political science and anthropology, she had a PhD in sociology and was an expert on library science and medieval Russian art. People who knew her looked curiously at this extraordinary CV, especially as its holder was a mere administrative assistant with no apparent ambitions. They didn't understand, she said to herself peevishly; they didn't understand the concept of *excellence*. How could they, in a world where things no longer meant what they were supposed to mean?

'Are you *his* new librarian?'

Startled, the applicant looked down. There, in the porch of what appeared to be the main entrance to the house, she met the gaze of a little boy with blond hair and a scowl.

'Are you or aren't you?' pressed the child.

'I think it's too soon to say,' she replied. 'I'm here because of the advertisement your father placed in the paper.'

'He's not a father,' the boy said simply, then turned and ran back inside.

Disconcerted, Miss Prim stared at the doorway. She was absolutely sure that there had been specific mention in the advert of a gentleman with children. Naturally, it wasn't necessary for a gentleman to have children: in her life she'd known a few without them. But when a paragraph contained both the words *gentleman* and *children*, what else was one to think?

Just then she raised her eyes and took in the house for the first time. She'd been so absorbed in her thoughts as she came through the garden that she hadn't paid it any attention. It was an old building of faded red stone, with a great many windows and French doors leading onto the garden. A solid, shabby edifice, its cracked and creviced walls were adorned with climbing roses that seemed never to have encountered a gardener. The front porch, supported by four columns and hung with a huge wisteria, looked bleak and imposing.

'It must be freezing in winter,' she murmured.

She glanced at her watch; it was almost mid-afternoon. All the windows were wide open, their curtains fluttering capriciously in the fresh September breeze, as white and light as sails. 'It looks just like a ship,' she thought, 'an old ship run aground.' And coming around the porch, she went up to the nearest French door, hoping to find a host who had, at least, reached adulthood.

Looking in, Miss Prim saw a large, untidy room, full of books and children. There were many more books than children, but somehow the way they were distributed made it look as if there were almost as many children as books. The applicant counted thirty arms, thirty legs and fifteen heads. Their owners were dotted about on the rug, lying on old sofas, curled up in dilapidated leather armchairs. She also noticed two gigantic dogs lying on either side of a wingchair that faced the fireplace, its back to the window. The boy who had spoken to her in the porch was there on the rug, bowed conscientiously over a notebook. The others raised their heads from time to time to answer a speaker whose voice seemed to spring straight from the wingchair.

'Let's begin,' said the man in the wingchair.

'Can we ask for clues?' said one of the children.

Instead of replying, the man's voice recited:

> *Ultima Cumaei venit iam carminis aetas;*
> *magnus ab integro saeclorum nascitur ordo:*
> *iam redit et Virgo, redeunt Saturnia regna;*
> *iam nova progenies caelo demittitur alto.*

'Well?' he said when he'd finished.

The children remained silent.

'Could it be Horace?' asked one of them timidly.

'It could be,' replied the man, 'but it isn't. Come on, try again. Anyone dare translate it?'

The applicant, observing the scene from behind the heavy curtains that hung on either side of a pair of lace panels, thought the question far too difficult. The children were too young to recognize a work from a single quotation, especially when the quotation was in Latin. Despite having read Virgil with pleasure, Miss Prim did not approve of the game; she didn't approve at all.

'I'll give you some help,' the voice continued from within the wingchair. 'These lines were dedicated to a Roman politician from the early years of the Empire. A politician who became friends with some of the great poets we've studied, such as Horace. One of those friends dedicated the lines to him for having mediated in the Treaty of Brundisium which, as you know, or should know, put an end to the conflict between Antony and Octavian.'

The man fell silent and stared at the children (or so Miss Prim imagined, from her hiding place) with a look of mute interrogation that received no response. Only one of the dogs, as if wanting to show its interest in the historical event, got up slowly and lazily, lumbered nearer to the fireplace and lay down once again on the rug.

'We studied all this, absolutely all of it, last spring,' complained the man.

The children, still looking down, chewed their pens

14

thoughtfully, swung their feet nonchalantly, rested their cheeks on their hands.

'Pack of ignorant brutes,' insisted the voice irritably. 'What on earth's the matter with you today?'

Miss Prim felt a wave of heat rise to her face. She had no experience whatsoever with children, this was true, but she was a mistress of the art of delicacy. Miss Prim firmly believed that delicacy was the force that drove the universe. Where it was lacking, she knew, the world became gloomy and dark. Indignant at the scene and growing a little stiff, she tried to shift quietly in her hiding place, but a sudden growl from one of the dogs made her stop.

'All right,' the man's voice softened. 'Let's try again with something a bit easier.'

'By the same author?' asked a little girl.

'By exactly the same author. Ready? I'm only going to recite half a line.'

. . . facilis descensus Averno . . .

A sudden forest of raised hands and noisy cries of triumph showed that this time the pupils knew the answer.

'Virgil!' they shouted in a shrill chorus. 'It's the *Aeneid*!'

'That's right, that's right,' laughed the man, pleased. 'And what I recited before was from the *Eclogues*, *Eclogue IV*. Therefore, the Roman statesman who was a friend of Virgil and Horace is . . .'

Before any of the children could answer, Miss Prim's clear, melodious voice came from behind the curtains, filling the room.

'Asinius Pollio, of course.'

Fifteen childish heads turned in unison towards the window. Surprised by her boldness, the applicant instinctively retreated. Only a sense of her own dignity and the importance of the reason for her presence stopped her from running away.

'I apologize deeply for making such an entrance,' she said, advancing slowly to the centre of the room. 'I know I should have announced myself, but the boy who answered the front door left me alone in the porch. So I thought I'd look in here, and that's when I heard you talking about Virgil and Pollio. I really am terribly sorry, sir.'

'Are you here about the post of librarian?'

The man spoke gently, and seemed quite unconcerned by the fact that a stranger had just burst into his sitting room. A gentleman, thought Miss Prim admiringly. A true gentleman. Maybe she'd judged him too hastily; and she'd undoubtedly been rash.

'Yes, sir. I rang this morning. I came about your advertisement.'

The man in the wingchair stared at her for a few seconds, long enough to realize that the woman standing before him was too young for the job.

'Have you brought your CV, Miss . . . ?'

'Prim. Miss Prudencia Prim,' she replied, adding apologetically: 'It's an unusual name, I know.'

'I'd say it has character. But if you wouldn't mind, before we go any further I'd like to see your CV. Have you brought it with you?'

'The advert stated that the applicant shouldn't have any qualifications, so I didn't think it would be needed.'

'Then I take it you don't have any higher qualifications. I mean, other than a basic knowledge of librarianship, is that right?'

Miss Prim remained silent. For some reason she couldn't fathom, the conversation wasn't taking the course she'd expected.

'Actually, I do have some qualifications,' she said eventually. 'A few ... quite a few.'

'Quite a few?' The tone of the man in the wingchair hardened slightly. 'Miss Prim, I thought the advert was clear.'

'Yes, it was,' she said quickly, 'of course it was. But please, let me explain. I'm not a conventional person from an academic point of view. I've never made use of my qualifications in my career. I don't use them, I never mention them and,' she paused for breath, 'you can rest assured that they will not interfere with my work in any way.'

As she finished, the librarian noticed that the children and dogs had been staring at her in silence for some time. Then she recalled what the boy in the porch had said about the man she was now speaking to. Could it really be that of this tribe of children not one of them was his?

'Tell me,' he said, 'what qualifications are we talking about? And how many?'

The applicant swallowed, wondering how best to deal with this tricky question.

'If you'd be so kind as to give me a sheet of paper, sir, I could draw you a quick diagram.'

'A quick diagram?' exclaimed the man in astonishment. 'Are you insane? Why would a person whose qualifications need a diagram apply for a post that specifically rules out qualifications?'

Miss Prim hesitated for a moment before answering. She wanted to tell the truth, of course, she had to tell the truth, she desperately wanted to; but she knew that if she did, she wouldn't get the job. She couldn't say that she'd had a hunch as she read the advert. She couldn't explain that her heart had beaten faster, her eyes had clouded over, that in the ad's few lines she'd glimpsed a new dawn. Lying, however, was out of the question. Even if she'd wanted to – and she definitely did not – there was the regrettable matter of the reddening of her nose. Miss Prim's nose was endowed with great moral sensitivity. It didn't redden when she was com- plimented, or when she was shouted at; she had never flinched at a rude remark, or even an insult. But at the prospect of a lie, then there was nothing to be done. An involuntary inaccuracy, a single exaggeration, an innocent deception and her nose lit up like a magnificent beacon.

'Well?' asked the man in the wingchair.

'I was seeking a refuge,' she said suddenly.

'A refuge? You mean, somewhere to live?' The man stared at his shoes anxiously. 'Miss Prim, I apologize in advance for what I'm about to say. The question I'm going to ask is rather delicate, and it's difficult for me to ask it, but it's my duty to do so. Are you in trouble? The victim of a misunderstanding? An unfortunate incident? Some legal irregularity, perhaps?'

The librarian, who came from a family strictly trained in the nobility of civic virtue, reacted strongly and heatedly to this accusation.

'Of course not, sir, definitely not! I'm an honourable person. I pay my taxes, I pay my parking fines, I make small donations to charity. I've never committed a criminal act or offence. There's not a single blot on my CV, or my family's. If you'd like to check . . . '

'There's no need, Miss Prim,' he replied, disconcerted. 'Please forgive me; I obviously misinterpreted your words.'

The applicant, perfectly composed a few minutes earlier, now looked very upset. The children meanwhile continued to watch her wordlessly.

'I don't know how you could have thought such a thing,' she lamented.

'Please, forgive me,' urged the man again. 'How can I make up for my rudeness?'

'We *could* hire her.' The voice of the tousled boy in the

porch came suddenly from somewhere on the rug. 'You're *always* saying that one should do the right thing. You're *always* saying that.'

For a moment the man in the wingchair seemed put out. Then he smiled at the boy, gave a little nod and approached the applicant with a look of contrition.

'Miss Prim, a woman who puts up with rudeness such as I've just inflicted without turning and leaving has my total confidence, whatever job she's to be entrusted with. Would you be so kind as to accept the position?'

The applicant was just opening her mouth to say no when she had a fleeting vision. She pictured the long, dark days at her office, heard the tedious chit-chat about sport, recalled mocking smiles and malicious glances, remembered half-whispered rude remarks. Then she came to and made a decision. After all, he *was* a gentleman. And who wouldn't want to work for a gentleman?

'When do I start, sir?'

Without waiting for a reply, she turned and went out through the French windows to fetch her suitcases.

2

Once inside the room that would be hers for the coming months, Prudencia sat down on the bed and stared out of the large window that stood open onto the terrace. There wasn't much furniture, but what there was was exactly as it should be: an ottoman covered in faded blue damask, a huge Venetian mirror, a Georgian cast-iron fireplace, a wardrobe painted aquamarine and two ancient Wilton rugs. 'Rather too luxurious for a librarian,' she thought. Although luxurious wasn't exactly the right word. It all looked extremely well used. It had all been lived with, mended, worn out. It exuded experience. 'This would have been considered the height of comfort – a century ago,' sighed Miss Prim, as she started to unpack.

A creaking sound made her look up, and her gaze landed on a painting leaning on the mantelpiece. It was a small board depicting three figures, painted by a child. The technique wasn't bad; superb for a child, she reflected as she admired with pleasure the young artist's brushwork.

'It's Rublev's *Holy Trinity*,' said a now familiar young voice behind her.

'Yes, I know, thank you, young man. By the way, shouldn't you knock before coming in?' she said, and saw that the boy wasn't alone.

'But the door was open, wasn't it?' he said to the three other children crowding behind him, who all nodded. 'This is my sister, Teseris. She's ten. This is Deka, he's nine, and Eksi is the youngest, she's *only* seven and a half. My name's Septimus. But they're not our *real* names,' he said with a confidential look.

Miss Prim stared at the four siblings and was surprised at how different they were. Though little Deka had the same untidy blond hair as his older brother, the mischievous yet absolutely innocent expression on his face was quite unlike the thoughtful look of the boy who had met her in the porch. Nor was it easy to tell that the two girls were sisters. One possessed a serene, gentle beauty; the other radiated vivacity and charm.

Teseris suddenly whispered something in her older brother's ear before asking softly: 'Miss Prim, do you think it's possible to step through a mirror?'

She looked at the child, dumbfounded, before realizing what she meant.

'I remember my father reading me that story before I went to sleep,' she said, smiling.

The little girl gave her brother a sideways glance.

'I told you she wouldn't *understand*,' said the boy smugly.

Not knowing what to say, Miss Prim opened another suitcase and took out a jade-green silk kimono that she hung carelessly in the wardrobe. So this was dealing with children, she thought, a little ruffled. This was what the advert had been referring to, quite simply. Not pranks, or sweets, or fairy tales, but – who would have thought it? – mysteries and riddles.

'Do you like Rublev's icon?' asked the boy, peering at some books poking out of one of the suitcases.

'Very much,' she said gravely, putting her items of clothing away one by one. 'It's a marvellous picture.'

Little Teseris looked up when she heard this.

'Icons aren't pictures, Miss Prim. They're *windows*.'

She broke off from hanging up her dresses and looked at the girl uneasily. The man who ran this house had definitely gone too far with these children. At ten years of age you shouldn't have such ridiculous ideas about icons and windows. It wasn't a bad thing, of course not, it just wasn't natural. Fairies and princesses, dragons and knights, poems by Robert Louis Stevenson, apple tart; in her opinion, this was what a child that age should take an interest in.

'So was it you who painted this *window*?' she asked, trying to appear casual.

The girl nodded.

'She painted it from memory,' added her brother. 'She saw it in the Tretyakov Gallery two years ago. She sat in front of it and refused to look at anything else. When we got home she started painting it all over the place. There are windows like this in every room.'

'That's impossible,' said Miss Prim briskly. 'No one could paint something like this from memory. Especially not a little girl of eight, as your sister would have been at the time. It's just not possible.'

'But you weren't there!' exclaimed little Deka with surprising vehemence. 'How do you know?'

Without a word, she went over to the picture, opened her handbag and took out a ruler and pair of compasses. There they were, there was no doubt about it: the octagon formed by the figures, the inner and outer circles, the shape of the chalice at the centre.

'How did you do it, Teseris? You can't possibly have painted it on your own, even with a reproduction to copy from. Someone must have helped you. Tell me the truth: was it your father, or your uncle, or whoever it is who looks after you?'

'No one helped me,' said the little girl quietly but firmly. Then, addressing her younger sister: 'Did they, Eksi?'

'No one helped her. She *always* does things on her own,' Eksi solemnly confirmed, while at the same moment trying to balance on one leg.

Stunned by this sisterly show of defiance, Miss Prim did

not insist. If these had been adults, her interrogation skills would have exposed the deception easily. But a child wasn't an adult; there was a big difference between a child and an adult. A child might scream, cry noisily, react in some ridiculous fashion. And what would happen then? An employee who provokes to anger the most vulnerable members of the family on her first day at work can't count on great prospects in the job. Especially – she shuddered – when she'd had the misfortune to enter the house in such an irregular fashion.

'And what were children as young as you doing in the Tretyakov Gallery? Moscow is a long way away.'

'We went there to study art,' replied Septimus.

'Do you mean with your school?'

The children looked at one another in delight.

'Oh, no!' said the boy. 'We've *never* gone to school.'

This, said as if it were perfectly natural, fell like a stone into the librarian's already agitated mind. Children who didn't go to school? It couldn't be true. A group of children who seemed half wild and didn't go to school – where had she ended up? Miss Prim recalled her first impression of the man who had hired her. A strange individual, no doubt about it. An outlandish character, a hermit; who knows, perhaps even a madman.

'Miss Prim.' Just then, the deep, cultured voice of the Man in the Wingchair himself floated up to her from the staircase. 'When you've finished unpacking, I'd like to see you in the library, please.'

She secretly prided herself on the tenacity with which she strove to do the correct thing at all times. And in the present situation, she reflected, the correct course of action was to make her excuses and leave immediately. Heartened by this conclusion, she quickly shut her suitcases, tidied her hair in the mirror, shot a final glance at the Rublev icon and prepared to do her duty.

'Of course,' she called out. 'I'll be straight down.'

The Man in the Wingchair was standing in the middle of the room, hands clasped behind his back. While the librarian had been unpacking, he'd been rehearsing how best to explain her duties to her. It wasn't an easy task, because what he required wasn't a librarian in the usual sense. Following the previous incumbent's departure, his library needed to be completely re-catalogued and reorganized. The volumes of fiction, essays and history were thick with dust, and those on theology had colonized all the rooms in the house to a greater or lesser extent. The day before, he'd found the homilies of St John Chrysostom in the pantry, between jars of jam and packets of lentils. How had they got there? It was difficult to know. It could have been the children – they treated books as if they were notebooks or boxes of pencils; but it could just as easily have been him. It wouldn't be the first time, and it probably wouldn't be the last. And he had to admit that these were the consequences of his own rules.

He vividly recalled his father's prohibition on the removal of books from the library. This had meant that he and his siblings had had to choose between fresh air and reading. Thus, he had spent the afternoons of his childhood with Jules Verne, Alexandre Dumas, Robert Louis Stevenson, Homer, Walter Scott. Outside, in the sunshine, the other children yelled and ran around, but he was always indoors, reading, immersed in worlds of which the others had barely an inkling. Years later, returning home after a long absence, he had abolished this rule. He loved to watch the children reading in the sun, stretched out on the lawn, perched in the comfortable old branches of a tree, munching on apples, devouring buttered toast, leaving sticky fingerprints on his beloved books.

'I hope you've settled in comfortably,' he said politely, to break the ice.

'Very comfortably, thank you,' she replied. 'But I'm afraid I won't be staying.'

'Not staying?'

'There are too many questions in the air,' said Miss Prim, raising her chin slightly.

'I don't understand,' he said amiably. 'But if I can satisfy your curiosity, I'm at your disposal. I thought we'd come to an agreement.'

At the word 'curiosity', her expression hardened.

'It's not curiosity. I just don't know what kind of family this is. I've seen several children not in school. Generally, several children would be a major challenge for anyone, but several children in a wild state is, I believe, sheer folly.'

'So you've been struck by the lack of schooling,' he muttered, frowning slightly. 'Very well, Miss Prim, you're right: if you're going to work here you're entitled to know what kind of household this is, though I must remind you that the children will not be in your charge. Their care is not part of your duties.'

'I know, sir, but the children – how can I put it? – *exist*.'

'Indeed they exist and, as the days pass, you'll grow increasingly aware of their existence.'

'Do you mean they're ill mannered?'

'I mean that the children are my life.'

His reply caught her off guard. Despite her first impressions, there seemed to be a glimmer of delicacy in the man, much more so than she could have imagined – a strange, austere, intense delicacy.

'Are ... are the children yours? I mean, some of them?'

'Are you asking if I'm their father? No, I'm not. Four of them are my sister's children, but I've been their guardian since she died about five years ago. The rest are from the village, and they come here for lessons two or three times a week.'

Miss Prim looked down tactfully: now she understood everything. Now she could see why the children were being educated at home instead of at school. This was clearly a case of what modern psychology called prolonged grief disorder.

A sad situation, undoubtedly, but absolutely no excuse for such behaviour. Homeschooling wasn't good for children and, though it might be difficult or even embarrassing to talk about it, she knew it was her duty to do so.

'I'm terribly sorry for your loss,' she said as if addressing a wounded animal, 'but you shouldn't shut yourself away with your grief. You have to think of your nephews and nieces, of them and their future. You can't let your own sorrow lock them up inside this house and deprive them of a decent education.'

He stared at her for a moment uncomprehendingly. Then he looked down and shook his head, smiling briefly.

Prudencia, who wasn't given to romanticizing, surprised herself by reflecting how an unexpected smile could light up a dark room.

'A decent education? You think I'm a sad man who's holding on to his nephews and nieces, not letting them go to school so as not to feel lonely, is that so?'

'Is it?' she replied with a note of caution.

'No, it isn't.'

The man went to the drinks cabinet by the window, in which a dozen fine crystal flutes and six heavy whisky tumblers stood alongside an array of wines and liqueurs.

'Would you like a drink, Miss Prim? I usually have one around this time. How about a glass of port?'

'Thank you, sir, but I don't drink.'

'Do you mind if I have one?'

'Absolutely not, you're in your own home.'

He turned and looked at her inquiringly, trying to gauge if there was sarcasm behind her words. Then he took a sip of his drink and set the glass directly on the tabletop, prompting an involuntary, barely perceptible expression of reproof to pass across her usually serene face.

'The truth is, I have rather particular views on formal education. But if you do decide to stay and work here, all you need to know is that I'm schooling my nephews and nieces myself because I'm determined they should have the best education possible. I don't have the romantic reasons you attribute to me, Miss Prim. I'm not wounded, I'm not depressed, I wouldn't even say I feel lonely. My only aim is that the children should one day become all that modern schooling is incapable of producing.'

'Producing?'

'That's the apposite word, in my opinion,' he replied, a gleam of amusement in his eyes.

She said nothing. Was this house really the right place for a woman like her? She couldn't say that the man was unpleasant. He wasn't rude, or insulting, nor was there any sign of the lingering gaze she'd had to endure for years from her previous employer; but there was no delicacy in the way he spoke to the children, or sensitivity in the frank, if courteous, tone with which he addressed her. Miss Prim had to admit that in her heart a little resentment persisted over the clumsy insinuation about her motives only half an hour

30

earlier. But there was something else; a troubling, hidden energy in his face, something indefinable that evoked hunting trophies, ancient battles and heroic deeds.

'So, your mind is made up to leave?' he asked, drawing her abruptly from her thoughts.

'No, it isn't. I wanted an explanation and I got one. I can't say I share your gloomy view of the education system, but I understand your fear that the brutality of the modern world might crush the children's spirits. If I could, however, speak candidly . . . '

'Please, go ahead.'

'Your approach seems a little extreme, but I believe you're guided by your convictions and that's more than enough for me.'

'So you think I'm going too far?'

'Yes, I do.'

The man went to the shelves and ran his hand over several books before stopping at a thick, ancient leather-bound volume and carefully withdrawing it.

'Do you know what this is?'

'I'm afraid not.'

'*De Trinitate.*'

'St Augustine?'

'I see you live up to your CV. Or do you perhaps have some, shall we say, spiritual concerns?'

Feeling awkward, she began playing with the amethyst ring on her right hand.

'That's a private matter, so if you wouldn't mind I'd rather not answer. I consider I have the right not to.'

'A private matter,' he repeated quietly, staring at the book. 'Of course, you're right. Again, I apologize.'

Miss Prim bit her lip before adding: 'I hope there'll be no problem concerning my personal beliefs, because if there is it seems to me that for both our sakes you should tell me now.'

'Absolutely none. You haven't been hired to give lessons in theology.'

'I'm relieved to hear it.'

'I'm sure you are,' he said with a smile.

There was a lengthy silence in the room, broken only by the distant laughter of children in the garden.

'I have to say I was very surprised that the children are named after numbers,' she said at last, in an attempt to navigate into less controversial waters.

'Actually they're nicknames,' he laughed, 'and they have a lot to do with my inability to remember birthdays. Septimus was born in September, his brother Deka in October, Teseris in April and Eksi, the youngest, in June. I'm a lover of classical languages, and this system has helped get me out of a fix more than once.'

As he spoke he gestured at the disorder in the room. A seemingly infinite quantity of books was piled on tables and shelves two, three and even sometimes four rows deep among towering stacks of papers, old maps, fossils, mineral specimens and seashells.

'I'm afraid the state of my library tells you all you need to know about my organizational abilities.'

'Don't worry, I'm not intimidated by mess.'

'I'm pleased to hear it. But I bet it bothers you.'

Miss Prim didn't know what to say and, once again, chose to change the subject.

'Young Teseris says she paints icons from memory.'

'But you don't believe her.'

'Are you implying that I should?'

The man said nothing, simply going to the bookshelves and replacing the heavy leather-bound volume. Then he went over to the fireplace, picked up a notebook from the mantelpiece and handed it to her.

'This is a list of all the books in the library. It's arranged by author and was drawn up by the previous librarian. If you're not feeling too tired, I'd like you to take a look at it this evening, so that you're ready tomorrow for me to explain what I want you to do with this dusty old chaos. How does that sound?'

Miss Prim would have liked to carry on chatting, but she realized that for her new employer the conversation had reached its conclusion.

'That sounds perfect.'

'Wonderful. Supper is at nine and breakfast at eight.'

'If you wouldn't mind, I'd rather have my main meals in my room. I can cook myself something simple and take it upstairs.'

'I'll have your meals taken up to you from the kitchen, Miss Prim. As far as feeding people is concerned, we run a tight ship in this house. I hope you sleep well on your first night here,' he said, holding out his hand.

She was tempted to object. She disliked the idea of a man who was a virtual stranger assuming the right to decide how, what and when she should eat. She disliked that domineering way of having the last word.

'Goodnight, sir,' she said meekly before going upstairs.

3

Miss Prim wasn't sure whether the crowing of the cockerel had woken her or if she'd been startled awake by a troubled dream. She'd been at the house almost three weeks, but still she felt disoriented every time she woke. Drowsy, she stretched lazily beneath the sheets and looked over at the clock. She had two hours before she had to get up and start work. She sighed with relief – up here she was safe. Safe from peculiar, incomprehensible orders, sudden smiles that in fact heralded yet more orders, disconcerting looks, questions whose ultimate meaning she couldn't fathom. Was he making fun of her? Actually he seemed to be studying her, which was almost more annoying.

Still half asleep, she glanced at the clock again. She didn't want to bump into him and the children on their way to or back from the abbey. Miss Prim had always considered herself an open-minded woman, but she didn't approve of forcing four youngsters to trudge to a monastery every morning before breakfast. True, on their return they did seem particularly cheerful, despite the long walk in the chill morning air on an empty stomach. But of course she knew that there were many ways of influencing children.

When she left the house half an hour later, the sun was already growing warm. She made her way quickly through the garden and opened the wrought-iron gate, which creaked long and loud. Why did the man refuse to repair anything? Miss Prim loved neatness, she loved beauty and because she loved it, it bothered her to see the rusty gate, it saddened her that the paintings were shabby and in need of restoration, it offended her to find butter-stained incunabula in the greenhouse.

'The man's hopeless,' she muttered grumpily.

Instead of taking the road, she decided to turn right and follow the narrow path to the village, cutting across fields and through a wood. That morning she urgently needed to buy notebooks and labels. The day before, she had had a small disagreement with her employer, the fifth since her arrival at the house. He'd come into the library and declared that he didn't want her to use a computer to catalogue the books.

'Very well, if that's what you want, I won't,' replied Miss Prim with forced humility.

He'd added that he was against typewriters too, however old or dusty.

'Well, I won't be asking for one,' she muttered between pursed lips.

And that's when she couldn't help saying: 'Maybe you'd like me to use a quill pen to catalogue the books?'

He had greeted her sarcasm with a pleasant smile of exquisite gentlemanliness and admirable refinement. But after three weeks at the house, Miss Prim was now perfectly well aware that his hypnotic masculine courtesy only served to get her to do things.

'If you insist on such archaic methods, I can do it all by hand, but I'm warning you I'll need labels. I won't compromise on this point. It's a question of method, and a librarian without method is not a librarian.'

'My dear Miss Prim,' he'd said, 'you may use all the labels you wish, of course you may. All I ask is that you don't use the kind that glow in the dark. I don't have anything against coloured labels, nothing at all, but I don't think the sermons of St Bonaventure should be catalogued in lime green, or the works of Virgil in fluorescent pink.'

The librarian had found this reply deeply insulting. With eyes blazing and her noble nose pointed skywards, she found herself explaining that she had never used luminous labels; a professional such as herself would not handle such materials; she didn't have to be told that a library like this was not the place for garish stickers. And then he'd laughed at her and said something even more offensive.

'Come now, Prudencia, I was only joking, no need to be so regal. You look just like Liberty leading the People.'

Flushing at the memory, Miss Prim's train of thought was interrupted by the need to brush aside the brambles that were blocking her path. She was about to leave behind the last stand of trees when she heard familiar voices. In the middle of a large clearing, seated on the grass, the two girls were animatedly watching their brothers fight with what looked like oars or wooden poles. She crouched behind some bushes so as to watch without being seen. The boys were wearing old fencing masks, but they afforded little protection. Once again she wondered if her employer was in his right mind. He was standing in the middle of the clearing, issuing precise instructions on battle strategy to the combatants.

'Typical,' she muttered contemptuously from her hiding place. 'First teach the children to fight and take them to church second.'

'He's not mad, if that's what you're thinking. And don't worry, he'd never do anything to endanger the children.'

Miss Prim whirled around in surprise and came face to face with a tall, elderly, smiling man.

'Who are you?' she asked, wondering if she should emerge from the undergrowth or whether it was safer to stay where she was.

'I'm sorry if I surprised you. You're staying at the house sorting out the library, aren't you? Miss Prim, I believe.'

She nodded, scrutinizing the man discreetly.

'I'm an old friend of the family. I've known them all practically since they were born. If he's like a father to them, I'm like a grandfather.'

'Delighted to meet you, Mr . . . '

'Horacio Delàs. Please, call me Horacio.'

Miss Prim thanked him for this courtesy, and then indicated the children.

'Could you tell me, Horacio, what on earth he is up to? Training them for war?'

'My dear, I've heard that you're overflowing with qualifications,' said the elderly man with mild irony. 'Watch, he's showing them how ancient knights fought. Most children nowadays have no idea how to grasp a sword, lance or pike. They don't even know what a knight is. Observe: if I'm not mistaken, he's now going to remind them of the six precepts of Geoffroy de Preuilly.'

'Geoffroy de Preuilly?'

'You're not from around here, so there's no reason why you should know about him. He was a knight who died in the mid-eleventh century and he's credited with being the inventor of jousting, no less. Some claim he formulated the first rules governing tournaments. The historical record isn't entirely clear on this, but they're beautiful, noble precepts.'

The clear, deep voice of the Man in the Wingchair interrupted their conversation: 'First precept: never stab your opponent with the point of your lance. Two, never stray outside your lane. Three, several men should never attack a single man. Four, do not wound your opponent's horse. Five, only strike the chest and face . . . '

'Sixth and final precept,' said the older man, turning towards Miss Prim and raising a hand triumphantly to the brim of his hat, 'never tilt at your opponent when he has the visor of his helmet raised. It's no laughing matter: that was how Henry the Second of France died. As you may recall, Gabriel de Montgomery's lance pierced his eye during a tournament.'

She nodded benignly, stretched out a hand to pick a late blackberry and then glanced at her watch.

'Please excuse me, Horacio, but I must be going. I need to do some shopping in the village and get back by midday. I suppose they'll stop jousting and head for the abbey.'

'Won't you be going with them?'

'I'm afraid I'm not a very spiritual person.'

'Don't worry, neither am I. I go straight home after my morning walk, so if you'd allow me, I'd be delighted to accompany you.'

The old man offered her his arm and she took it gratefully. For the first time since her arrival she felt relaxed and at ease. She had a feeling she'd met an ally. A reasonable, sensible, level-headed man; a person with whom one could talk. A gentleman, she thought happily as they walked together in the pleasant morning sun. And who wouldn't want a gentleman as an ally?

Three hours after this enjoyable encounter, Miss Prim returned from the village. She was a little late, but was confident that the elegant white labels and navy-blue leather notebooks would more than make up for her tardiness. Didn't she think her employer a delightful man, the stationery shop owner had asked when she found out that she worked at the house? Miss Prim did not. He was different, she'd admit that. He'd been very generous in taking in his sister's children and teaching classical languages to half the children of San Ireneo, she was happy to acknowledge that too. But he wasn't delightful; at least, not when defending his ideas. He wasn't delightful in arguments, or in debates: he wouldn't yield an inch concerning what he believed to be true, and he had no mercy with opponents when he saw they weren't on his level. Miss Prim had not been at the house long, but she'd already had occasion to see him in action. He could be the nicest man in the world, but he could also be the hardest.

'How strange to hear you say this!' said the owner of the stationer's. 'I've never heard a woman say such a thing about him. Hard? You must be mistaken.'

He definitely wasn't hard with the children, Miss Prim reflected as she left the shop, though he did exert discipline –

loving discipline, but discipline nevertheless – and, as the headmaster of that peculiar homeschool, he demanded a great deal from them. Miss Prim had spent several mornings working in the library while the children were having their lessons. Sheltered by the huge rows of books she was cataloguing, she'd observed the passion with which he explained the most complex matters to them, the clarity with which he expressed himself, the way he taught them to think. But she'd also seen him when he questioned them. She couldn't say that they feared him, though they obviously wanted his attention and desperately sought his approval. It was touching to watch how they played and joked with him, laughing and shouting, but less so to witness them sidle up to him contritely when they got a Greek conjugation wrong and their mentor frowned and bowed his head in disappointment.

'Don't you think he's too strict?' she had asked her new friend that morning. He had invited her to have breakfast with him in his garden as an agreeable conclusion to their walk to the village.

'Too strict? I'm a fan of the scholastic method, Miss Prim. Don't expect me to be critical of educational rigour. To be honest, I don't have a very high opinion of the education system of the past fifty years.'

'But it's more than rigour, Horacio. His methods are archaic and outlandish, just like him. I assume you know that when he's not giving the children their lessons, or playing at medieval tournaments with them, he spends hours shut up by himself. Sometimes he cloisters himself away almost all day, and it's not unusual for him to miss lunch and dinner. Do you really believe that's part of some educational strategy?'

Her host laughed with relish. He got up and went into the house, returning with two books. He sat down at the table again and poured himself a second cup of coffee before opening one of the volumes.

'My dear Miss Prim, I'm going to explain something to you. I presume you've read *Pantagruel* by Rabelais?'

'Of course.'

'Well then, I want you to understand that our Man in the Wingchair, as you call him, is very like Gargantua in his method of educating the children.'

'How do you mean?'

'Let me explain. There's a passage in *Pantagruel* where Gargantua tells his son all the things he wants him to learn. I'm sure you know it. Let me see ... yes, here it is. Would you care to read it and see if it reminds you of anything?'

Miss Prim took the book from him and began reading aloud.

'*I intend, and will have it so, that thou learn the languages perfectly; first of all the Greek, as Quintilian will have it; secondly, the Latin; and then the Hebrew, for the Holy Scripture sake; and then the Chaldee and Arabic likewise.*'

'Don't tell me he's teaching the children Hebrew, Arabic and Chaldaic?' she asked, aghast.

'Oh no, though he's a great linguist himself, especially in the dead languages. No, he's not teaching them Arabic, but he is teaching them Greek, Latin and some Aramaic, the latter more for sentimental than academic reasons. But please, continue reading.'

Miss Prim took up the book again obediently.

'*And that thou frame thy style in Greek in imitation of Plato, and for the Latin after Cicero. Let there be no history which thou shalt not have ready in thy memory; unto the prosecuting of which design, books of cosmography will be very conducible and help thee much. Of the liberal arts of geometry, arithmetic, and music, I gave thee some taste when thou wert yet little, and not above five or six years old. Proceed further in them, and learn the remainder if thou canst. As for astronomy, study all the rules thereof.*'

'I don't wish to tire you; please let me summarize the rest. In civil law, Gargantua wants his son to "*know the texts by heart, and then to confer them with philosophy*". And as for nature, he teaches him that the world is one big school. He wants there to be "*no sea, river, nor fountain, of which thou dost not know the fishes; all the fowls of the air; all the several kinds of shrubs and trees, whether in forests or orchards; all the sorts of herbs and flowers that grow upon the ground; all the various metals that are hid within the bowels of the earth; together with all the diversity of precious stones that are to be seen in the orient and south parts of the world*".'

'Impressive,' she murmured.

'Yes, it is. He requires that he learn about medicine and man. He wants to see in his son an "abyss of knowledge".'

'Is this what *he* wants from the children? It's ridiculous, they're too young.'

'I won't lie to you; I think it's wonderful. For me, it's an exciting academic adventure. But allow me to show you another of the texts that have inspired his teaching of philosophy and you'll understand a little better what it's all about. You may not be familiar with this one. It's the letter from Jerome of Stridon to Laeta. St Jerome, as you know, is the author of the magnificent translation . . .'

'The Vulgate.'

'That's right. He spent many years as a hermit in the desert studying the Scriptures before returning to Rome and finally settling in Bethlehem. He's unquestionably an intellectual giant, a man with a prodigious mind and a temperament and will of iron. He was extremely strict with himself, extremely demanding. Well, at one point during his time in Bethlehem, he received a letter from a woman called Laeta, asking for advice about her young daughter's education.'

'And did he recommend that she punish her by making her kneel with her arms outstretched?' asked Miss Prim with a smile.

'No, absolutely not,' replied her host vehemently. 'In my opinion, he gave her some admirable advice. In his letter he explains to Laeta that he believes it essential for children to learn foreign languages, especially Greek and Latin, from an early age because, as he writes: "*For, if the tender lips are not from the first shaped to this, the tongue is spoilt by a foreign accent*". This is no more and no less than one of your young employer's guiding principles, my dear. St Jerome recommends, of course, daily reading of the Scriptures.'

'So, in fact, it all has a purpose?'

'One day we'll discuss purposes. Meanwhile, enjoy what you see . . . and join in. I'm sure you can answer little Eksi's questions on the character flaws of the heroines of English literature much better than he can.'

Back at the house, Miss Prim opened the garden gate and proceeded along the stately autumnal hydrangea path with a distracted air. She'd never considered the possibility of teaching any child anything. Or any adult, for that matter. She didn't even know if she could, and besides, he hadn't asked her to and probably wouldn't even approve. She could still remember the look of disappointment that passed across his face on the afternoon she arrived, when she'd confessed that she had a considerable number of qualifications.

'Damn him and his arrogance,' she muttered indignantly.

She was not going to concern herself with the children. She had quite enough to do with her own work.

4

A little over a month after her meeting with Horacio, Miss Prim began to notice the undertaking of the first attempts to remedy her unmarried state. At first she didn't attach much importance to them; after all, it was rather flattering to know that she was the focus of village gossip. It was an exceptionally traditional community and, as such, its members probably wondered why a good-looking young woman like her wasn't married, or at least engaged. So when, one morning, Madame Oeillet, owner of the biggest flower shop in the village, asked with a wink where she'd left her wedding ring, Miss Prim was not surprised.

'I'm not married, if that's what you mean,' she said with a smile, examining a bunch of *Papaver rhoeas*, which was how the librarian referred to what the rest of the world calls poppies.

Madame Oeillet confirmed that this was exactly what she meant. Women in San Ireneo de Arnois tended to have husbands. It wasn't compulsory, but it was advisable. And women like Miss Prim seemed naturally suited to marriage. An attractive face, good figure, refined manners, cultured mind – all these gifts indicated that the end for which Miss Prim had been created, the ultimate purpose of her existence, was none other than matrimony.

'You're very kind, but I have no intention of ever getting married,' she said firmly. 'I'm not in favour of marriage; for me, it makes no sense.'

The florist smiled very sweetly, surprising the librarian. She had not expected a smile in reply. An angry look, an exclamation of astonishment, a shocked, cutting remark, these would have been appropriate. Women like Madame Oeillet, who came through their middle years splendidly and sailed on into old age with the solid dignity of a steamship, tended to be scandalized by public declarations of opposition to marriage. This was the natural response, the decent reaction in such situations. And Miss Prim, who had been brought up in a household rigidly shaped by discipline, liked people to react as they should.

'I quite agree!' exclaimed the florist at last after a lengthy sigh. 'Marriage nowadays has become a simple legal agreement, with all the red tape, those chilly municipal offices and registries, all those prenuptial agreements and laws that debase everything. If I were you and had to get married in this day and age, I would not sign *that*. Definitely not.'

Miss Prim, now focusing her attention on a centrepiece of *Zinnia elegans*, wondered if the florist was in her right mind. Hadn't she just said she considered her made for marriage? Hadn't she made mention of her obvious vocation for conjugal life? Hadn't she praised her attractive face, good manners and the fact that she was hugely cultured?

'Please don't take offence,' the lady continued with the utmost courtesy, 'but I often wonder how anyone could imagine public officials being involved with marriage in any way. It seems almost like a contradiction! Marriage can be many things, both good and bad, but you must agree that none of them has much to do with bureaucracy.'

Miss Prim, who couldn't decide whether to buy the zinnias as well, agreed that bureaucracy and marriage were indeed mutually exclusive realities. As she was paying for the bunch of *Papaver rhoeas*, she reflected on the extraordinary fact that she and Madame Oeillet were in absolute agreement on the matter, despite approaching the problem from completely different angles. They disagreed about marriage, that was clear. But so was the fact that they agreed completely on what marital union was not and could never be.

She was just coming out of the florist's when she bumped into the Man in the Wingchair. Surprised and annoyed, she mumbled something about some business at the post office, a remark he seemed to decide to ignore.

'Miss Prim with poppies ... it sounds like the title of a painting. Please, let me help you with those. I'll come with you, if you like.'

'You're very kind,' she replied coldly.

The Man in the Wingchair took the bunch of flowers and walked beside her.

'I see you've been chatting with Hortensia Oeillet. And naturally she'll have asked you why you're not married. Am I right?' he said with a smile.

'That woman has strange ideas about marriage,' she replied.

'What you mean by that cryptic remark is that they differ from yours, I suppose.'

'Of course they do. I'm totally opposed to marriage.'

'Really?'

'I consider it a useless institution and one in decline.'

'Interesting you should say that,' he reflected. 'Because I have the opposite impression. It seems to me that nowadays everyone wants to get married. I don't know if you're aware, but all kinds of people are claiming their right to marry, not to mention all the people who declare their faith in the institution while marrying as many times as possible in their lifetime. I can't get over how interesting it is that you're against it. In my opinion, it's proof of a touching innocence.'

'You're in favour, of course.'

'Completely in favour. I'm a staunch supporter of marriage; that's why I'm emphatically opposed to the civil authorities being involved in it. I'm in the same camp as Hortensia – I find it surprising to see a public official at a wedding. Unless he's one of the betrothed or a guest, of course.'

Miss Prim looked down to hide her smile.

'And does everyone around here think like you and Madame Oeillet?'

'I'd say they're all here because they think like me and Madame Oeillet, which is something quite different.'

She did not understand what was meant by this reply, but she refrained from commenting. She didn't want to start another argument. Her instinct for self-preservation told her that when she argued with her employer, she was bound to lose. She'd always considered herself an excellent debater – people often feared her debating skills – but now she had met someone who comprehensively bettered her in this area. Someone irritating, who knew how to steer arguments into difficult territory and twist them to unlikely extremes, making her feel ridiculous and unsure of herself.

'"San Ireneo Feminist League",' she read aloud on a small notice beside a house that was almost completely concealed by a vast tangle of ivy. 'I'm surprised there are any feminists in San Ireneo. It's all a bit too modern for this place, isn't it?' she asked in a teasing tone.

Her companion stopped, lowered his gaze to meet hers and burst out laughing.

'Do you really think so? Do you really think that feminism is something modern?' he asked, grinning. 'Really, Prudencia, you are quite delightful.'

Miss Prim opened her mouth to object to this show of disrespect, but thought better of it.

'It depends what you're comparing it to,' she said, rather put out. 'There are more modern movements, but you can't deny that feminism was liberating in its early days. And I say this even though I don't number myself in its ranks; you'll never see me flying the flag for it.'

'I'm relieved to hear it.'

She blushed but said nothing.

'Even so, I can't say I share your view of the supposedly liberating origins of the movement,' he continued. 'You've obviously never heard of Carrie Nation and her famous hatchet.'

Miss Prim bit her lip. She knew exactly what was coming. She knew the man well enough by now; that the reference to the hatchet and its owner was simply bait, so that he could proceed to give another of his masterclasses. She wanted to deny him that satisfaction, wished it fervently, was absolutely determined; but in the end curiosity got the better of her.

'Carrie Nation and her hatchet?'

'You don't know who she is?'

'No. Are you making her up?'

'Making her up? How could you think such a thing?' he protested in an offended tone. 'For your information, Carrie

Nation was the founder of the Temperance Movement, a tiny group that opposed the drinking of alcohol even before Prohibition. I'm sure she was a lovely old lady, but she and her friends had the bad habit of bursting into bars brandishing hatchets, with the noble aim of smashing every bottle in their path. Newspaper reports of the time describe her as almost six feet tall and weighing around twelve and a half stone, so you can imagine how liberating a scene that was. Apparently, when she died, her followers had this moving epitaph carved on her tombstone: "Faithful to the Cause of Prohibition, She Hath Done What She Could".'

'And what has any of this got to do with feminism?' snapped Miss Prim, realizing that she was beginning to enjoy the conversation.

'Let me finish. You've the diabolical habit of interrupting your elders. Carrie Nation's movement claimed that alcoholism led to domestic violence. It was therefore closely linked with the early leagues in defence of women's rights. Many of those fanatical bar-smashers were committed feminists, the kind you call liberators. Believe me, I consider Carrie Nation one of the noble forebears of the movement. All the absurdity came quite a bit later.'

Miss Prim, indignant, again chewed her lip.

'And yet you still allow feminists in this lovely village?' she asked with cold sarcasm as they reached the post office.

The Man in the Wingchair squinted in the sunlight and shook his head thoughtfully.

'Would you like to meet them? I'm warning you, they're not exactly what you'd expect.'

'And how do you know what I might expect? I would like to meet them, if that's all right with you. I'm sure it would be an interesting experience,' she replied, bouncing on tiptoe as she snatched the bunch of poppies from him.

'Actually,' he said before crossing the street, 'I think you had the honour of meeting their chairwoman today: our mutual friend, the amiable Hortensia Oeillet.'

Hortensia Oeillet soon sent a formal invitation to Miss Prim. The note stated that the Feminist League of San Ireneo would be delighted if she would attend their next meeting, to be held the following Tuesday. On the morning the invitation arrived, however, she was occupied with another matter. For a little more than three decades, though no one actually knew how much more, her birthday had been celebrated on that very day. It was a solemn occasion, because Prudencia Prim was of the opinion that, since only the living celebrated birthdays, this advantage over the dead should be suitably commemorated. On her birthday Miss Prim would rise at exactly seven in the morning and begin making her special birthday tart. She tied an apron round her waist, scraped back her hair and faithfully followed the recipe her grandmother had handed down to her mother who, convinced that she would enjoy great longevity, had decided to bequeath it in life to her daughter.

Miss Prim's tart was very popular with her small circle of friends, colleagues and acquaintances. Even so, no one had ever been able to find out exactly what she used to create its delicious, subtle flavour. 'It's made with love,' she'd say, making light of it. Yet they all suspected that it wasn't love so much as an ingredient foraged in the wild and added to the mixture. 'If they can't identify it, they don't deserve to know what it is,' she said, justifying herself on those occasions – very rare – when she was assailed by pangs of guilt for guarding her secret so jealously.

'Miss Prim, did you know that Emily Brontë studied German while things were baking in the oven?' asked little Eksi out of the blue that morning, as she busied herself shaping a tiny portion of pastry taken from the main tart.

'No, dear, I had no idea, but it sounds very interesting. I suppose your uncle told you about it?'

'No, he doesn't know much about that sort of thing. Uncle Horacio told me. He says she used to pace up and down the kitchen with a German textbook in her hand while she was keeping an eye on the bread in the oven. Isn't that lovely?'

Miss Prim did not think that studying languages in front of a bread oven in a freezing nineteenth-century kitchen was lovely, but she refrained from saying so. That morning she felt very happy. In an unexpected gesture, the Man in the Wingchair had given the children the day off their lessons so that they could help her with the tart. Following her instructions, the three eldest were at that moment in the garden gathering the leaves of aromatic plants for decoration, while the youngest was helping in her own way by making a miniature version of the birthday tart. The cook too had been bustling about for several hours, determined to produce a birthday menu that would make it quite clear to an outsider who was in charge of the kitchen.

The librarian, her arms dusted in flour to the elbows and cheeks flushed by her efforts, contemplated the handsome old range, which was as ancient and worn as everything else in the house. The range suggested an idyllic childhood. A childhood rich with the scent of freshly baked bread, of sweet sugary fritters, chocolate cake, biscuits and doughnuts. The kind of childhood she herself had not had but which, in this somewhat chaotic house, she had to admit was a daily reality.

'Miss Prim, do you think anyone like Mr Darcy exists?' asked Eksi, who, at the age of only seven and a half, wrote serial novels for her siblings.

Prudencia, who, a few weeks earlier, would have been surprised to learn that a child so young read such literature, put down the rolling pin and wiped her hands on her apron.

'I think Jane Austen deserves our admiration for having created the perfect man. But as you're a very clever little girl, Eksi, you'll know that the perfect person does not really exist, so . . .'

'There's no one in the world like Mr Darcy,' declared the child cheerfully.

'I wouldn't be so sure.' The sudden arrival of the Man in the Wingchair gave Miss Prim a start, but she managed to hide it skilfully.

'So there is someone like that?' the little girl asked her uncle, who greeted her with an affectionate dab of flour on her nose.

'I have no idea, Eks, and I have to confess I'm rather bored of hearing about it. What I'd say is that I very much doubt that Darcy is the perfect man. And what's more, I doubt his creator ever thought her character even remotely perfect.'

Miss Prim, who had begun furiously rolling the pastry, looked up, steeling herself to intervene.

'I'm afraid you've got it slightly wrong. You may not be able to see the character clearly because you're the same sex as he is and, as everyone knows, this can make you blinkered, but any woman can see that Darcy is a man who always says exactly the right thing.'

'Which is quite natural,' he replied, 'if we allow for the fact that he's a fictional character and that there's a hand behind him writing his dialogue.'

'Exactly. And that's why I was reminding Eksi that he doesn't exist, that no man like that could exist,' cried Miss Prim triumphantly, her nose pointed higher than ever in the air.

'My dear Prudencia, that's cheating,' replied the Man in the Wingchair, tasting a bite of the little girl's pastry as she came to sit on his lap. 'As I've said, I'm not discussing whether a man like Darcy exists, what I'm questioning is whether the character of Darcy represents the perfect man. The novel, as I'm sure you don't need me to remind you, is called *Pride and Prejudice* because Mr Darcy is proud and Elizabeth Bennet is prejudiced. Ergo, Miss Prim, Darcy is not perfect because pride is the greatest of all character flaws and a man who is proud is deeply imperfect.'

'As you yourself, no doubt, know from experience,' she blurted, and then clapped a hand over her mouth, horrified by what she'd said.

A frosty silence filled the kitchen. Not even Eksi, who had been watching fascinated as the grown-ups crossed swords, dared break it.

'I'm . . . I'm so sorry, I didn't mean that. I don't know what possessed me,' the librarian said, her voice trembling.

The Man in the Wingchair lifted his niece off his lap before addressing his employee.

'I may have deserved it, Miss Prim,' he said calmly. 'And if so, I apologize.'

'Oh no, please! Don't apologize, I beg you,' she said, burning with shame. 'I didn't mean to say it. I didn't intend to, please believe me.'

He stared at her in silence.

'Actually, I believe you,' he said at last. 'What you were probably intending to say was that I'm domineering, arrogant and stubborn, wasn't it? And you may be right, I wouldn't deny it.'

Miss Prim put a hand on her forehead and swallowed before speaking.

'Please, I'm begging you to stop. What can I do to excuse myself?'

The Man in the Wingchair made his way round the enormous wooden kitchen table and slowly approached his employee.

'Come now, Prudencia, I'm perfectly well aware that you didn't mean to offend me, or not much, at least. You only had to see the look of horror on your face to know that. Why don't we forget this unpleasant misunderstanding and sign a truce?' he said, holding out his hand.

Prudencia, head bowed, wiped her hand on her apron before extending it.

'That's very generous of you. But will you really be able to forget this? You'd have every right in the world to dismiss me for such a remark.'

'I'd have every right, that's for sure, but I'm not going to. You're too good with books. And something tells me that this won't be the last time I have to forgive you,' he said, taking advantage of the confusion of the moment to have a spoonful of the tart filling.

'Congratulations, this is absolutely delicious. Has it got poppy seeds in it?'

Miss Prim, distressed, opened her eyes wide.

'How did you know?'

Instead of replying, the Man in the Wingchair grabbed an

apple and, with a wink at his niece, headed towards the door.

'You should be pleased I've discovered your secret ingredient,' he said before leaving. 'Now we can truly say we're quits.'

Once the door had closed behind him, the librarian sighed deeply. She glanced out of the window before rubbing her hands in flour and getting back to shaping her pastry.

'Miss Prim,' said Eksi from across the table, 'don't you think our uncle always says exactly the right thing?'

'Possibly, dear, possibly,' murmured Miss Prim, still very worked up. Then she went to the oven, opened it carefully and, with some impetus and one might even say a touch of euphoria, placed her wonderful tart inside.

5

The headquarters of the San Ireneo Feminist League was approached along a narrow path lined with tuffets of chrysanthemums. At five o'clock precisely on Tuesday afternoon – the date and time stated on the invitation – the graceful figure of Miss Prim could be seen ringing at the doorbell, ready to encounter at last the hub of female power in the village. To her surprise she was greeted by a tiny, rosy-cheeked maid in a white cap and starched apron. Miss Prim had not expected such formality at a meeting of feminists. True, she had no experience in these matters, but the idea of a maid at this sort of gathering seemed incongruous. However, her feeling for old-fashioned beauty allowed her to appreciate the smile of welcome, the courtesy with which she was ushered upstairs and the way she found herself, as if by magic, in the middle of the living room.

'My dear, we're delighted you're here!'

Hortensia Oeillet came up to her in the company of a group of women — the librarian counted ten of them — who crowded round her and, with astounding speed, settled her on a chair and furnished her with a cup of hot chocolate and two cream cakes. Miss Prim thanked them for the honour, but politely turned down their invitation to say a few words before the chairwoman opened the meeting. As she was introduced to them in turn, she learnt that many of the guests were professional women, which seemed perfectly natural at a gathering that advocated female liberation. But she soon noticed something rather odd. The librarian was used to the convention by which, when talking about their occupation, people made reference to their qualifications, whether in medicine, law, finance, or university teaching. At the meeting of the Feminist League, however, conversations took a different course. Each time Miss Prim asked one of the other guests what she did, the reply was not what she was expecting.

'So you're a pharmacist,' she said to one woman. 'Where do you work? I think I've seen a pharmacy in the square.'

'Oh yes, I am, but I don't have a pharmacy. I run a small art school. In San Ireneo one pharmacy is plenty, but when I arrived here there was no one who could teach art, do you see?'

Miss Prim, who certainly did not see, then spoke to an elegant woman who, she had been informed, once ran one of the most expensive and fashionable slimming clinics in the country.

'Tell me,' she said with friendly interest, 'how does a professional woman with all your experience come to settle in such a small place?'

'Actually it's very simple,' the woman replied with a smile, 'though I don't think you've been told the whole story. That chapter of my career ended some time ago. You've probably seen my bakery, in the square next to Hortensia's flower shop? Yes, I see you're surprised. I closed the clinic five years ago, just before moving here. I'd achieved almost everything I set out to do, I no longer had much to occupy me and at that time I craved a simpler life. And what could be simpler than baking? I must say I'm tremendously lucky that here in San Ireneo I'm mistress of my own time. I've been able to specialize so that I only bake for afternoon tea. All I make are buns, choux pastries, cakes, dainty bites.'

'It must take great courage to make such an extreme change to your life,' murmured Miss Prim without great conviction before resuming her seat by the fireplace.

She had just sat down when a tall, heavy blonde woman came up to her and shook her hand energetically.

'Allow me to introduce myself. My name is Clarissa Waste, proprietor of the *San Ireneo Gazette*. You may already have met my business partner, Herminia.'

She replied that she hadn't yet had that pleasure, adding that she'd never spoken to a journalist before.

'Well, I think you'll have to wait a little longer. I'm not a journalist. Let's say I'm more of a small businesswoman. Emma Giovanacci, that curvy woman you see with Hortensia, is a journalist, or at least she was before she came here. Now she's concentrating on setting up our Institute for Research into Medieval Iconography, as well as teaching around twenty village children at her home. Don't ask me how she manages, it's a mystery.'

Miss Prim agreed that, indeed, the capacity for multitasking of some members of their sex was a mystery, which, in her opinion, had yet to be fully studied by scientists. She then asked the woman what she had done before working in the newspaper business.

'I was a busy housewife. I still am; it's not something I want to give up, but I combine it with running the newspaper. Before coming to live here, that would have been unthinkable. Oh, but I see you don't know! It's an evening paper. We put it together in the mornings, while the children are attending Miss Mott's school or your employer's wonderful classes on Homer and Aeschylus. You see, here our philosophy is that everything important happens in the morning.'

'And what if something important happens in the afternoon?' she asked, surprised.

'Well, we'd have to report it in the following evening's edition. What else could we do?'

Intrigued, Miss Prim continued to move around the room. In this way she found out that many families in San

Ireneo invested all their time and expertise – in some cases, very finely specialized – in personally seeing to their children's education and giving classes to the children of others as well, an activity that provided great social prestige. Many of the women there owned their own businesses, small establishments that were almost all located on the ground floor of their houses so as not to disrupt family life too much. Working hours didn't seem to be a problem. Everyone was of the opinion that women, if anything more than men, should be able to organize their time freely. This meant that no one was surprised that the bookshop opened from ten till two, the solicitor's office was open from eleven till three and the dentist's surgery began its day at twelve and ended it on the dot of five in the afternoon.

Miss Prim had just poured herself a third cup of hot chocolate when Hortensia Oeillet's voice rose above the hubbub.

'Ladies, ladies, please take your seats! We must begin, it's almost five-thirty.'

All the guests – the librarian counted nearly thirty of them – sat down to listen to the chairwoman, who began by reading out the agenda from a sheet of paper.

'The first matter we need to deal with is the untenable situation of our dear Amelia and Judge Bassett.'

A murmur of approval went round the room. The woman beside Miss Prim whispered that young Amelia was in a position of semi-slavery at the house of a retired magistrate whom she'd been helping to complete his memoirs for the past six years.

'Imagine, the girl's working over eight hours a day. It's anachronistic and intolerable.'

Hearing this, it dawned on the librarian for the first time that her own working day, at the house of the Man in the Wingchair, never lasted longer than five or six hours. In the beginning she had attributed the relaxed timetable to her employer's eccentricity, but she was now starting to see that it was a core value in San Ireneo.

'Our friend Amelia,' Hortensia was saying, 'is obliged to work hours that are unacceptable according to the principles we in San Ireneo hold dear. The judge has been warned on several occasions, but he turns a deaf ear. As you know, the girl is getting married in April next year,' another murmur, this time of congratulation, ran around the room, 'and will no doubt soon become a mother. It is therefore urgent that we do all we can to resolve the situation.'

Applause accompanied by a few cheers greeted the chairwoman's words. Next, a slight woman with large eyes and an extraordinarily expressive face stood up to speak.

'That's Herminia Treaumont,' whispered Miss Prim's neighbour, 'the editor of the *San Ireneo Gazette*. Before settling here she held the Chair in Elizabethan Poetry at the University of Pennsylvania.'

Herminia spoke in a clear, calm and well-modulated voice.

'Dear friends, I think our chairwoman has clearly explained Amelia's situation. As some of you know, I've often been her confidante and I'm fully aware of the problems she faces at the judge's house, though I also know that she's very fond of him. Not only is it impossible for her to have a social life while working such hours, but she has also been unable to devote any time to reading and study which, as you know, is one of the main principles upon which our small community is based.'

The speaker paused for a sip of water before continuing.

'When Amelia arrived here, as I'm sure many of you remember, she was a young lady with a high opinion of both herself and her love of literature. That all changed when, within a few months of coming to live in the village, she discovered that what the *world* called literature, San Ireneo considered a waste of time. I still recall the morning when she entered my office, eyes shining with emotion and an old anthology of John Donne's poetry in her hand. This was where she discovered that intelligence, this wonderful gift, grows in silence, not in noise. It was here too that she learnt that a human mind, a truly human mind, is nurtured over time, with hard work and discipline.'

More applause, noisy and animated, reverberated around the room.

'Isn't she wonderful?' whispered the woman next to Miss Prim. 'I never miss her column on a Tuesday. Be sure to read it, you'll love it.'

'The motion that the Chair proposes to the Feminist League,' continued Herminia Treaumont, 'is as follows. As you know, Amelia has exquisite taste. Give her a remnant of fabric, a teapot, half a dozen roses and a chipped mirror and she can create a work of art. So we thought we could organize a collection to help her start a small interior-design business. We don't have anything like that here in San Ireneo, and I think we could all benefit from it. It would liberate her from the restrictions endured by all employees. I'm afraid her husband-to-be is not showing much of a talent for gardening. They won't be able to live off his salary alone, not for the time being.'

'But who'll help the judge with his memoirs?' objected one of the women anxiously.

'His memoirs? His memoirs? To hell with his memoirs!' replied the speaker with unexpected vehemence, seconded immediately by a chorus of applause.

Once the votes had been cast, unanimously supporting the motion that a collection be started, the meeting continued uneventfully. The next item on the agenda, proposed by Hortensia Oeillet, related to the feasibility of setting up a theatre company to complement the village children's literary education. All those present were in agreement. You couldn't study Shakespeare, Racine or Molière unless you left behind the pages of the book, explained the chairwoman firmly. Nor could you understand Aeschylus or Sophocles from the confines of a school desk. (At this, Miss Prim, absolutely delighted, could not refrain from murmuring with feeling: *Who knows what is considered righteous below?*) It was unimaginable that someone could come to love Corneille or Schiller, continued Hortensia energetically, without having had the opportunity to witness the violent beauty and hero-ism of their characters on stage.

'Bravo! Bravo!' cried the librarian, on her feet amid the thunder of applause, foot-stamping and spoon-rattling. A few minutes later, as Miss Prim was drinking her fourth cup of chocolate, a plump, jolly woman, whom her neighbour identified as Emma Giovanacci, stood up to present the final item on the agenda.

'The third and final matter to be addressed concerns the advisability of finding a husband for the new resident in San Ireneo, young Miss Prim.'

She gave a violent start. Pale and trembling, she stood up, placed her cup on the table and sought the chairwoman's eye.

'I'm sorry, Hortensia,' she said icily, 'I don't understand.'

A weighty silence filled the room.

'My dear Emma, what were you thinking?' stammered the chairwoman, looking at the woman who had read out the last item on the agenda. 'Are you unaware that Miss Prim is here, *here*, with us today?'

Horrified, Emma Giovanacci stared at the paper in her hands.

'But it's on the agenda!' she wailed after being informed that the woman referred to was the attractive young lady who had been sitting by the fireplace all evening and was now frantically searching for her handbag.

When she had found what she was looking for, the librarian hurried to the door, intent on leaving without waiting to be seen out by the rosy-faced maid in the white cap who, like many of the other women of the village, had taken a seat and joined the meeting. Emma's apologies and Hortensia's distressed pleas were to no avail. Nor were the soothing words of Clarissa Waste, who explained to Miss Prim that finding husbands for people was quite customary for the feminist ladies of San Ireneo.

'You call yourselves feminists?' Prudencia exclaimed indignantly, turning on them. 'Surely you don't believe that a woman should still depend on a man?'

'But, my dear, look at yourself for a moment.' Herminia Treaumont's clear, mild voice froze Miss Prim to the spot. 'You live in a man's house, you work all day obeying a man's orders and you receive a salary from that same man, who pays all his bills punctually on the first of every month. Did you really imagine that you'd freed yourself from dependence on a male?'

'It's not the same, and you know it,' replied the librarian in a hoarse undertone.

'Of course it's not the same. Most of the married women in this village don't even remotely depend on their husbands the way you depend on your boss. As owners of their own businesses, some are the main breadwinners in their households, and many others save a great deal of money by educating their children themselves and turning into disposable income sums that the rest of the world squanders on mediocre schools. None of them has to ask permission to carry out personal business, as I hazard you have to at work. None of us has to keep our opinions to ourselves, as I'm sure you frequently have to in conversations with your employer.'

Miss Prim opened her mouth to object, but something in the other woman's expression caused her to close it again.

'It wouldn't occur to any of them,' continued Herminia, 'to present a medical certificate when they're ill, or expect to endure condescension when they announce something as natural as a pregnancy. Do you see that quotation in the little frame above the fireplace?'

Prudencia reluctantly turned her gaze towards the wall.

'It was written many years ago by the man to whom I owe most thanks in my life, after my academic mentor and my father. And unfortunately I think it's the most profound truth ever spoken on the matter. Read it. Read it closely, and tell me it's not true.'

In silence, Miss Prim read.

Ten thousand women marched through the streets of London saying: 'We will not be dictated to,' and then went off to become stenographers.*

---

* G. K. Chesterton

'Believe me, ladies, if I really wanted a husband I would look for a husband myself,' she said before she left the room, her nose pointing higher in the air than ever, and slammed the door behind her.

'Come now, Prudencia, don't upset yourself, it really isn't worth it.'

Horacio Delàs poured Miss Prim a steaming cup of lime-blossom tea, which she gently refused.

'You can't imagine how unpleasant it was for me,' she murmured, 'how embarrassed I felt.'

Following her hasty departure from the Feminist League, the librarian had gone to the house of the only other man she knew in the village apart from her employer.

'This is a strange place, full of very odd people,' she said with a sigh.

'I hope you don't think of me in that way. Remember, I'm one of them,' replied her host, offering her a glass of brandy. This she accepted gratefully.

Miss Prim assured him that she didn't mean to include him. Since her arrival in San Ireneo she had tried to fit in, but her efforts had been in vain. There were too many unanswered questions, and the first of these was about her employer: who was he? What did he do for a living? Why did he go to the abbey first thing every morning? Why did he spend whole days immersed in old books, forgetting mealtimes? Was he some kind of urban hermit? Miss Prim had heard of such people. Madmen devoted to a life of prayer, mystics who lived in the city in a state of constant worship just like the original hermits in the desert, or the mysterious Russian *starets*. Perhaps the Man in the Wingchair was an urban hermit.

'For the record, I don't have anything against hermits, much less urban ones. I've always respected all forms of spirituality,' she pointed out.

'Of course you have, my dear. But believe me, *he* is not a hermit.'

'What is he, then? Because you can't deny that his religious zeal goes beyond the norm.'

'Well beyond. I can't believe you're so unobservant. Haven't you realized that you're working for a convert?'

'A convert?'

'I was sure you knew.'

'Absolutely not. A convert from what?'

'From scepticism, of course. What else? You have to agree that of all dragons, it's the only one worth fleeing.'

Perplexed, the librarian wondered if the brandy wasn't going straight to her head.

'You must at least have observed that he's not an ordinary man,' insisted her host.

Miss Prim agreed that it wouldn't be easy to consider the Man in the Wingchair an ordinary man.

'What does he do with his time?' she asked before raising her glass to her lips again.

'Study.'

'No one can make a living from studying.'

'He's also a teacher.'

'To fifteen children whom he doesn't even charge for their tea.'

'True, but that's only one of his occupations. If you want to know what his main source of income is, I can tell you that he's very highly regarded as an expert in dead languages; he contributes to a great many publications, and once or twice a year he gives series of lectures at various universities. As well as all that, which brings more prestige than money, he manages a large part of his family's assets. Actually, he doesn't need much to live on. He's a frugal man, as you've no doubt noticed.'

'Series of lectures? I didn't know that Latin and Greek were such a big deal,' said Miss Prim with a giggle.

Horacio gave her a look of surprise and consternation.

'Latin and Greek? My dear Prudencia, once again you leave me speechless. Your Man in the Wingchair is fluent in around twenty languages, half of them dead. And when I say dead, I don't mean just Aramaic and Sanskrit. I'm talking about Ugaritic, Syrio-Chaldean, Carthaginian Punic and old Coptic dialects such as Sahidic and Fayyumic. As I said, you're in the employ of a man who's far from ordinary. You see him go to the abbey every morning because he's devoted to the ancient Roman liturgy. And he lives isolated in this small place occupying himself with parochial concerns

74

because he was inspired by the old man in the abbey – who now almost never ventures outside – and is in fact the founder of this colony of sorts.'

'Colony? What do you mean?'

For the second time Horacio stared at his guest in amazement.

'Prudencia, are you telling me that you had no idea that San Ireneo was a refuge for exiles from the hustle and bustle of modern life? It's precisely what attracts such diverse people from so many different places! I'm beginning to think you accepted the job absolutely blind. I can't believe you hadn't seen that there was something unusual about our way of life until now.'

Emboldened by the brandy, Miss Prim confessed that she had noticed something. She'd been there long enough to take stock, form an opinion and build up a mental picture of the place, if only a rather impressionistic one. Admittedly, she'd really only managed a rough sketch. She had, however, observed one or two peculiarities. In that one remote village, families of very different backgrounds had settled. They all owned their own houses, land or small businesses. Primary goods were produced in the village and there was a flourishing, prosperous local trade. She hadn't spotted it at first, partly because she hadn't had to buy much. If she wanted tights, shoes or any other personal items she simply made a note of it and bought whatever she needed on her fortnightly visits to the city. She then aired her flat, watered her plants, chatted with her mother, had coffee with friends, did some shopping and returned in the evening.

Gradually, however, she began to sense that there was something hidden beneath the surface of the community. In the area around San Ireneo de Arnois there were no factories, large businesses or offices. All the shops sold high-quality goods, produced locally. The clothes and shoes bore the signatures of three or four tailors and shoemakers; the small stationery shop, charmingly, sold goods made to order; the food shops were friendly establishments bursting with produce, handmade preserves, fresh milk and bread just baked at the bakery on the corner. At first, Miss Prim thought she detected an environmentalist zeal, but soon realized she was wrong. Whatever was nourishing this village, it was far from green in hue. A quiet, peaceful community of home and business owners, that's what it was. Life in San Ireneo was small-scale and, Miss Prim thought to herself, also unusually harmonious.

'Are they Distributists, or something?'

'They are, as well as many other things. Really, I am amazed, Prudencia. I'd have expected you to inform yourself before coming here,' admonished her host.

'Do people who believe that sort of thing still exist? I thought those old ideas of returning to a simple, traditional, family-based economy had vanished long ago.'

'They definitely still exist. You're in the place where almost all of them live in this country. And they're not only from this country. Or hadn't you also noticed the intriguing variety of surnames we have here?'

'I'm surprised you're one of them. I'd never have dreamed you were a utopian.'

Horacio took a generous gulp of brandy and regarded her affectionately.

'It would be utopian to imagine that the present-day world could go into reverse and completely reorganize itself. But there's nothing utopian about this village, Prudencia. What we are is hugely privileged. Nowadays, to live quietly and simply you have to take refuge in a small community, a village or hamlet where the din and aggression of the overgrown cities can't reach; a remote corner like this, where you know nevertheless that about a couple of hundred miles away, just in case . . . ' he smiled, 'a vigorous, vibrant metropolis exists.'

Pensively, Miss Prim placed her empty glass on the table.

'This does seem like a very prosperous place.'

'It is, in all senses.'

'So you're all refugees from the city, romantic fugitives?'

'We have escaped the city, you're right, but not all for the same reasons. Some, like old Judge Bassett and I, made the decision after having got all we possibly could out of life, because we knew that finding a quiet, cultured environment like the one that's grown up here is a rare freedom. Others, like Herminia Treaumont, are reformers. They've come to believe that contemporary life wears women out, debases the family and crushes the human capacity for thought, and they want to try something different. And there's a third group, to which your Man in the Wingchair belongs, whose aim is to escape from the dragon. They want to protect their children from the influences of the world, to return to the purity of old customs, recover the splendour of an ancient culture.'

Horacio paused to pour himself another glass of brandy.

'Do you understand what I'm trying to tell you, Prudencia? You can't build yourself a world made to measure, but you can build a village. In a way, all of us here belong to a club of refugees. Your employer is one of the few inhabitants with family roots in San Ireneo. He came back a few years ago and set it all up. You may not know it, but his father's family has lived here for centuries.'

Miss Prim, who had been listening closely to her friend's explanation, now sighed in resignation.

'Horacio, is there anything else I should know about this village?'

'Of course there is, my dear,' he replied with a wink before draining his glass. 'But *I'm* not going to *tell* you what it is.'

6

'Well? Why did you take the job?' the Man in the Wingchair asked Miss Prim a few days later. He was nonchalantly eating a slice of pineapple.

She did not reply. Busy cleaning and labelling a five-volume edition of the Venerable Bede's *Ecclesiastical History of the English People*, she pretended not to hear the question. It was a luminously bright day, and sunbeams lit up the thick layer of dust on the books and the subtle honey tones in her hair.

'Come now, Prudencia, you heard me perfectly well. Tell me, why would a woman with all your qualifications accept an obscure little job like this?'

Miss Prim looked up, realizing she wasn't going to be able to avoid a conversation. Apart from what was essential to her duties as librarian, she hadn't said a word to her employer since the incident in the kitchen on her birthday. She didn't want to speak to him, she really didn't. Deep down she felt a profound conviction that she *shouldn't* speak to him. For some reason, she became absurdly nervous and could hardly conceal her annoyance if they came across each other in a room or passed in the corridor. She peered at him from the corner of her eye as he calmly ate his piece of fruit in the November sun. Then she looked down and decided to answer him.

'I think it was to escape the noise.'

The Man in the Wingchair couldn't help smiling.

'Miss Prim, since we first met you've never disappointed me with any of your replies. It's a wonderful thing to ask you questions. There's not the slightest trace of small talk in you. So it was the noise . . . Do you mean the noise of the city?'

Prudencia, a volume of the Venerable Bede still clasped in her hand, looked at him with pity.

'I mean the noise of the mind, the clamour.'

He looked at her with interest.

'The clamour?'

'That's right.'

'Go on, be a little more specific,' said the Man in the Wingchair, offering her a slice of pineapple.

Miss Prim untied her apron, put down the book and the feather duster and accepted the fruit. Meanwhile, he moved two old armchairs over to the window and politely invited her to sit down.

'Please tell me about the clamour, Miss Prim. I would never have imagined that a head as neat and delicate as yours might have contained any turmoil.'

'Have you never experienced a kind of inner noise?'

Before answering, he carefully cut another slice of pineapple, divided it in two and handed her a piece.

'Actually, I've heard it almost all my life.'

Surprised, she stopped eating.

'Really? You don't seem like that sort of person. How did you manage to silence it?'

Dazzled by the sunlight, the Man in the Wingchair closed his eyes and rested his feet on an old planter.

'I haven't managed to.'

'So you still hear it?'

'I didn't say that. All I said was that *I* haven't managed to.'

'But if you haven't, that means you still hear it,' insisted Miss Prim, puzzled.

'Let's say I've largely stopped hearing it, but it's not an achievement I can ascribe to my own efforts. A woman as well educated as you ought to recognize the distinction.'

'You seize every opportunity to criticize my education, don't you?' she said tartly. 'Why do you do it?'

He turned his head and looked at her for a moment before answering.

'Can't you guess? You're the perfect product of the modern education system, Prudencia. For someone in permanent opposition to that system, like me, it's an irresistible provocation. Also,' he added teasingly, 'I'd like to remind you that I'm quite a bit older than you.'

Miss Prim took another piece of pineapple and regarded the man beside her with a mischievous glint in her eye.

'I estimate you must be at least as old as the Venerable Bede.'

'Let's say I'm a good few years older than you.'

'Let's say you're five years and six months older, to be precise.'

The Man in the Wingchair opened his eyes just in time to see her rise quickly and cross the room. He followed her, with half a pineapple in one hand and a knife in the other.

'Tell me about the noise, Miss Prim.'

'Why should I?' she snapped.

'Because I'd like to get to know you. You've been here almost two months and I hardly know anything about you.'

Turning away, the librarian climbed the old wooden library ladder and began reshelving the *Ecclesiastical History*.

'There's not much I can tell you.'

'You could at least try.'

'If I do, will you leave me in peace to get on with my work?'

'You have my word.'

With a sigh, Miss Prim turned round and sat down cautiously on the third rung.

'I'm warning you, I don't know, really, how to explain it,' she began. 'Let's just say there are days – fortunately not many – when it feels as if the inside of my head is whirling like a spin-dryer. I'm not very pleasant to be with then, and

I don't sleep too well either. It's as though there's a void in my mind, a void where there should be *something*, but where there's *nothing*, absolutely nothing, just a deafening noise.'

She paused, saw her employer's look of concern and smiled gently. 'Don't make that face, it's not serious. Lots of people have it. It can be controlled with pills. But you say you've felt it. You should know what I mean.'

'Why do you think it doesn't go away?'

'I don't know.'

'You don't know?'

The librarian tied her hair back neatly at the nape of her neck before responding.

'Sometimes I think it has to do with loss.'

At this she hesitated, but his intently interested look made her go on.

'How shall I explain it? In some ways I've always considered myself a modern woman – free, independent, highly qualified academically. You know, we both know, that you look down on me for it.' The Man in the Wingchair made a gesture of polite protest which she ignored. 'But I have to admit that I've also always felt burdened by nostalgia, by a desire to stop time, to recapture things that have been lost. A sense that everything, absolutely everything, is on a journey from which there's no return.'

'What does *everything* mean to you?'

'The same as it does to you, I assume. All of life, beauty, love, friendship, even childhood, especially childhood.

Before, not so long ago, I used to think I possessed a sensibility from another century. I was convinced I'd been born at the wrong time and that that was why vulgarity, ugliness, lack of delicacy all bothered me so much. I thought I was longing for a beauty that no longer existed, from an era that one fine day bade us farewell and disappeared.'

'And now?'

'Now I'm working for someone who effectively lives immersed in another century, and it's made me realize that *that* was not what my problem was.'

The Man in the Wingchair gave a burst of such happy, infectious laughter that she flushed with pleasure.

'I should fire you for that. I told you I knew what I was doing when I said I'd have to forgive you on more than one occasion.'

Smiling, Miss Prim stood up and began meticulously dusting a battered edition of St Anselm of Canterbury's *Monologion*.

'Your turn now,' she said. 'Why did you hear the clamour?'

He took a few moments to reply.

'For the same reason everyone does, I suppose. It's the sound of war.'

'That metaphor is so typical of you,' she interrupted, laughing. 'But what caused your war? You have to admit there's always a cause: an illness, a moral failing, sometimes an unmanageable temperament or unstable personality, or fear of death or the passing of time . . . What is it with you?'

'You're wrong, Prudencia, it's just due to one thing, not many. And it's not something but rather the absence of something, a missing piece. And when a piece is missing, from a puzzle, for instance, when the key piece is missing, nothing works. Do you like puzzles?'

'I'm like most people when they're not good at something; I don't enjoy what I can't master.'

'People who love puzzles,' he went on, 'can spend whole nights trying to fit a single piece. My sister used to do that. You could wake up at dawn and find her still engrossed in a puzzle. Obviously I don't mean a child's jigsaw, but one of those wonderful pictures with thousands and thousands of tiny pieces. Do you know what I mean?'

'Of course I do.'

'Well, what I'm trying to explain is that there are people, Prudencia, who suddenly realize that they're missing a key piece of the puzzle and can't complete it. They feel that something won't work, or maybe that absolutely nothing will work, until they find or, better still, are allowed to find the missing piece.'

'That sounds like esotericism or Gnosticism,' she murmured.

'Not at all; it's not about obscure knowledge, wisdom only for the initiated. Instead, it's the kind of discovery that Edgar Allan Poe describes in *The Purloined Letter*. Have you read it? Yes, of course you have. Well, in the story, the missing piece or purloined letter *is there*, in the room with you, *right in front of you*, but you can't see it, you're not aware of its presence. Until one day . . . '

Miss Prim shifted uncomfortably on the stepladder.

'I must get back to the *Monologion*,' she said, recovering her calm, distant professional tone.

The Man in the Wingchair regarded her with curiosity.

'As usual, Miss Prim scuttles back into her shell as soon as she senses the threat of the supernatural. Why does it bother you so much to talk about things you don't believe in? It's not very reasonable.'

Already engaged in dusting another book, she was silent. What could she say? Talking about things she didn't believe in didn't bother her at all; she had no doubt that something that didn't exist could have no effect on her. It wasn't the supernatural that she feared, it was the influence that the conversation and conviction of the Man in the Wingchair might have on her. How could she explain that what she feared was coming to believe in something that didn't exist simply because he believed in it?

'Don't worry, Prudencia. No man can convert himself or another by the power of the will alone. We're second causes, remember? Hard as we might try, the initiative isn't ours.'

'I'm not a Thomist,' she said abruptly, annoyed at feeling that she'd exposed her fears.

Astonished, he looked at her much as a father would at a daughter who'd just boasted of not being able to read.

'That, Miss Prim, is your big problem.'

7

A few days later, an apology from the Feminist League arrived in the shape of a dozen Comte de Chambord roses. A dozen roses would have been quite sufficient as a means of conveying apologies, but a dozen Comte de Chambord was more than an apology, it was an exquisite peace offering. The librarian immediately detected the expert hand of Hortensia Oeillet in the choice of flower, and that of Herminia Treaumont – who else? – in the Elizabethan verse on the card.

> *Go and catch a falling star,*
> *Get with child a mandrake root,*
> *Tell me where all past years are,*
> *Or who cleft the devil's foot,*
> *Teach me to hear mermaids singing,*

Or to keep off envy's stinging,
And find
What wind
Serves to advance an honest mind.

Beneath the poem, she read:

Dearest Prudencia,

Will you ever be able to forgive us? We wouldn't blame you if you couldn't. Devastated, repentant and deeply ashamed, we're sending you some old-fashioned *bellezza* wrapped in our most sincere apologies.

Hortensia Oeillet

PS Herminia thought the lines from John Donne would brighten your day. Aren't they wonderful?

'They are indeed,' murmured Miss Prim, pleased, plunging her dainty nose into the blooms.

Since the day of the unfortunate incident, Miss Prim had not stopped thinking about the peculiar idiosyncrasy of the feminist group that had welcomed her to San Ireneo. And the more she thought about it, the less serious the offence seemed. That didn't mean she approved, but, somehow, forgiveness had started to alter her view of the women. It was true that their conduct had been thoughtless and rude, and it was also true that delicacy and tact had been conspicuous by their absence, but the librarian had begun to suspect that beneath the slightly inept conspiracy lay a form of *love*.

Love? The first time this thought occurred to her she was astounded. She wasn't a sentimental woman, but she couldn't help sensing a kind of love – brash, clumsy, maternal – in the way the women had set out to provide her with a husband. As she deftly arranged the roses in a crystal vase, she told herself that if the ladies of San Ireneo considered a husband the greatest good to which a woman could aspire and were determined to obtain one for her, who was she to judge them? If they were prepared to expend time and effort to that end, who was she to treat as an insult something intended as, and which couldn't in any way be seen as other than, a warm, sincere gift?

Moreover, she had to admit that the idea of marriage did not entirely repel her. Certainly, in public she'd always claimed otherwise, but like many women of her kind, Miss Prim tended to scoff at what she secretly feared she would never have. Once again she cast her mind back and recalled the distraught faces of Hortensia Oeillet and Emma Giovanacci, and Herminia Treaumont's serene speech. If someone as beautiful and intelligent as Herminia considered marriage essential to a woman's well-being, who was she to cast doubt on it so emphatically? Had she ever looked into the matter in depth? Had she ever sat down with pencil and paper to list the pros and cons of the marital state? Had she? Miss Prim had to admit that she had not.

At the same time, she couldn't say she was fully in favour of marriage, either. Marital union, she reflected as she swathed herself in a woollen blanket and stepped out onto the balcony to watch the sunset, was definitely for women of a different kind. Women with a certain flexibility of character, biddable women, women who were comfortable with such concepts as *compromise* or *accommodation*. Miss Prim was definitely not one of those. She couldn't see herself compromising over anything. It wasn't that she didn't want to – she'd always valued the concept in the abstract – she just couldn't imagine it *in practice*. She had a certain resistance, she'd realized in various situations throughout her life, to relinquishing, even in part, her view of things.

While she found this resistance tiresome, in some ways she was also inwardly proud of it. Why should she concede that a certain composer was superior to another, she told herself, remembering a heated argument about music at the house of friends, when she was absolutely sure that he wasn't? Why should she accept, as a friendly compromise, that the respective talents were probably difficult to compare when she considered them eminently comparable? Why should she feign, in an even more abject spirit of accommodation, that the superiority of one or other composer depended largely on the listener's mood? Miss Prim believed that compromises of this kind constituted a sort of intellectual indecency. And though she sometimes forced herself to make them for the sake of her relationships, the fact was that to do so was repugnant to her.

The sky was growing tinged with pink when there was a knock at the door.

'Prudencia,' said the Man in the Wingchair, 'I have some business to do in the village and I'm afraid it's the staff's day off. Would you mind keeping an eye on the children? They're playing in the garden. I'm sorry to ask, but I've no choice.'

Conscious that her sunset had just been ruined, the librarian assured him pleasantly that she would look after the children. They weren't normal children, she thought as she made her way downstairs. They didn't read normal books, or play normal games, or even say normal things. It wasn't that they were unpleasant, or rude – actually, she had to admit that they were delightful – but they were quite unlike any children she'd encountered at friends' houses, in the street or in restaurants. When she spoke to them, she often had the uncomfortable sensation that she was being interrogated. It was the children who steered the conversation. It was they too who peppered the chats with strange items of information that the librarian considered quite unsuitable for children of their age.

'Today we learnt about Russian archimandrites and *starets*, Miss Prim. Do you know the story of Starets Ambrose and the turkeys?' Teseris had asked one morning in the kitchen as the librarian was making herself some cheese on toast behind the cook's back.

91

Miss Prim solemnly confessed that she knew a little about the elders of the Russian Orthodox Church, but that she had never heard of Starets Ambrose or any turkeys. No sooner had the librarian made this sincere admission of ignorance than the child launched into a disquisition on Starets Ambrose and the monastery of Optina, the similarities between him and Starets Zosima and the story of the turkeys that refused to eat.

'One day, a peasant woman who tended turkeys for a landowner went to see the *starets*,' explained the little girl. 'She was very sad because the turkeys were dying and the landowner was going to evict her. When the pilgrims at the monastery heard her crying, they laughed and told her not to bother the monk with such trivial nonsense. But Starets Ambrose listened to her very carefully and when she'd finished, he asked what she fed the turkeys. He advised her to change their feed and gave her his blessing. Once the woman had left, they asked the elder why he'd wasted his time over some turkeys. Do you know what he said?'

'I have no idea,' replied Miss Prim, bewildered.

'He said they were all blind if they couldn't see that those poor turkeys were the woman's whole life. Starets Ambrose didn't divide problems into big and small like everyone else does. He always said that angels are in the simple things; you never find angels where things are complicated. He believed that the small things are important.'

They definitely were not normal children, she sighed as she trotted down to the garden. She made her way along the path lined with now leafless hydrangeas and turned right into a bower formed by the branches of six large plane trees that were also starting to shed their leaves. This was where, on two aged wrought-iron benches, the children of the house had their headquarters. When they saw Miss Prim enter their sanctuary, their tousled heads sprang apart.

'Your uncle asked me not to let you out of my sight, so I came to see what you were up to,' she said truthfully.

'We weren't doing anything, just reading a book from when we were small,' said Septimus.

'And what book is that?' she asked, peering discreetly at the small yellow volume the boy was holding.

'It's the story of a toad who loves driving,' he said with the superior air of someone who believes he has a secret that can't be guessed.

Miss Prim smiled benevolently.

'A toad who's friends with a mole, a rat and a badger?'

Taken aback, the children nodded.

'You know it? It's a pretty old book. It was already around when our grandmother was small. It's fairly ancient,' said Septimus with absolute seriousness.

The librarian suppressed another smile.

'I've read it and studied it.'

'Studied it? But it's just a children's story!' cried Teseris, eyes wide.

Miss Prim crossed her arms and gazed over the children's heads at the horizon.

'It's more than a children's book, it's literature. And literature is to be studied, analysed. One traces its influences and researches what it's intending to convey.'

The children stared at her while the mild evening light, filtering through the yellowing leaves of the trees, threw flickering shadows on their faces.

'Our uncle says if you do that to books it spoils them,' declared Septimus eventually. 'He *hates* all that text analysis stuff. He's never made *us* do it.'

A cold wave of indignation washed over her.

'Oh really?' she muttered sourly. 'That's what he says, is it? In that case, I can't believe he got you to recognize Virgil from a single line. How can you do that without studying or analysing? Don't you know parts of the *Aeneid* by heart? I seem to remember that's what I heard the afternoon I arrived.'

'We know lots of parts of poems and stories by heart – it's the first thing we do with all books,' said Teseris in her gentle voice. 'He says it's how you learn to love books, it's got a lot to do with memory. He says that when men fall in love with women they learn their faces by heart so they can remember them later. They notice the colour of their eyes, the colour of their hair; whether they like music, prefer chocolate or biscuits, what their brothers and sisters are called, whether they write a diary, or have a cat . . .'

Miss Prim's expression softened a little. There it was again, the strange, dark, concentrated delicacy, the infuriating male ego combined with unexpected streaks of grace.

'It's the same thing with books,' continued Teseris. 'In lessons we learn bits by heart and recite them. Then we read the books and discuss them and then we read them again.'

The librarian removed her jacket with neat gestures and sat down on a bench.

'So your uncle believes you should enjoy books, not study them?'

'Yes, and he says it about other things, like music and paintings. Do you remember the day you arrived? You saw the Rublev icon and you measured it with a compass, remember?' asked Teseris.

Miss Prim flushed, suspecting that the child was about to question her approach to art.

'I remember,' she said curtly.

'You didn't take any notice when I said no grown-ups had helped me paint the icon. Grown-ups would have told me to use a compass. My uncle says an icon is a window between this world and the other one, it's what he learnt from the old *starets*. It's also how old Athonites do it, and it's how they've always been painted.'

Miss Prim shifted uneasily on the bench. There was something troubling about these children, though she couldn't quite put her finger on it. Something unsettling that coexisted with a sunny, luminous innocence and their fond veneration of the Man in the Wingchair and every word he uttered.

'You love him very much, don't you? Your uncle, I mean.'

'Yes,' said little Deka, and his siblings nodded. Straight away he added: 'He always tells the truth.'

'So, do other people lie?' she asked, astonished by his statement.

'People lie to children,' said Septimus solemnly. 'Everyone does it, and no one thinks it's wrong. When our mother died everyone told us she'd turned into an angel.'

'But she didn't,' murmured Miss Prim, moved.

Septimus glanced at his sister, who shook her head firmly.

'No one can turn into an angel, Miss Prim. People are people and angels are angels. They're different things. Look at trees and deer. Do you think a tree could turn into a deer?'

She shook her head.

'Maybe it's a way of explaining it, or maybe it's a legend. And what's wrong with legends? What about fairy tales? Don't you like fairy tales?' she asked, trying to change the subject.

'We like them,' said Eksi shyly. 'We like them a lot.'

'What's your favourite?'

'The story of the Redemption,' replied her older sister simply.

Astounded, Miss Prim couldn't think how to respond. The

child's strange statement showed that despite his efforts, despite his insistence and his arrogance, the Man in the Wingchair hadn't succeeded in instilling even the most basic rudiments of the faith that was so important to him. He hadn't managed to explain the historical background of his religion. How could this be? All those morning walks to the abbey, all that reading of theology, all that ancient liturgy, all that playing at medieval jousting and what had he achieved? Four children convinced that the texts he so loved were just fairy tales.

'But Tes, it's not exactly a fairy tale. Fairy tales are stories full of fantasy and adventure, they're meant to entertain. They're not set at any specific time and aren't about real people or places.'

'Oh, we know that,' said the little girl. 'We know it's not a normal fairy tale; it's a *real* fairy tale.'

Miss Prim, pensive, adjusted her position on the old iron bench.

'What you mean is it's *like* a fairy tale, is that it?' she asked, intrigued.

'No, of course not. The Redemption is nothing like a fairy tale, Miss Prim. Fairy tales and ancient legends are *like* the Redemption. Haven't you ever noticed? It's like when you copy a tree from the garden on a piece of paper. The tree from the garden doesn't look like the drawing, does it? It's the drawing that's a bit, just a *little* bit, like the real tree.'

Miss Prim, who had begun to feel hot – feverishly, suffo-catingly hot – remained silent for a long moment. The sun had almost set in the distance when at last she got to her feet and gave the children permission to go and play by the carp pond for a while, before slowly heading back to her room.

Part 2

It's Winter on the Russian Steppe

1

In the middle of November, Miss Prim had the opportunity of meeting her employer's mother. She arrived without warning, wearing an elegant hat and followed by a maid weighed down with luggage. The children greeted her jubilantly, signifying to the librarian that behind the imposing aspect was concealed an attentive, devoted grandmother. An opinion Miss Prim held on to even after she observed that the children's joy was due in large part to the pet bulldog and the numerous presents she had brought with her. Miss Prim was immediately struck by her extreme beauty. An attractive, refined woman is a work of art, her father had always said. If this was true, and the librarian believed it was, the lady who had just entered the house was a Botticelli, a Leonardo, even a Raphael.

'Where is my son?' she asked briskly as the maid helped her remove her beautiful silver-fox fur stole.

'At the abbey, I'm afraid,' replied the librarian.

'The abbey,' the old lady echoed in a disapproving tone. 'If he thought less about the abbey and more about this house, everything would go much better. And you are?'

'I'm sorry, I should have introduced myself. My name is Prudencia Prim, and I'm here to sort out the library.'

The lady stared at her for a few moments without a word. She looked closely at her face and examined her figure minutely, finally bringing her gaze to rest on her neat hair. Finally she asked the maid to bring her a cup of coffee and sat down in an armchair.

'And him too? Are you here to sort him out?'

The librarian blushed furiously. Miss Prim loved beauty, and the woman was beautiful, but that did not mean she was prepared to put up with certain insinuations. And of all possible insinuations, this was the one she was least able to tolerate.

'I don't know what you mean,' she replied curtly.

The visitor looked up at her with a sardonic grin.

'First of all, Miss Prim, I must tell you that I don't like having to crane my neck when holding a conversation. Do sit down. In my father's time, a librarian wasn't considered an employee, exactly; it was a position of trust, so it wasn't customary for them to remain standing when spoken to. I'm an old-fashioned woman, and I don't like to change my habits.'

Miss Prim obediently sat down in an armchair. She'd abandoned her work and was painfully aware that Herodotus' *Histories* awaited her in the library.

'I didn't mean to offend you, but you can't deny that your employer is rather peculiar. Or hadn't you noticed? Don't be afraid to speak freely, my dear, he is my son. If there's a woman in the world who knows him thoroughly, it's me, Miss Print.'

The librarian opened her mouth to correct the pronunciation of her name but thought better of it. It was plain that this lady was not accustomed to being interrupted, much less contradicted. She had probably never in her life had that salutary experience.

'He's a pleasant, generous employer. I have no cause for complaint. With regard to his character, you'll understand if I say that I don't consider it right or appropriate to give my opinion.'

The old lady, removing her gloves, was silent for a moment.

'It's a relief to hear it, Miss Prim. I'm pleased to see that you're exactly as they say you are. I'd like to make a confession: I have a bad habit of testing people before I trust them in the slightest. You must be aware that in the space of half a minute I made a malicious insinuation about your intentions in this house, prompted you to gossip about your employer's character flaws and deliberately mispronounced your name. You, however, responded to my insinuation with dignity, politely rejected my prompting and overlooked my mistake. As my son says, you're impeccable. There is absolutely no doubt about it.'

Hearing this, the librarian felt confused. The idea that this stranger had been testing her was not pleasant, and yet she wasn't offended. Not only because she had evidently passed the test but because, despite his prejudice against highly qualified people, the Man in the Wingchair had described her to his mother as impeccable.

'You're very kind,' she stammered.

'I'm simply being honest.'

The maid came back into the room with a tray and, while the old lady took her first sip of coffee, she set about lighting the fire and drawing the curtains to shut out the dull, grey outdoors.

'Do you like autumn?' the lady asked, out of the blue.

'I find it romantic,' replied Miss Prim, then blushed, this time at the thought that the woman might misinterpret her words. 'I mean Romantic in the sense of the artistic movement, not the emotion, of course.'

Appearing to ignore this last comment, the mother of the Man in the Wingchair offered Miss Prim a steaming cup of coffee.

'I detest it. I've always thought T. S. Eliot was quite wrong. April is not the cruellest month, it's November, without a doubt. April is a wonderful month, full of sun, light and wisteria in flower. Do you know Italy?'

Somewhat bewildered by the twists and turns in the conversation, the librarian replied that she did indeed know Italy.

'Do you mean you've lived there?'

Miss Prim clarified that she had not lived there.

'Then you should. Right now, before it's too late.'

'I don't think it would be possible at the moment,' the librarian replied, worried that this sudden recommendation concealed a wish to dispense with her services.

The visitor's laughter, jolly and tinkling, broke the silence.

'When you get to my age you'll realize that anything's possible. Look at my son. A few years ago a brilliant academic career lay ahead of him. He was a charming, intelligent man with a dazzling future. And what remains of it? Here he is, buried in this tiny village, holed up in his father's family's house, looking after four children and traipsing to an old monastery every morning before breakfast. Believe me when I tell you anything's possible.'

'But he seems very happy here,' Miss Prim ventured.

'He is, he definitely is. That's the most annoying thing about it. And I have to admit that he's done a great job. You can't imagine what it was like here only a few years ago.'

The librarian, who had by now put the distressing image of the volumes of Herodotus lying on the desk quite out of her mind, made herself comfortable in the armchair, looking forward to hearing some things that would satisfy her endless curiosity about the village and her employer.

'What gave him the idea of setting up this community? Few people would undertake such a daunting enterprise.'

The old lady put down her cup, leant her head back and half-closed her eyes, as if trying to remember.

'If only I knew. Actually I don't think it was down to one single factor. Obviously it had something to do with meeting the old Benedictine monk. I expect you've heard about him already.'

Miss Prim settled deeper into the armchair and drank some more of her coffee.

'As I recall, he'd just finished giving a series of lectures,' the old lady continued, 'and he took a break to attend a university seminar in Kansas. He found something there, don't ask me what. That summer he travelled to Egypt, then to Simonos Petras on Mount Athos, and he also spent time at the Benedictine abbey in Le Barroux. On his return he said he'd decided to live at the abbey here in San Ireneo for a few months. Imagine: he, who hadn't stepped inside a church in twenty years, in a monastery of traditionalist Benedictine monks. I thought he wouldn't be able to stand it, but a year later he asked if he could open up the house again and, as far as I can tell, that's how this whole thing started. But you shouldn't be surprised. Life is surprising.'

The librarian thought for a moment before asking: 'But what about the children? Aren't you worried about his influence on them?'

'Worried?' exclaimed the old lady, taken aback. 'My dear

'Miss Prim, my grandchildren are the only children I know who can recite Dante, Virgil and Racine, read classical texts in the original languages and recognize most of the great pieces of classical music from a few chords. Not only am I not worried, I'm actually proud, frankly proud. It's one of the few things I truly approve of in this hermit's retreat my son has chosen and which, I won't lie to you, I detest profoundly.'

'I wasn't referring to culture, but to religion. Aren't you concerned that they might be too religious, as it were? Too precociously religious? You know what I mean.'

The woman regarded the librarian incredulously before giving a happy laugh.

'My dear, I see you know very little about the house you live in,' she said, eyes shining with mirth.

Miss Prim peered at her, confused.

'What do you mean?'

The lady smiled.

'I mean that it wasn't my son who instilled his beliefs in the children. He had already taken a step or two when he took charge of them after my daughter's death. He'd discovered the depths of Christian thought and culture and he was delighting in the beauty of worship. But he hadn't taken the final step. He was still, so to speak, on the threshold. Don't you understand? It wasn't him, it was them. It was the children, the children *themselves* who guided him to where he is today.'

*

The arrival of the Man in the Wingchair's mother marked a turning point in Miss Prim's life. From the day of their first meeting, the librarian found that her social life was considerably enriched. The old lady immediately adopted her as an inseparable companion. Soon she considered it perfectly natural to take Miss Prim with her to all the social engagements that filled her diary.

'Today we must go and drop in on poor Miss Mott,' she said as they walked to the village one afternoon. 'You don't know her, of course – she's our schoolteacher. I was a member of the selection panel, several years ago now, and I feel a certain responsibility, so I visit her whenever I'm in San Ireneo. This is the place. Obviously in spring it's much prettier than it is now, but isn't it charming?'

Miss Prim admitted that she had never seen a school like it. Standing in the centre of the village right on the main square, Eugenia Mott's schoolhouse was encircled by a wooden fence literally sagging beneath the weight of numerous rose bushes whose luxuriance had now been checked by the onset of autumn. A pair of huge plane trees flanked the entrance. On a sign above the lintel hung an ancient Latin motto that proudly exhorted the young pupils: *Sapere aude*.

It was five o'clock in the afternoon. The children had finished their classes some time ago, and Miss Mott was busy polishing the old brass plaque which the school kept as a reminder of past glories. She was a woman of around sixty, with a plump figure and friendly smile. Her cheeks flushed and hands covered in metal polish, she greeted the two visitors solicitously and bustled them inside. Did Miss Prim like the school, she asked as she led the two ladies into the large schoolroom? How very kind! She couldn't take the credit, of course, the school had been there for many years. But now that Miss Prim mentioned it, she had to confess that everyone asked how she managed to grow such perfect roses in a garden full of boisterous children. Naturally, she had a little trick, a teacher couldn't manage in life without one. Hers consisted in allocating a rose bush to each child at the beginning of the school year. This small distinction made them feel proud and important, and helped them to develop a sense of responsibility. She only had the children for three years; she taught them little more than reading and writing, a smattering of geometry, some arithmetic and maybe even the rudiments of rhetoric.

While Miss Mott's chatter filled the classroom, battering the librarian's sensibilities, the mother of the Man in the Wingchair kept quiet. Apparently absorbed in her thoughts, she walked slowly around the room before coming to a stop in front of an old wooden coat rack filled with the children's paint-spattered overalls. Then she turned and directed her beautiful, worldly-wise gaze at the teacher.

'Are you happy here, Eugenia?'

Caught off guard, Miss Mott blushed and had to clear her throat before replying.

'What a funny question! Yes, I would say so. Of course I am. Why wouldn't I be?'

The mother of the Man in the Wingchair sat down at one of the desks and peered at something carved into the wood.

'I'd say that it wasn't my question that was funny but your answer. Why shouldn't you be? I could give you many reasons. First, because happiness is not the natural state of human beings. Or perhaps because teaching so many children for all these years would exhaust anyone. Or even,' the lady lowered her voice almost imperceptibly, 'because he hasn't returned, after all.'

The librarian suddenly felt uncomfortable. Her employer's mother's remark seemed to refer to some disappointment in love. Miss Prim disapproved of both heartbreak and its consequences. She disliked what it did to people, didn't enjoy seeing the havoc it wreaked and didn't appreciate witnessing its victories. For this reason, before Eugenia could reply, she hastily announced that she would like to go out and take a stroll among the laurels and chrysanthemums in the gardens.

'How delicate you are, Prudencia! Don't worry, it's an old story and I don't mind people knowing it now. Actually I've learnt to live with it and be reasonably happy. No, my husband hasn't returned. He definitely hasn't returned. But I'm no longer waiting for him. I couldn't live my life like that.'

'I'm glad to hear it,' snapped the old lady. 'There's something sinister about the idea of waiting. I have never waited for anybody. My son, however, considers it a virtue.'

'He considers waiting to be a virtue?' asked Miss Prim with interest. 'In what sense?'

'Oh, he means something else,' exclaimed Eugenia sadly. 'Nothing as silly and sentimental as the love of an abandoned woman.'

'I don't know if he means something else or not, but what I do know is that *you* have done the right thing in ceasing to wait around,' said the mother of the Man in the Wingchair severely. 'And now, tell me, Eugenia, do you know Italy?'

The librarian jumped at this. The woman, one couldn't help noticing, seemed obsessed with having people know Italy. Miss Prim had nothing against Italy, a wonderful country in every way, but why the insistence? To her, there was something almost impolite about continually urging everyone to travel halfway across Europe.

'As I said to Prudencia the day I met her, in my view a woman's education cannot be complete unless she has lived for a time in Italy. There's a certain lack of polish to the minds of women who haven't had that experience. It's vital to the development of the female intellect.'

'Only female? What about men?' asked the librarian.

The old lady looked at her with a sardonic expression.

'Men? Men can take care of themselves. We've got enough to be getting on with, don't you think? You're very young and inexperienced, Prudencia, but let me tell you something: the day that most dinner parties in mixed company stop splitting into two camps – one male, where they discuss politics and economics, the other female where gossip and chit-chat dominate – is the day when we'll have the authority to pronounce on men's education. What I'm going to say now will undoubtedly shock you, but I will say it anyway: most women have no conversation. And the worst thing is, it's not because they're incapable of it, it's because they don't bother trying.'

The librarian exchanged a glance of resigned understanding with Miss Mott, who quickly changed the subject, saying that, in her opinion, the Ancient Greek and Roman classics were the cornerstone of any education, male or female.

'Would you mind if I asked you something about your son? Where did he complete his studies?' asked Miss Prim.

'I like to think that my son educated himself. Of course, we gave him all the tools, first-rate tools: wonderful schools, excellent teachers. But it's to his credit that he made use of them as he did.'

'He's a brilliant man,' said Miss Mott.

'He's a brilliant man who's wasted his talent,' declared the old lady bitterly as she stood up to leave. Miss Mott saw the two women to the garden gate and said goodbye with a smile.

The old lady and the librarian walked for some time, side by side, each deep in thought. Though Miss Prim was keen to ask more about her employer's education, she didn't dare draw her companion from her silence. It was the latter who resumed the conversation. She explained that Eugenia Mott's husband had left her one morning without a word, three months before she moved to San Ireneo. Then she asked Miss Prim what she thought of the teacher.

'She seems like a good, simple woman, though not excessively bright. I'm surprised you selected her. I thought education was highly prized in San Ireneo.'

'You mean, you find her average?'

Prudencia looked at the old lady in dismay. How could such an elegant woman refer to others with so little tact or respect? However much she pondered, she could not understand it. She couldn't get used to the coldness of the older woman's remarks, her abrupt frankness, her habit of speaking, looking and even listening with an air of incontrovertible authority.

'What I mean is that I was expecting someone ... less simple. Is she well qualified, academically?' she asked, treading carefully.

'Absolutely not, she's an ordinary teacher. Extremely ordinary.'

'But the education in the classics that the children here receive ... not everyone is qualified to teach it.'

The old lady turned to her with a weary shrug.

'My dear Miss Prim, do you still not understand how things work here? Eugenia Mott is a simple, extremely simple teacher because what San Ireneo wants for its children is exactly that: a teacher without intellectual aspirations.'

'Forgive me for pressing you on this,' said Prudencia, puzzled, 'but I can't understand how a place where children perform *Antigone* in Greek could want a schoolteacher with no intellectual aspirations.'

For the second time the old lady stopped and stared at her companion gravely.

'Because, in actual fact, they don't need anyone to teach the children anything. Because it's they who educate their children themselves, who teach them to recite poems by Ariosto before they can read; explain Euclidian geometry using the *Elements* as a textbook; play them a fragment of a Palestrina motet for them to guess which one it is. It's they, my dear, who regularly cross half of Europe to sit their children before Fra Angelico's *Noli Me Tangere*, show them the high altar of St John Lateran, bring them face to face with the capital of the Temple of Aphrodite.'

'So why do they want a teacher at all?'

'To safeguard all that work, to preserve and protect it. In other words, to ensure it doesn't get spoilt. Does that shock you? If they hired a teacher bursting with theories on education, sociology, child psychology and all those other modern sciences, they'd be letting the fox into the henhouse. Look at it this way: if you were convinced that the world had forgotten how to think and teach, if you believed it had discarded the beauty of art and literature, if you thought it had crushed the power of the truth, would you let that world educate your children?'

'Now I understand why your son didn't want someone with a degree for a librarian,' sighed Miss Prim.

The lady smiled at her sweetly.

'Ah, but he hired you, didn't he? He must have seen something special in you, isn't that so? Tell me, what do you think it was?'

Miss Prim said she didn't know, though she suspected that it had something to do with the misunderstanding that had occurred on the day of her arrival at the house.

'Don't delude yourself,' insisted the old lady. 'My son isn't sentimental. Believe me when I say he must *really* have seen something interesting in you.'

And with her usual sharp tone, she added: 'I wonder what it *was?*'

2

$\mathcal{I}$n the past ten days, Miss Prim had exchanged no more than a few words with the Man in the Wing-chair. Busy with the children, lessons, visits to the abbey and his mother's company, he had been an elusive presence. As she nibbled on a piece of toast at breakfast, the librarian told herself she didn't need his company. And it was true. A woman like her, who enjoyed robust mental health and glorious independence, was perfectly capable of keeping herself amused without the need to chat. Nevertheless, she had to admit that she did slightly miss the masculine humour that enlivened the work of cataloguing the endless rows of books.

That afternoon, Miss Prim received a note from Herminia Treaumont inviting her to join the San Ireneo Christmas committee. She read the note silently as she finished her coffee. Since she didn't have a lot of work to complete that day, she decided to fetch her hat and coat and attend the meeting at the village tearoom.

It was cold out, and the librarian hurried down the garden path towards the wrought-iron gate.

'Are you going to the village, Prudencia? I can give you a lift if you like.'

The Man in the Wingchair was already at the wheel of his car. Miss Prim hesitated, but a glance at the low grey sky prompted her to accept.

'Thank you,' she said, climbing into the passenger seat. 'I think it's going to start snowing any minute.'

He smiled pleasantly but didn't reply.

'Would you like me to turn up the heating?' he asked.

The librarian assured him that the temperature inside the car was perfect.

'Tell me, if I'm not being nosy, what are you doing going to the village on such a cold afternoon?'

'I'm meeting Herminia Treaumont and the other residents to discuss the Christmas festivities.'

'I see you've fitted in fully with our small community. So, have you forgiven them?'

Miss Prim, who had taken special care to prevent news of the contretemps at the Feminist League from reaching her employer, blushed.

'I didn't realize you knew so much about my adventures in San Ireneo. I suppose it was your friend, Mr Delàs, who told you.'

'I'm afraid you put too much faith in the discretion of thirty witnesses. I've been told the story about five times, and I must say in every version your reaction has seemed magnificent.'

Prudencia laughed gratefully, but dismissed his praise with a wave of her hand.

'Believe me, I'm not too proud of myself. But I've realized that what happened, though it was mortifying for me personally, was done with the best intentions. It wasn't very polite of me to behave as I did, especially to Miss Treaumont, a wonderful woman.'

'She is splendid,' was all the Man in the Wingchair replied.

Prudencia, huddled in the front passenger seat, suddenly felt strangely uneasy.

'She's very beautiful, don't you think?' she asked, glancing sideways at her employer, who was concentrating on the road.

'Definitely. She's one of the most attractive women I've ever met. And highly intelligent.'

For a moment neither said anything more. Miss Prim simply looked out of the window in silence. The ancient, leafless trees that lined the road and the cold grey light made the landscape look sombre and dramatic.

'She must have been a great beauty,' she said at last with a strange tightness in her stomach.

'What was that?'

'I said,' she repeated patiently, 'that she must have been a great beauty.'

'Do you mean my mother?'

'Your mother? No, why would I mention your mother now? I meant Miss Treaumont.'

'She isn't that old,' he said, bemused. 'Not so old as to say that she must *have been* a great beauty.'

'Don't you think so?'

'Of course I don't. She's younger than me, and probably only slightly older than you.'

'Oh,' said Miss Prim.

He glanced at her, intrigued, and then looked back at the road.

'You don't believe me? She really is.'

'Of course I believe you,' she said, 'though it is surprising.'

'What is?'

Miss Prim, who had started to feel better, relieved of the tension in the pit of her stomach, lowered the window slightly, letting in a gust of icy air.

'Some women are unfortunate in that they wither before their time,' she murmured.

'Wither before their time? What nonsense. In my opinion Herminia is a young, attractive woman.'

Miss Prim, suddenly feeling the same tiresome tightening in her stomach, was silent.

'Why don't you say something?'

'What can I say?'

'I suppose you could make a comment on what I just said.'

'I'd rather not.'

'Why?'

'Because it wouldn't be tactful.'

'What wouldn't be tactful?'

'It wouldn't be tactful to continue talking about another woman to a man, especially about things he doesn't understand.'

'So that's it,' he said, trying not to smile.

They continued the journey without another word until the car drew up outside the tearoom, where the Christmas committee was waiting.

'Would you like me to pick you up when you've finished?' he asked politely, leaning across to open her door.

'There's no need, thank you,' she said coldly.

'Miss Prim, look at the sky: it's about to snow heavily.'

'I'm perfectly well aware of that, thanks.'

'Well, if you're perfectly well aware of it, then I've got nothing further to say. Enjoy your afternoon,' he said, frowning, before restarting the engine.

Miss Prim straightened her hat in the tearoom window. She felt annoyed, she couldn't conceal it. The excessive praise of Herminia Treaumont had bothered her deeply, it would be absurd to deny it. But surely it would bother any woman? Surely any woman would find it disagreeable to be stuck in a car with a man who wouldn't stop showering compliments on another person? What kind of man insisted over and over on the extreme beauty of one woman in the presence of another? It was an intolerable lack of courtesy and, without courtesy, all was lost. She knew it because she'd seen it in her own home. Year after year she'd watched courtesy evaporate from her parents' marriage. She'd experienced first-hand the effects of the lack of courtesy in her relationship with her sister. And now, when she seemed to have arrived at a place where formality still had a raison d'être, precisely now she had just endured the company of a man who couldn't stop talking about the sublime qualities and dazzling beauty of another woman.

Herminia was an interesting woman. So what? Wasn't she, too? Herminia was attractive – fine. Couldn't the same be said about her as well? He was perfectly free to be enchanted by the woman if he wanted, she had no objection, but did he have to show it so obviously? Miss Prim had always been against public displays of sentiment. In her view, in civilized societies people had private homes in which they could give free rein to their feelings without others being obliged to witness it. Emotional excess, she reasoned as she adjusted her coat collar, was characteristic of primitive societies and equally primitive individuals. And anyway, wasn't she an employee? Was it necessary to subject an employee to a show of feelings as he had just done in the car? Miss Prim did not believe it was. And not only did she not believe it, but she was convinced that there must be some kind of regulation prohibiting such behaviour.

Still annoyed, she entered the tearoom, where small lamps at every table created a warm, welcoming atmosphere.

'Miss Prim, how lovely to see you again!' The calm, gentle tones of Herminia Treaumont, who had risen to greet her, brought her back to reality.

'It's lovely to see you too, Miss Treaumont.'

'Please, call me Herminia. And may I call you Prudencia? We're neither of us old enough to be so formal, are we?'

'Definitely not,' replied Miss Prim, blushing to the roots of her hair.

Despite her bad mood, she soon managed to join in the conversation. In addition to her hostess, there were three other women and two men at the table. One was introduced as Judge Bassett, a short, thickset man with bushy eyebrows and moustache, whose eyes would only focus when he found the conversation of interest. The other was a young man answering to the name of François Flavel, who was the only vet in the area. The women were Mrs Von Larstrom, owner of the San Ireneo Hotel; the elderly Miss Miles, a walking encyclopedia on the subject of folk customs; and young Amelia Lime, the judge's secretary. After discussing the principal matters bearing on the Christmas preparations, ranging from the choice of hymns to the fabulous candle illuminations and the street decorations, which would consist of garlands of foliage and wild berries, the committee moved on to the main events of the festivities. More than an hour was spent itemizing all the details yet to be settled. Then the conversation became more personal. This was when Miss Prim moved her chair closer to the vet's and, with the memory of the Man in the Wingchair's behaviour still painfully vivid in her mind, prepared to deploy all her charm.

'I adore animals,' she said with her most beguiling smile.

The target of this remark grinned back at her and was about to respond pleasantly when Judge Bassett's deep voice interrupted.

'That must be because you've never been on a farm. I wager you've never seen a cow give birth. Ask him, ask our vet if it's pleasant sticking your arm up to the shoulder inside a cow's private parts. Tell me, my dear, have you ever had occasion to see a cow calving?'

Miss Prim straightened her back and squared her jaw.

'Of course not, but my understanding is that you can love animals without having witnessed such a spectacle.'

The young vet hastened to concur. You could definitely love animals without having to undergo the experience of exploring their reproductive systems. Millions of people throughout history had done so.

'You may both be right, but I think it important to distinguish between a love of animals, which is a strong and noble thing, and the cloying sentimentality that some people confuse it with. Naturally, I take it as given that that's not your case, young lady.'

'Naturally,' chimed in the vet amiably.

Miss Prim said nothing.

'Do you have a dog?' the judge asked.

Miss Prim replied that she did not, unfortunately, have a dog.

'A cat, perhaps? You look like a cat owner. I thought it the moment I saw you.'

'I thought so too,' said the younger man cheerfully. 'There's something feline about you, if you don't mind me saying.'

Miss Prim assured him warmly that she was delighted to accept this compliment, but her sense of honour obliged her to make it clear that, despite appearances, she had never had a cat.

'A canary?' said Judge Bassett.

She shook her head.

'A tortoise?' suggested François.

Miss Prim had to confess that she had never lived with any shelled creature either.

'A fish, maybe?' Judge Bassett persisted, now with a noticeable edge of impatience to his voice.

'I've never owned an animal,' she said in an attempt to bring the interrogation to a halt. 'I've always been of the opinion that the absence of the object of one's love purifies that love.'

'That's a good theory,' exclaimed Judge Bassett with satisfaction. 'If most men believed the same, divorce probably wouldn't exist and, if pushed, I'd say marriage wouldn't either.'

François looked at Miss Prim in silence.

'Do you mean that you love dogs in the abstract?'

'Exactly,' she said with a smile.

'And cats?'

'Exactly the same.'

'And fish, canaries and hamsters?'

Miss Prim, who was starting to lose patience herself, was grateful when the judge interrupted, emphatically ordering young François to cease with his questions.

'But that's almost inhuman,' said the vet. 'I can't believe a woman as sweet as you could love in the abstract.'

Miss Prim tucked back a stray lock of hair and lowered her eyes.

'I didn't say that,' she murmured.

'Yes, you did,' cut in Judge Bassett. 'You said that the absence of the object of one's love purifies that love. It's a splendid theory, as I said, so don't spoil it now with a lack of backbone.'

Miss Prim shifted in her seat. The other women at the table were discussing how to shield the Christmas-tree candles from the wind. She glanced at them enviously before returning to the fray.

'If there's one thing I pride myself on, Judge Bassett, it's having backbone. But I have to say that when I spoke of the absence of the object of one's love, I was making a reference to courtly love. It was poetic licence. I wasn't referring to real love.'

The young vet gazed into her eyes before speaking.

'Do you mean that the love of animals is like courtly love? Sublimated love?'

'I mean that the love of animals isn't love.'

The judge greeted this with a roar of laughter.

'Yes, sir,' he said in his deep voice, 'yes, sir. You're quite a woman. That's the greatest truth on the matter I've heard in a long time. But tell me something: if you think the love of animals isn't love, and you've never owned an animal yourself, then why the blazes did you say you adored animals?'

Miss Prim looked at François and what she saw in his eyes prompted her to be candid. It was useless to go on pretending. The current of sympathy that had sprung up between them when they were introduced had completely disappeared. What had she expected? The afternoon had started badly with that unpleasant exchange with her employer. She shouldn't be surprised that it had continued in the same vein.

'I was just trying to be friendly,' she said to the vet, who quickly averted his gaze and stared down at the plate of toast with butter and honey that sat on the table.

'Here in the village we're in the habit of being frank, you know. It's one of the reasons some of us have come here, to escape the small talk,' the old judge said curtly.

At these words, Miss Prim's back stiffened once again.

'May I point out, Judge Bassett, that being friendly is not the same as making small talk.'

'You're right,' said François, his gaze meeting hers, 'you can be friendly and tell the truth. There's nothing preventing it.'

Miss Prim reddened, and at that moment realized something that filled her with amazement: she had told a lie without being aware of it. She, who prided herself on being incapable of lying, had lied without batting an eyelid. She hadn't blushed, hadn't been perturbed, hadn't felt her heart race. She'd tried to impress the young man with a ridiculous, silly lie, and she'd done so without turning a hair. Was this the first time it had happened? Deeply ashamed, she had to admit to herself that it wasn't. And then, silently within her, a huge question formed: could it be that everything she had so proudly throughout her life termed her *delicacy* was simply a discreet, efficient cover for her lies? She'd never tolerated deception regarding her strong opinions, that much was true. But wasn't it also true that when it came to trying to please in matters that weren't crucial to her, that didn't compromise her sense of things, she had been dishonest?

'I'm sorry,' she said, quickly rising to her feet, 'but I think I have to leave.'

Everyone at the table stood up.

'I hope you weren't offended by what I said,' enquired the

vet anxiously. Seeing Miss Prim so flustered seemed to have reawakened his sympathy towards her.

'Offended? Why would she be offended?' asked Herminia Treaumont.

'Don't worry, Herminia, we were just bantering,' said Miss Prim, trying to make light of the situation. 'We were discussing animals and small talk, nothing that could offend anyone.'

'Our guest has been a revelation, Herminia. She's delighted us with her conversation,' said Judge Bassett. 'I wonder if she'd like to work for me, now that Amelia is thinking of leaving and I'm being accused of enslaving young women.'

'Now, now, don't talk nonsense,' replied Herminia fondly.

Miss Prim laughed, flattered.

'It's a tempting offer,' she said. 'But I'm afraid I already have a job I love.'

'Fine, fine, but think it over. I like women who have their heads screwed on.'

After saying goodbye to everyone, and agreeing to visit Herminia Treaumont at the newspaper office the following Wednesday, Miss Prim left the tearoom. Turning up her coat collar and putting on her gloves, she prepared for the walk back to the house.

Outside, the streets were slowly disappearing under a blanket of white.

*

She had gone barely half a mile and was about to enter the woods when she heard a car behind her.

'Prudencia, I have to warn you that if you walk through the woods in those shoes you run the risk of losing your feet and we'll have to come and rescue you. Can I give you a lift home? I promise not to say anything that could bother you. In fact, I promise not to speak at all.'

Miss Prim turned and looked at him with a mixture of relief and gratitude. She had chosen the wrong shoes for snow. Her feet were hurting, they were starting to go numb, she didn't want to lose them and she definitely didn't want to have to be rescued.

'I'd be very grateful. I have to admit you were right when you said I shouldn't walk back.'

'Miss Prim admitting I'm right, I can't believe it! You must be unwell. Probably the effects of the cold,' he said, leaning over to open the door and offering her a blanket for her legs. 'You're frozen. Would you like some brandy? I know you think I'm a hopeless alcoholic, but try to set aside your unpitying judgement for a moment and have a sip. It'll warm you.'

She obeyed without a word while he started the engine and turned up the heater. She was too cold to argue, but something in his words compelled her to respond.

'Unpitying judgement? Do you really think my judgement is so unpitying? And I thought it was your religion that condemned drinking. I find it surprising that you should accuse me of being judgemental. I've always considered myself a tolerant person.'

'A tolerant person?' he laughed. 'Come on, Prudencia, I'd say you were actually extremely strict. I grant you, it's a wonderful quality for your job, and I'm the main beneficiary, but it must be a heavy burden for your slender shoulders.'

Miss Prim bit her lip, remembering her afternoon at the tearoom and her distress at discovering her facility as a social liar.

'And as for my religion and drinking, you're a little confused on the matter, though in your defence the confusion is common. Drink, like all the other gifts of Creation, is a good thing, Prudencia. It's its misuse, or abuse, that accounts for its negative effects.'

For the second time that day, Miss Prim recognized that her companion might be right. But she wasn't really concerned with drinking or religion just then.

'So you think I'm strict? I thought I was, too, but today I found out that not only is that not true but I'm a deeply hypocritical woman with a tendency to lie.'

The Man in the Wingchair looked across at her, taken aback.

'I was tempted to respond with a joke to what you've just said, but I can see you're upset. May I ask what's happened? I promise to be tactful, if that's possible for me.'

After hesitating a moment, Miss Prim decided to tell

him all about it. She was very tired and she longed to pour it all out, to unload the burden of her anguish onto other shoulders. Throughout her life she had made huge efforts to be virtuous and to overcome her faults, and had emerged victorious from many battles, but now she had to admit defeat and acknowledge that her delicacy, the quality she had elevated to the status of an art, was simply a cover.

'So you see,' she said, after recounting the story of her love of animals, the vet and Judge Bassett, 'I'm a common hypocrite, a liar.'

'I'd say you're more of a fool,' was her companion's succinct reply.

Miss Prim looked at him aghast, then abruptly unfastened her seat belt.

'Stop the car immediately,' she said with barely contained rage.

'What?'

'I said, stop the car immediately. I'm not staying in here with you a moment longer.'

The Man in the Wingchair pulled over, turned off the ignition and lifted both hands from the steering wheel.

'Why the hell must you always be so extreme?'

'Extreme? You think I'm extreme? You get me to open my heart to you, you promise to be tactful and then when I fall into your trap and confide my concerns, you respond with an insult. Do I need to remind you that you called me a fool? You, who pride yourself on being gentlemanly. You, no one else.'

'Yes, me,' he replied abruptly. 'Make no mistake, Prudencia, I'm a man like any other, maybe worse than others. I hope it doesn't come as a shock to you because it definitely doesn't to me.'

She made to open the car door, but he put out an arm and firmly held her back.

'Listen carefully. I called you a fool because I think getting upset over what you told me is to behave like a fool. I'm a frank man, probably a little too frank, and you're right, I'm not very tactful. But you should know me well enough by now to understand that though I may not be a model of tact, I'm a decent person. If I tell you to confide in me it's because I want to help. So let me speak and listen to what I have to say.'

'Only if you take back your insult,' she said stonily.

'Fine, I take back what I said. But, for the record, it wasn't an insult. I was describing your behaviour, I wasn't describing you.'

'Please, don't start with your theological distinctions. You're not going to trick me again.'

'Would you please just listen?' he insisted, pronouncing the words slowly and deliberately.

Miss Prim raised her eyes and looked at him. The day had started badly. It had been a mistake to attend the meeting at the tearoom. It had also been a mistake to let him give her a lift to the village. Had she not accepted his offer, she wouldn't have had to listen to all that praise heaped upon the beauty of another woman. Nor would she have got carried away flirting with the young vet, much less spouted all that nonsense about how much she liked animals. She, who had always been afraid of dogs and disliked cats. How could she have been so stupid?

'No, you're right, I am a fool,' she said with tears in her eyes.

He took her tenderly by the hand and looked at her with an expression that she didn't know how to interpret.

'Come on, you're not a fool, Prudencia. You just act like one. Please don't cry. People like me can't handle tears; we haven't been granted that gift. Listen to me: the fact is, there are some things that make you suffer, and they make you suffer because you don't fully understand them, that's all.'

She wiped away her tears and smiled.

'Between us it always boils down to that, doesn't it? You understand things that I don't.'

'No, that's not right, at least not quite. Will you listen to me now?'

Miss Prim assured him that she would. He switched on the engine, offered her another sip of brandy and shifted in his seat before speaking.

'First of all, there's no such thing as definitive victory over one's faults, Prudencia. It's not an arena in which mere willpower works. Our nature is defective, like an old, broken locomotive, so however hard we try, we're bound to fail. Getting upset about it is absurd and, though it might make you angry to hear it, arrogant too. You won't like this but, when we fail, what we have to do is ask for help from the machine's maker. And always allow the maker to improve things with a good application of oil from time to time.'

'That's a religious explanation, and I'm not a religious woman. Please don't use that argument with me, it's not valid,' she said, her nose red from crying as well as from the cold.

He leant his head back and laughed.

'That answer isn't worthy of a lucid mind, Prudencia. And it's a product of the anti-Thomist education you're so proud of. The question here, and in any other discussion, is not whether my argument is religious, but whether it's right. Can't you see the difference? Give me your counterargument, Prudencia. Say you think that what I've said is wrong and explain why, but don't tell me that my argument fails because it's religious. The only reason it might not work here or anywhere else is simply because it's wrong.'

'All right then, I'm telling you it doesn't work because it's wrong.'

'Really? That means you think human beings can achieve perfection and maintain moral excellence through their own efforts. Don't you think that to err is human? Do you really think man never fails?'

'Of course I don't, I know perfectly well that it's human to make mistakes and that nobody's perfect.'

'In other words, deep down you think that a large part of what I've said is true. The thing is, you only recognize the truth when it's dressed up as secularism.'

Miss Prim looked at the Man in the Wingchair through the growing darkness and wondered bitterly why, even at such gloomy moments, a conversation with him was so much more interesting than any she had with other people; why the most obstinate and odious of his species was also the most stimulating to talk to.

'I'm cold. Would you mind taking me home now?'

'Mind? I'm always happy to take you home, Prudencia.'

On Tuesday and Friday mornings the two youngest children of the Man in the Wingchair's household attended Miss Mott's school. The older ones, though too advanced for the teacher's lessons, also received part of their education outside the home. Three times a week they had language classes at Herminia Treaumont's house; there were two weekly biology sessions at the village doctor's surgery; they studied history with Horacio Delàs; botany with Hortensia Oeillet; music with Emma Giovanacci, and so on. It was on a Tuesday morning that the two little ones burst into the sitting room full of news.

'Grandmama! Miss Prim! Miss Mott's husband's come back!' shouted Eksi as she rushed into the room, where the two women were busy, one dealing with her correspondence, the other cataloguing the works of Swift.

'And he's brought sweets for all the children!' added Deka who ran in after, loaded down with his sister's books.

The Man in the Wingchair's mother arched her right eyebrow and continued writing, telling her grandchildren that they should wait till she'd finished what she was doing. It was Miss Prim who turned round and expressed her delight at this latest development. She knew she herself lacked experience with children, but she didn't understand the grandmother's cool reserve and ability to put rules and manners before her grandchildren's spontaneity. Though at the same time, something inside her told her that the children probably owed their charm and good manners, at least in part, to her military discipline.

'Miss Mott's husband? Are you sure? How exciting!' she cried, gently closing a third edition of *The Battle of the Books*.

'That's right, tell Miss Prim all about it and let your poor grandmother finish her letters,' said the old lady with a glance at the librarian.

The children couldn't give many details about what had happened at the school. At break time, when they were playing in the garden, they'd heard the teacher murmur: 'My God, he's come back.'

They had all turned to see, standing at the gate, a tall, heavily built man in an old coat and muddy boots, smiling, full of emotion.

'His eyes were *swimming* with tears,' said Eksi, whose

precocious love of reading exceeded her verbal fluency by quite a margin.

'You mean brimming, dear,' her grandmother corrected her, peering at the child fondly over her reading glasses.

'Miss Mott's husband is as big as one of the giants in Gulliver, Grandmama,' said Deka.

The old lady said she hoped that Mr Mott's apology to his wife for all his years of absence would be at least half as big as Swift's giants, and that Miss Mott would make him pay an equally large penance.

'Grandmama, if Miss Mott is married, why isn't she called Mrs Mott?' asked Eksi.

'Well, because Mr Mott left the house one day and never came back. You're much too young to understand, but if there's one thing worse than being a widow it's being married to a man who's disappeared. Poor Eugenia Mott,' said the older woman to Miss Prim, 'couldn't bear people continually asking where her husband was, so one day she decided to become a "Miss", start a new life and forget all about trying to explain.'

'A very sensible decision,' said the librarian.

'My thoughts exactly.'

As the weeks passed, Miss Prim had felt increasingly at ease in the old lady's company. She didn't approve of her patrician rudeness – to do so would have been contrary to her own nature, and Miss Prim never did anything that was contrary to her nature – but she was starting to appreciate the some-what sharp-edged candour that showed itself in merciless judgements as well as in deliciously sincere praise. In the older woman's character the librarian had found an elucidation of the amazing toughness she'd always admired in venerable dynastic families; the cast-iron capacity to preserve one's own opinions and habits through wars, reversals of fortune and revolutions. The skill of remembering at all times who one was and where one came from rather than bothering, as modern people did, with trying to guess where one was headed.

'Prudencia,' said the old lady, 'maybe we should go and visit Eugenia. Women like her often don't know how to react to such changes. I wouldn't want that swine to make a fool of her again.'

Miss Prim agreed that the possibility of Eugenia Mott being made a fool of again was something to consider, and she gladly accepted the old lady's suggestion. They both rose, leaving aside their respective tasks, and prepared to go out into the cold winter afternoon, with the maid as their chauffeur.

Eugenia Mott's house was on the outskirts of San Ireneo. It was a small stone building with white window frames and a small front door, and shutters in bright red that stood out like brushstrokes in an oil painting. Clumps of beautiful late chrysanthemums lent the house the old-fashioned charm typical of most of the homes in San Ireneo. As they approached,

Miss Prim was lost in thought when a line unexpectedly came to mind:

What beauty will save the world?

Who had said that? It must have been a Russian; it sounded just like the kind of thing a Russian would say. It definitely wasn't obscure, she was sure she'd read it and heard it on countless occasions and in different forms, but she couldn't remember the author. As she watched the maid struggle with the latch on the garden gate, it occurred to her that the Man in the Wingchair would probably know.

'The front door's open, madam. Should we go in?'

'Of course we should. The poor woman must be in the arms of grief,' replied the old lady firmly, pushing the door open and stepping into the narrow hall.

'*What beauty will save the world?*' the librarian repeated to herself as she followed the old lady to the door of Miss Mott's living room. The Man in the Wingchair would know the quotation; she'd ask him as soon as she got back to the house.

'For the love of God, Eugenia!'

Startled by the old lady's exclamation, Miss Prim peered over her shoulder into the room. There in the middle, Miss Mott could be seen sheltering in someone's arms. Arms that looked nothing like Prudencia's idea of the arms of grief, arms that were wrapped around her in a gesture of consolation.

'Hello, Mother, I'm glad you've arrived,' said the owner of the arms, gently detaching a tearful Miss Mott from around his neck.

Miss Prim was stunned to see Miss Mott in the arms of the Man in the Wingchair. Naturally, she wasn't alarmed; she wasn't a woman prone to alarm. Nor did she jump to conclusions; Eugenia Mott's age, together with her natural slow-wittedness, made even a glimmer of romance between the two parties inconceivable. But Miss Prim definitely felt *something*. It wasn't jealousy; Miss Prim was contemptuous of people who were tormented by jealousy. Nor was it repulsion; if she was honest with herself, there was nothing about the Man in the Wingchair that even remotely inspired repulsion. She would even allow that, aesthetically speaking, her employer was the kind of human being who was pleasing to the eye. Miss Prim wasn't ashamed of this opinion, nor did she draw any conclusions from it. Her deep-rooted appreciation of beauty led her to arrive at her opinion with just the same ease as she would about a swan or a horse.

So what was she feeling? The answer came to her as she silently observed his unhurried explanations and his mother's stiff attempts to console the afflicted Miss Mott: she felt *envy*. Envy of the middle-aged village schoolteacher? Miss Prim had to admit that it was so. It wasn't the fact of seeing Miss Mott in her employer's arms, but the display of attention and sensitivity that he had never shown *her*. The librarian was inwardly ashamed by the idea that anyone might read in her eyes what she was thinking. And also, for the first time, she wondered if the moment hadn't come to ask the ladies of San Ireneo to help her find a husband. After all, a reaction such as this could only be the product of what psychotherapists called transference. Maybe she did need a husband. Maybe she needed one urgently.

'Eugenia, I trust you're not going to say yes,' said the old lady sternly, drawing Miss Prim out of her marital fantasy.

'Mother . . . ' the Man in the Wingchair admonished.

'You think I shouldn't forgive him?' asked the teacher plaintively. 'Maybe I shouldn't, but I've dreamed so many times of him returning, and he seems so sorry.'

'Nonsense,' snapped the old lady. 'Of course he's sorry. When he left he was still young and full of life, and the world was exciting. Now he's reaching the age when we all realize it no longer is exciting.'

'Stop it, Mother, that's enough.'

'You think I should say no?' whimpered Eugenia Mott.

The Man in the Wingchair approached his mother before she could reply and said quietly but audibly: 'May I remind you it's her decision. It's not your life, or mine.'

'She has no experience of this sort of thing, nor do you. I know exactly how to resolve such a situation. She mustn't take him back. She mustn't let that man into her house ever again.'

'Why not?' he asked in a low, harsh tone that Miss Prim had never heard him use before. 'Because you didn't?'

The old lady gave her son such a terrible, icy look that Miss Prim thought the door must have blown open and let in a blast of cold air.

'How dare you!' the old lady hissed before rising from her seat, snatching her coat and rushing from the room, followed by her maid.

He didn't try to stop her, but once the door had closed he sank down onto the sofa and rested his forehead on his hands.

'It's all my fault,' moaned Miss Mott, anxiously twisting the belt of her dress. 'I should never have called you, I should never have involved you in all this. Now your mother's angry. I'm so stupid! I don't have any strength of character, I never had, but I shouldn't let my problems . . .'

'Please, Eugenia, don't worry. None of that is your fault, and in any case it's not important. Right now we have to discuss how to resolve this, what you want to do with your life and whether there's a place in it for your husband.'

At this, Prudencia cleared her throat quietly.

'Yes, Miss Prim?' he asked, raising his head and looking at her for the first time since she'd entered the room.

'Would you like me to go after your mother?'

'I'd be very grateful. I can't leave Miss Mott in this state, but I was a little abrupt with Mother. I'm sorry you had to witness it.'

Again she felt a pang of envy, a strange, inopportune envy combined in equal measure with something very like compassion.

'That's OK,' she replied, 'I'll go and talk to her.'

As she came out of the house she saw the old lady sitting with her maid on a bench beneath a camellia. Miss Prim approached slowly and sat down beside her. The maid slipped away to fetch the car. Once she'd gone, the old lady spoke.

'I expect you're wondering why my son said what he did, aren't you?'

'Definitely not,' she replied. 'It's a family matter.'

'It is indeed.'

'Although, since you've asked, there is one thing I don't understand.'

The old lady turned towards her, interested.

'Tell me, what don't you understand?'

'It's just that I'm surprised at your son mentioning something so personal in public. It's not like him.'

The elderly lady picked up a pale pink camellia blossom from the ground and began sorrowfully to pluck the petals.

'No, it isn't, but he couldn't help it.'

'Why not? I've never met anyone with his gift for avoiding discourtesy.'

'Why not? Because he blames me, my dear, and when a son blames his mother, much as he might want to avoid it, the feeling surfaces sooner or later.'

Miss Prim now picked up a flower herself and stared at it as she spun it round between her fingertips. It was beginning to grow dark and the air was becoming colder. All of a sudden, she removed her scarf and slipped it round the old lady's shoulders.

'People sometimes say things without thinking. They're not expressing what they feel but rather the tension of the moment, or even a desire to win the argument. I don't think your son was showing his grief or resentment when he said what he did; I think he simply wanted to put an end to the conversation.'

The old lady shivered in a gust of cold wind and then looked straight into the librarian's eyes.

'My dear Prudencia, there are times in life when we're all faced with a dilemma we'd rather not have to deal with. For each person the dilemma might come in a different guise, but in essence it's always the same. There's a sacrifice to be made, and you have to choose the victim: yourself or those around you.'

In her turn, Prudencia slowly began to strip the petals from the camellia flower.

'Of course, when your children are involved the decision shouldn't be difficult. They always come first. You live, you watch, you listen, play, teach, all the while thinking of them. But then one day the great dilemma arrives, the one that touches your heart, crushes your spirit, threatens your self-esteem. It turns up one day and presents you with a choice between two paths, each ending in sacrifice. If you take the right-hand path, you have to sacrifice yourself; if you take the left, it's your children who suffer. Are you following me?'

'Please, go on.'

'Put like that it sounds rather cold-blooded, doesn't it? You must be wondering how anyone could choose the left path and sacrifice their children. But it's not that simple, my dear, because when you decide to take the second path you never allow yourself to see reality as it is, without excuses. You tell yourself that if you don't pursue your own happiness, they'll suffer too; that you have a right to be happy and you only get one life; that it'll be better for them, they're young, they'll get over it. But the truth is, you make a choice and there is always a price to pay.'

Miss Prim turned towards the old lady and took her cold hands in her own. For the first time she appeared hunched, small and fragile.

'I was faced with just such a dilemma, Prudencia. The details don't matter now. All you need to know is that I could have chosen the right-hand path. But I chose the left. That's the one I chose.'

Their conversation was interrupted by the sound of the horn as the maid pulled up to the house. As the two women rose and Miss Prim walked her companion to the car, tiny snowflakes started falling on the garden.

'You need to get home, you're frozen. I'll stay and wait for your son, don't worry.'

'I'm not worried, dear, I stopped worrying a long time ago,' she replied as Miss Prim helped her climb in.

Once the car had driven off, Prudencia went to join the Man in the Wingchair, who was taking his leave of a smiling, composed Miss Mott. As they walked to his car, she asked gently: 'So, has everything been sorted out?'

He took off his coat and placed it round his employee, who was silently grateful.

'Yes, all sorted out.'

'Is she going to take him back?'

'She is, as long as he meets certain terms, which he assures her he's prepared to do. I've spoken to him on the phone and I think he means it, but I want to see him in person and explain the plan to him more clearly.'

'The plan? There's a plan?'

'Of course there's a plan.'

'But you're not going to tell me what it is, are you?'

'Quite right.'

They walked on in silence. The paths of San Ireneo were becoming blurred under snow when he asked: 'Is she all right?'

Miss Prim searched for her words before replying.

'I think so, but she seems very sad. She believes you blame her for something that happened many years ago.'

The Man in the Wingchair was silent for a moment.

'I don't. I forgave her many years ago, when I was still a boy. It's she who blames herself, but she can't see that. It's easier to project blame into the eyes of others and defend yourself against that than to find it within yourself, where there's no possible defence.'

'But you said something very harsh to her this afternoon. I was staggered that you could say such a thing in front of everyone.'

While her employer took out his keys and unlocked the car, she wondered if she had said too much. Once he'd started the engine and switched the heating on full blast, he turned to her and spoke.

'My mother's problem is that she can't submit to any authority. She lost her parents years ago, and she lost her husband. She takes no account of her relatives' views – she never has – and especially not her children's. There's no human or spiritual discipline to which she'll subject her will. She just has her own opinions, and they're the only tribunal that's permitted to judge her when she makes a mistake. Can you imagine what you would be like if you didn't have anyone close who was capable of influencing you? Anyone to point out your flaws, to confront you when you went too far, to correct you when you did something wrong?'

Miss Prim said that she certainly couldn't imagine.

'My mother doesn't have the blessing of someone to tell her what she absolutely doesn't want to hear. This evening she was about to make a mistake and a weak, innocent person would have paid for it. I couldn't let it happen, that's all. There's no bitterness or blame or accusation whatsoever in it. Quite the contrary: I love my mother deeply, believe me.'

Miss Prim again experienced the envy that had lingered all afternoon. They were almost back at the house when she remembered that there was something she wanted to ask him.

'*What beauty will save the world?*' she murmured.

He peered at her through the gloom inside the car.

'Dostoyevsky, Prudencia? Dostoyevsky? If I were you, I'd start worrying.'

Miss Prim, snugly wrapped in her employer's coat, gave a happy grin, unseen in the darkness.

4

*I*n the following weeks, the inhabitants of San Ireneo gradually learnt the details of the plan that would turn Miss Mott's husband into a resident spouse. As the mystery plan was revealed, enthusiasm spread throughout the village. The solution negotiated by the Man in the Wingchair and approved by both husband and wife was designed to ensure that San Ireneo's teacher overcame the major and most serious obstacle to restoring her marriage: loss of trust. Two conditions were considered essential to achieving this objective. The first, to find a job for the penitent Mr Mott; the second, that the job should enable his wife to feel secure and not fear that he would leave again. How was this to be achieved? The answer surprised Miss Prim in its simplicity. San Ireneo de Arnois didn't have a newsagent's; there was nowhere to buy newspapers, magazines, children's books, newspaper supplements, part-works, picture cards, colouring pencils or penny sweets. And the right place for it was the village square, close to all the main businesses and a stone's throw from the school.

At first, Prudencia didn't grasp the key to the plan. She agreed that a decent job was essential for any man, especially a profoundly repentant man who wanted to rebuild his life, but she couldn't comprehend why a simple newsagent's was so important to the success of the undertaking. Hortensia Oeillet enlightened her.

'It's so she can *see* him, Prudencia, don't you understand? He's only a few yards from the school. All she has to do is look out of the window and there he is, right in front of her, selling the *San Ireneo Gazette*, thrillers, sweets and sewing patterns. Isn't it perfect?'

Miss Prim did not agree. She thought it undignified for a man to be cooped up within four walls just so that his wife could keep tabs on him. She thought it unhealthy for a wife to be confident her husband would not run away perhaps only because it was impossible for him to do so. She thought it inappropriate that a married couple should have their private business on display in the village square in front of all their neighbours. Soon, however, she changed her mind. As the days passed, it became apparent to the residents of San Ireneo that a current of love had begun to flow between the newsagent's and the school. It didn't escape anyone's notice that Mr Mott's smiles to his customers became distracted whenever his wife appeared at the window or came out into the garden. Nor could anyone fail to observe the teacher's new hairstyle, her increasingly close-fitting dresses, or that she had exchanged her comfortable rubber-soled boots for dainty, high-heeled shoes. Thus married love bloomed in San Ireneo before everyone's eyes, enfolded by the cold, sunny days that preceded Christmas in the region.

This was what was in the air when Miss Prim reaffirmed her decision to place her marital future in the hands of the ladies of the village.

'My dear, are you sure?' asked Hortensia Oeillet the morning she told her of her intentions over a cup of tea at the back of the flower shop.

'Not really. Who could be? But if I haven't met the right man before now, perhaps it's due to negligence on my part.'

'Oh, but it's not your fault. That's not how it works,' objected Emma Giovanacci, who had also been invited to have tea.

'Emma's right, Prudencia, it's not a matter of negligence, not entirely anyway. It's more like ... have you read *The Purloined Letter* by Edgar Allan Poe?'

'Again? Don't tell me that story is relevant to falling in love as well? You all apply it to everything. I don't understand what's going on in this place.'

'To everything? I'm not sure what you mean,' said the florist, surprised, 'but what I do know is that it perfectly describes the discovery of love. Isn't that right, Emma?'

Her friend hastened to confirm this. She herself had observed the truth of Hortensia's statement. Two years after her first husband died, she had become friendly with one of his old colleagues, a quiet, affable man called Edmundo Giovanacci, and had had coffee with him occasionally.

'It was many years ago. I was still young and hadn't yet moved to San Ireneo. I was busy carving out a future for myself. I had to work hard because my first husband, God forgive him, had squandered all our money behind my back. Edmundo knew how draining it had all been, and that I barely wanted to go on living. He would simply take me somewhere nice and order two cups of coffee. And it's what he did week after week for eight years.'

'Eight years? That's such a long time,' said Miss Prim.

'Of course it's a long time. Emma's always been a bit lazy,' laughed Hortensia, giving her friend a humorous pinch.

'The truth is, I've never liked change,' replied Emma Giovanacci, bristling slightly. 'That's why I live here.'

The florist cut each of her guests a large slice of apple tart and then filled their cups with steaming hot China tea.

'But in the end you changed, did you?' asked the librarian.

'Oh yes, I had no choice.'

'Why not? Did he give you an ultimatum?'

'Not exactly. Edmundo moved here to San Ireneo, and eventually I came after him. Don't imagine it happened instantly – in real life things rarely happen instantly. I hadn't seen him for weeks. Then one day I woke up and realized that something was missing from my life, something seemingly tiny but actually hugely important. The coffees, the chats, the walks, the pleasant afternoon outings were missing. It sounds silly but, as you grow older, it's the little things that matter.'

Miss Prim sipped her tea and nestled down into the storeroom armchair. She too believed in the value of the little things. Her first coffee in the morning drunk from her Limoges porcelain cup. Sunlight filtering through the shutters of her room, casting shadows on the floor. Dozing off over a book on a summer's afternoon. The look in the children's eyes when they told you about some fact they'd just learnt. It was from the little things that the big ones were made, it definitely was. And suddenly she thought of Starets Ambrose and the turkeys.

'It's like a detective novel, Prudencia. Just like one,' the florist was saying.

'What do you mean?'

'Love, I mean love. It already exists, you can be sure. You just have to find out where, follow the trail, investigate. Exactly like a detective.'

Miss Prim laughed and replied: 'But that's ridiculous. What you're telling me is that a candidate – the Candidate – already exists and I just have to find out who he is, is that right?'

The other two women smiled indulgently and said it was.

'Well, I've never heard such a thing before, but let's assume for a moment that it is so, just for a moment. How can I find him? What are the clues?'

'Ah, the clues. There's only one clue. Only one,' said Hortensia.

Prudencia gathered her hair at the nape of her neck and drew her chair closer.

'And that is . . . ?' she asked.

'Harmony, of course. The Ancient Greeks' ἁρμονία, the Romans' *harmonia*. Herminia would explain it better, she knows so much about this sort of thing . . . Well, how to express it? I think the classical definition refers to balance in the proportions of parts of a whole. As in the sculpture of a beautiful face or body, in the manner in which you arrange flowers in a vase, combining them in ten different ways until you achieve something that satisfies your soul. As a highly qualified woman, you no doubt know that harmony comes from the Greek ἁρμόζω, which means "to fit together", "to connect". That's the definitive clue, dear, the one that'll help you solve your detective story.'

Miss Prim considered this as she took a bite of apple tart.

'But wouldn't it be boring? Wouldn't it be monotonous to be married to harmony?'

The two friends gazed at her benevolently.

'I don't think we've explained it very well, Prudencia,' said Hortensia. 'It's not the husband who has to be the source of harmony. It's not in him that you have to seek harmony. No, it's in the marriage, in the combination of the two of you, that you've got to look for it.'

'And not just that,' said her friend, 'but in routine as well, especially in routine. Isn't that so?'

'Definitely. Of course, in this, poor Balzac got it completely wrong. He really knew nothing about it,' said the florist, refilling the teapot.

'Balzac?' asked Miss Prim, a little confused.

'It's strange that the people who spit the most caustic words over marriage are precisely the ones who know least about it. All his life pursuing it, yearning for it ... and for what? To get it at the end when he was ill and without hope. A dreadful woman, that Madame Hanska. She's always seemed like the worst of our sex. So, tell me, how could he know anything about marriage?'

'But what did Balzac say about marriage?' insisted the librarian.

'He said that marriage always has to battle against a dark monster,' said Emma with a wink.

'He was referring to routine,' added her friend.

'And doesn't it?'

'Absolutely not. Not only is this not true but it's the biggest lie in the world, Prudencia. The cause of much suffering, believe me.'

Emma Giovanacci cleared her throat quietly and moved her chair closer to the table before speaking.

'Have you ever seen the flowers that grow on the Russian steppe?'

Miss Prim replied that, regrettably, she had never visited the Russian steppe.

'Well, you should. The Kalmyk steppe, near Stalingrad, is a bleak place, arid and featureless. If you go there in winter, it's devastating to the soul. But try going in spring and see what you find.'

Prudencia raised her eyebrows expectantly.

'Tulips,' whispered Emma Giovanacci.

'Tulips?'

'Tulips. Fresh, delicate, wild tulips. Tulips that come up every year and cover the steppe, without anyone planting them. And that's exactly what it's about, Prudencia. Routine is like the steppe: it's not a monster, it's nourishment. If you can get something to grow there you can be sure that it will be real and strong. It's the little everyday things that we mentioned earlier. But poor Balzac with all his dark, romantic sentimentality couldn't know that, could he?'

'The little everyday things,' echoed Miss Prim. 'Well, let's suppose I follow your advice. Can you help me with the investigation? Or do I have to do it all on my own?'

The other two women looked at each other, amused. Then the florist spoke.

'The investigation is up to you. We can only provide a little guidance. To start with, you could draw up a list of all the men you know who, objectively, possess the minimum qualities for a potential husband. We'll add a few more names to the list – there are always possible candidates who go unnoticed and, in that respect, due to our age, we've got more experience than you. You can use it as a starting point. How does that sound?'

Miss Prim, who had begun to feel a fizzing excitement at the idea of solving this old-fashioned detective mystery, assured her that it sounded good, wonderfully good.

The first name that came to Miss Prim's mind was that of her former employer, Augusto Oliver. Though her initial reaction was a shudder, she was forced to concede that if this was all about applying a scientific method of investigation, she couldn't make a list of possible husbands without including him. Had he ever wanted to marry her? Miss Prim maintained that he had not. Augusto Oliver was the kind of man who enjoyed making promises he had no intention of keeping. For three long years he had claimed to be sympathetic to his employee's wish for more reasonable working hours – Miss Prim worked from ten till ten – and had promised again and again to do all he could to change them. But it became apparent that this was the last thing on his mind. Mr Oliver liked to be alone with his most efficient employee at the end of their working day. He would emerge from his office and come to stand behind her, pretending to read over her shoulder. Sometimes, when he'd been at a business lunch and had had a little too much to drink, he'd come right up close and lean over so that he was almost whispering in her ear, making Miss Prim recoil. He was an attractive man, or at least he would have been if his manner had not been so overbearing.

Very soon, what had begun as a minor nuisance, the kind any female employee experiences when her boss is attracted to her, ended up becoming untenable. Compliments were followed by invitations on dates, and invitations on dates – always politely refused – eventually led to tensions between them. Would things have been different if she had ever agreed to go out with him? It was difficult to say. Would employer and employee have married if Miss Prim had replied in the affirmative to the ridiculous proposal he made her on the day she announced she was leaving?

'So was the swine really in love with you?' asked the mother of the Man in the Wingchair, who had listened attentively to the librarian's musings as they unpacked Christmas decorations from large white cardboard boxes.

'Of course not. It was his hunting instinct, the kind that makes a cat toy with a mouse, even if it isn't hungry. No, I don't think he wanted to marry me. He just wanted to win the chase, that's all.'

Thoughtfully, the Man in the Wingchair's mother unrolled a bright crimson velvet ribbon.

'Was he attractive?'

'I suppose so.'

'Intelligent?'

'Not especially.' Miss Prim thought fleetingly of the Man in the Wingchair.

'Honest?'

'Just enough.'

'Amusing?'

'In his own way.'

'And in yours?'

'I'm afraid not.'

'Did he have money?'

'Lots.'

'Then you can cross him off,' said the old lady firmly. 'A man who's not completely honest can keep within the bounds of decency if he's lucky enough to be unattractive and of slender means. But add money and good looks, and the road to ruin is clearly signposted.'

The librarian nodded and scored through the first name on the list.

'Come, my dear, let's not waste time. Who's next?'

The next one, Miss Prim explained nostalgically, had been her great love for several years, the first man she had fallen in love with and the first to have loved her. At the time, he was just a quiet young teacher, devoted to Husserl, amateur fencing and the instruction of German.

'I don't recommend this one. I know the type. Do you really think you could feel fond of him again?' asked the Man in the Wingchair's mother scornfully.

Miss Prim was sure she couldn't, though she had to admit she'd wondered about him more than once.

'Why did it end?' asked the old lady.

'I suppose because what we felt for each other wasn't love,' replied the librarian, weighing a Christmas star in her hand.

'And how do you know that?'

'Because I thought more of my own well-being than of his. And I think he, in his way, did the same.'

'Such altruism! You're starting to sound like my son,' said the old lady sardonically.

Miss Prim blushed but did not reply.

'So do we dispose of the disciple of Husserl as well?'

'We do.'

The old lady's maid entered the library with the tea tray and went around the room turning on the lamps, closing the heavy curtains and stoking the fire. Her silent, methodical movements passed almost unnoticed by the other two women, who were absorbed in unpacking fragile Nativity figures and conjuring further ghosts of men from the past.

'I think I should cross out these three,' said Miss Prim pensively once the door had closed behind the maid.

'I think so too, Prudencia. The fact that you refer to them as "these three", lumping them together, should give you a clue. Trust me, no woman should marry a man she sees as part of a group; it doesn't bode well.'

Miss Prim laughed wholeheartedly, admitting that none of the three men was at all likely to be a potential husband, and crossed off their names. When she reached the sixth name on the list she saw that it was one of those added by Hortensia and Emma.

'The vet?' Miss Prim burst out laughing once again. 'The vet? What possessed them to include him?'

'As far as I know it was Herminia's suggestion. She claimed to notice some interest on your part the day you met him.'

The librarian recalled her flirting at the tearoom and again blushed. Couldn't you do anything here without all the neighbours knowing? Admittedly she had found the young vet attractive, but from that to its being the talk of the village was quite a leap. True, she had smiled at him, paid him attention and tried, unsuccessfully, to charm him, but wasn't that every woman's prerogative without it becoming the subject of public discussion? And anyway, what none of the ladies of San Ireneo knew was that part of the vet's allure that afternoon had sprung from her rage at the Man in the Wingchair. Would she have noticed the vet if she hadn't been absolutely furious over her employer's discourteous behaviour? Would she have smiled as much? Miss Prim knew the answer perfectly well.

'Don't you want to give him a chance?' asked the old lady curiously. 'I know Hortensia well enough to sense she'd be happy to arrange a date and even make the poor man think that it was his own idea.'

'I'm pretty sure the poor man, as you call him, won't want to have anything to do with a woman who believes that a love of animals isn't real love. I think I said the wrong thing the day Hortensia introduced us. I'm afraid I offended him.'

The Man in the Wingchair's mother peered at her in surprise over her glasses.

'Offended him? For the love of God, what is the matter with men nowadays? In my husband's day, my father's, my brothers', the idea that a man might be offended by a bit of idle chat with a woman would have been thought ridiculous. A man who feels wounded by a conversation in a tearoom is simply a wimp. I can't imagine what you saw in him.'

Miss Prim said nothing as she went on carefully unwrapping the figures that decorated the living room every December.

'These are wonderful,' she said with admiration.

'They're over four centuries old. They were made by Irish monks. My husband, who had no sisters, inherited them from his mother, who inherited them from her mother, and so on for several generations. I was going to leave them to my daughter, but that wasn't to be. They'll go to Teseris, of course,' she said with sadness in her voice.

Miss Prim kept a respectful silence.

'So what about the wounded vet?' asked the old lady, making an effort to emerge from her introspection. 'Would you go out with him?'

'Maybe. It would depend how he asked,' she replied,

smiling. 'Let's see, there are two more names here and . . . a question mark. What does that mean?'

The Man in the Wingchair's mother cleared her throat and suddenly appeared intensely interested in the Christmas decorations.

'It must be a mistake. There's no name, just a question mark,' murmured Miss Prim.

'I don't think it's a mistake. I'd say our dear Hortensia and Emma know exactly what they are doing,' said the old lady with a wry grin.

'What do you mean? Who does the question mark stand for? Is it an actual man?'

'You do have an outlandish turn of phrase sometimes, Prudencia. Is there such a thing as a man in the abstract? At least, one whom you can go out with?'

Miss Prim did not reply.

'Of course the question mark stands for a specific man. Our two ladies obviously know of a prospective husband whom you haven't yet identified.'

'Do you mean I haven't met him yet?'

'Why would they bother to conceal his identity with a question mark if you hadn't met him? Of course you know him, my dear, that's the point – to hide from you a man you haven't yet considered as a candidate, or maybe are refusing to consider. Can you think of any man who fits that description?' asked the old lady, looking inquiringly into her eyes.

Miss Prim lowered her gaze and began nervously rummaging through the box of Nativity figures, eventually pulling out a little shepherd carrying a sheep.

'Would you mind handling those figures a little less energetically,' said the old lady coldly. 'A husband may last a lifetime, but those figures have survived several lifetimes. And I'd be grateful if they could continue to do so.'

5

The *San Ireneo Gazette* occupied one of the few office blocks in the village, if that's what you could call the old three-storey stone and timber building. It was so narrow that the staircase took up almost half of each floor. Like all the commercial establishments in San Ireneo, it had a neat metal sign and a small garden, but everyone agreed that its most valuable asset was, without a doubt, its editor. Miss Prim arrived at the appointed time in the early afternoon carrying a tray of freshly baked cakes. After almost three months in the village, she knew that tea, coffee or hot chocolate, fine pastries and a good liqueur were essential to any social gathering there.

'It surprised me too at first, but I've come to see it as a mark of civilization,' said Herminia Treaumont after thanking the librarian for her edible gift and inviting her to look around the tiny newspaper premises.

'Really? It seems like a relic to me,' said Miss Prim. 'Who has time nowadays for these leisurely teas?'

The editor of the *Gazette* showed her the antique rotary press on which the newspaper's four hundred copies were printed daily.

'What a beautiful thing! So it still works?'

'Of course it does. It's a relic, as you would say, but the concept of memory is inherent to civilization. Primitive peoples perpetuate barely more than a handful of traditions. They can't capture their history in writing. They have no sense of permanence.'

'That can apply to tea, macaroons and pastries.'

'And to conversation too, of course. We modern primitives also have our limitations. We no longer find the time to sit around a table and chat about the human and the divine. And not only do we not find the time, we don't even know how to any more.'

Miss Prim examined a copy of that evening's paper.

'What you mean, Herminia, is that traditions are a bulwark against the decline of culture, is that it?' she asked. 'I quite agree, but I would never have thought of extending that to the mountains of cake consumed at social gatherings in San Ireneo.'

They laughed as they entered Herminia's office, which was screened off from the minuscule editorial department behind a glass partition. Two paces from a desk piled with books and papers, there was a tea table spread with an immaculate cloth upon which were set out a tray of cupcakes and macaroons, a pot of hot chocolate, a jug of cream and a bowl of fruit.

'You're an extremely civilized woman,' said Miss Prim with a smile. 'Tell me, what do you report on around here? Is there any news in San Ireneo? Or do you make it up?'

'Of course there's news in San Ireneo,' replied her hostess. 'Wherever there's a group of human beings there's news. What constitutes news and the criteria you use to establish that is another matter. This is a newspaper in the old tradition, Prudencia. We don't only report small events in the community – above all, we are a forum for debate.'

'Really? Who takes part? And what do you debate?'

'We all take part. We debate anything and everything: politics, economics, art, education, literature, religion . . . Are you surprised? Look around you, at your own life, your relationships. Isn't life a continual debate?'

For a moment Miss Prim thought of herself in the library telling the Man in the Wingchair about the clamour in her head. Then she recalled discussing marriage with Hortensia Oeillet, feminism with the ladies of the Feminist League, education with her employer's mother, fairy tales with the children of the house. Yes, in a way, life was indeed a continual debate.

'From time to time – about once or twice a month, in

fact – we organize public debates at our Socratic Club and then we publish them.'

Prudencia took a macaroon and nibbled at it.

'What's a Socratic Club? Do you mean a debating society?'

'You can't imagine how popular it is. People come from all around. Sometimes it's not a live debate but happens in instalments. One day someone publishes an article, a second person responds, then a third writes something, a fourth, even a fifth, and we all watch the cut and thrust.'

Miss Prim asked if her employer joined in.

'Of course he does. And he often wins.'

The librarian replied that this didn't surprise her in the slightest.

'Well, I doubt he's ever used all his ammunition against you. Watching him in discussion with Horacio Delàs is quite a spectacle.'

'Horacio is a charming man,' said Miss Prim.

'I'm delighted you've noticed.'

The librarian regarded her hostess with interest. The editor of the *San Ireneo Gazette* had the indefinable charm of someone who said little but thought much. Miss Prim had always felt that such people were at a marked advantage. They never said anything tactless, never spouted nonsense, never had cause to regret their words or justify themselves. She had always tried to behave like this, tried not to say anything that might hurt other people or herself, but it wasn't easy. Herminia Treaumont was a master of the art. Reluctantly, she could now see what the Man in the Wingchair had meant when he'd said Herminia was attractive.

'I'm concerned about the two girls,' Miss Prim said suddenly, remembering something she'd wanted to raise for some time.

The editor looked at her, taken aback.

'What do you mean?'

'I mean their education. Not their religious beliefs – that's far too extraordinary a matter for me to engage with. I'm talking about delicacy.'

'You think they're being brought up without delicacy? Their uncle is a gentleman, a wonderfully sensitive and courteous man. I can testify to that.'

Miss Prim felt a slight discomfort in her stomach that made her wonder if the cakes were as fresh as they might be.

'I don't doubt that he possesses those qualities, but you've said it: he's a man. He's immersing those girls in Ancient Greek and Latin, medieval literature and Renaissance poetry, Baroque painting and sculpture.'

'It's funny you should say that, because he detests the Baroque. I myself find it wonderful,' said Herminia Treaumont, taking a piece of fruit from the bowl.

Miss Prim searched for the right words. Had she been one of those people who said little but thought much, she'd have found them, but she wasn't. And as she wasn't, the best option was probably to be direct.

'There's no sign of *Little Women* in the house.'

'*Little Women*?'

'*Little Women.*'

'But that's impossible. I can't believe it.'

Prudencia smiled with relief. For a moment she'd feared that Herminia Treaumont was one of those uncouth souls who didn't appreciate that a well-used copy of *Little Women* was essential to an education.

'You must be mistaken, Prudencia. There must be a separate library for the girls. I can't believe you haven't realized that. As far as I know, Eksi's already read Jane Austen.'

'That's true, but Jane Austen is Jane Austen. Even he couldn't ignore her, she's too important. Though I have to say, the only time I've heard him mention her it was to criticize Mr Darcy.'

Herminia offered another cup of hot chocolate to Miss Prim and poured one for herself.

'All the men I know are critical of Mr Darcy. They find him annoying and arrogant.'

'Why?' asked Miss Prim, intrigued.

'I suppose it's because they realize they seem rather lacklustre by comparison.'

Miss Prim said nothing, remembering the conversation in the kitchen.

'We'll have to have a word with him about it,' said her hostess.

'In my humble opinion, *Little Women* is hugely important,'

she insisted. 'I've always believed that a girl's childhood is like a wasteland without that book.'

'I agree.'

They both fell silent. One of the newspaper's contributors knocked at the door. Herminia dispensed some brief, precise instructions before closing the door and sitting down again with her guest.

'Let me tell you something, Prudencia. Those girls are receiving an exceptional education, academically quite unique. In fairness, I ought to make that clear.'

Miss Prim drew her chair closer to the table and spoke firmly.

'No education is complete without visiting that little corner of Concord. I'm sure its literary merit doesn't stand up next to many other books but, as we both know, this is not what it's about. It's about beauty, delicacy, security. When they grow up and life treats them badly – as it certainly will – they'll always be able to look back and take refuge for a few hours in that familiar sentimental story.

'They'll get back from work, stressed by the traffic, aching with tension and problems and there, in their minds, they'll be able to open a door into the parlour of Orchard House with its rather cloying, puritanical transcendentalism, its piano, cheerful fire and blessed Christmas tree.'

'I always wanted to be like Jo,' murmured Herminia nostalgically.

'Best I don't tell you who I wanted to be.'

'Why not?'

'Because it shows the kind of childhood I had.'

'Come on, Prudencia, tell me. Meg?'

'No.'

'Amy?'

'No.'

'Not poor Beth?'

'No.'

'Surely not Aunt March?'

'No, not Aunt March. Mrs March.'

'Mrs March? Really? Why?'

Miss Prim pondered a moment. It had something to do with the personality of her own mother, a sensitive, artistic woman but quite unlike the mother of the March girls. She bore not the slightest resemblance to the strong and steady, sweet and understanding woman in the novel. The librarian had often thought that if she had to choose an adjective to describe her mother it would be *consolable*.

'Consolable?'

'My mother's always been a highly dramatic person. She's the kind of woman who demands emotional support even when misfortune befalls others, not her. When my father lost his job a few years ago, it was she who shut herself up for days crying and wailing. He sat alone, quietly, in the living room, head bowed. When I lost my university scholarship she wouldn't come to the dinner table for two weeks. It was the same when my older sister's husband left her. Virginia couldn't cry because beside her she had a woman in sackcloth and ashes, bemoaning her misfortune.'

Herminia placed her hands over Miss Prim's.

'I'm so sorry, Prudencia. But why Mrs March? Wouldn't it have been more logical to identify with one of the daughters?'

Miss Prim squeezed her hostess's hands.

'I've always been a realistic woman, Herminia, and realistic women were once realistic little girls. I was very young when I read the book. At the time I didn't like my mother, but I knew I had one. I couldn't pretend I didn't have one, but I could imagine the kind of mother I'd be when I grew up. And that mother was Marmee.'

The editor of the San Ireneo newspaper stood up, went to her bookshelves and took down a small brown volume with its title embossed in gold letters on the spine.

'I'm sure there's a reasonable explanation for all of this,' she sighed.

'There is,' said Miss Prim. 'There's no woman in the house. None at all.'

After reflecting for a moment, Herminia approached Prudencia and resolutely held out to her the book, an 1893 edition of *Little Women*.

'You say there's no woman in the house? I think there is, Prudencia. Now there is.'

*

Miss Prim had just left Herminia Treaumont at the newspaper office when she heard a pleasant, familiar voice behind her.

'Prudencia, I've been meaning to call you for days. How are you? It seems incredible in a place as small as this, but I'd completely lost track of you.'

She turned to find a smiling Horacio Delàs, dressed in a red scarf and shabby navy-blue coat and loaded down with parcels.

'I was expecting you to kiss my hand, Horacio, but I see that's not possible,' she joked.

He bowed courteously, indicating all the parcels with a nod of his head.

'I'd like nothing more than to kiss your hand, my dear, and would do so if I weren't burdened with a terrible chore.'

'Chore?'

'What would you call the task of buying useless gifts for fifteen children and a dozen adults?'

Miss Prim smiled. She found the man very likeable. There was something in his manner, something warm and reassuring, that made her feel very much at ease.

'A skill, maybe?'

'Skill? Wait until you see your present before being so generous.'

'You haven't bought me one too, have you?' she asked, touched.

'Of course I have. You wouldn't expect us to leave you out

at Christmas, as if you'd been a naughty child? Don't be surprised if you receive a number of presents. I know for a fact that you've become very popular in this funny little community of ours.'

Miss Prim shivered, with pleasure rather than from the cold, in her soft cashmere coat.

'I'm sorry, Prudencia, I'm a swine keeping you outside in this cold. Why don't you come to the bookshop with me? I've got to buy something for that old monk who keeps himself hidden away from us in his cell.'

Miss Prim said she'd be delighted to spend some time shopping herself. The streets of San Ireneo were already adorned with Christmas decorations. Windows hung with garlands of holly and heather, lit candles, Nativity scenes and poinsettias drew passers-by into the shops. Inside, shopkeepers offered customers cups of tea and hot chocolate, biscuits, doughnuts and cupcakes dusted with sugar to look like snow.

'What are you thinking of buying him?' asked Miss Prim once they were in the bookshop.

'I'm a sentimental old man, you know,' sighed her friend. 'I went to see him at the abbey the other day and we talked about our childhoods. He told me about his schooldays, his mother's love, the catechism ...'

'You're going to buy him a catechism? Of the Council of Trent, I assume,' she interrupted with a smile.

Without a word, Horacio went to a shelf and withdrew a

small red book with a very worn cover. The librarian peered at the spine.

'Abbé Fleury?'

'The *Historical Catechism*, 1683, a first edition. A real gem.'

'Quite,' said a soft, polite voice behind them. 'You can't imagine how hard it was to get hold of. It only arrived from Edinburgh this morning.'

Miss Prim turned to see an extremely thin, severe-looking woman with mischievous, intelligent eyes.

'You must be the famous Prudencia Prim. Please, allow me to introduce myself: I'm Virginia Pille, San Ireneo's book-seller.'

'Delighted to meet you, Mrs Pille,' said Miss Prim, holding out her hand.

'Please, call me Virginia. Everybody does.'

'I think I should tell you, Prudencia, that you're talking to the most powerful woman in the village,' whispered Horacio.

The owner of the bookshop laughed, a clear and crystalline sound.

'Nonsense, Horacio, everyone knows that Herminia is the most powerful woman in San Ireneo. Not a leaf stirs in this village without her knowledge.'

'Maybe, but all the leaves that stir in this village belong to your books,' he said affectionately.

Virginia laughed happily again.

'You have a lovely bookshop,' said Prudencia, looking round. The old shelves were painted blue, charmingly rickety tables piled high with books bore penknife inscriptions, reading lamps were dotted about in corners and there was a vintage silver samovar on the counter.

'Thank you, I think so too. Can I offer you both a cup of tea?' asked the bookseller.

While she was making the tea, Miss Prim inhaled deeply and asked: 'Krasnodar?'

Virginia lifted her gaze and peered at her with curiosity.

'Yes. What a keen sense of smell! I have it picked, dried and packed for me specially. I have some good friends in old Russia.'

'In Sochi?'

'That's right. You know how it's prepared?'

Prudencia nodded with a smile, savouring the intense aroma of the tea as it pervaded the shop. She sat down at the small table behind the counter and contentedly admired the antique Meissen tea service and exquisitely mismatched silver teaspoons. For a woman like herself, she reflected, this was bliss.

'I'm afraid you ladies are too refined for me,' sighed Horacio. 'Please enlighten a poor man who's been drinking ordinary tea all his life.'

'As I understand it, in Sochi they pick only the top three leaves from the plant and discard the rest. It's the secret of the flavour,' explained Miss Prim.

'That, and the fact that it's only harvested from May to September. The climate does the rest,' added the bookseller.

Horacio took a sip of tea and warmly praised its quality. Then he indicated the ancient edition of the catechism. 'So, how difficult was it to get hold of?'

'For him, nothing could be too much trouble,' said the bookseller simply.

Miss Prim, who had been leafing through some children's books, turned to ask: 'What's so special about this monk? Why is he so popular?'

Virginia looked at her friend in mute interrogation.

'Doesn't she know him?'

He shook his head. Virginia looked down at the samovar lid, with which she was toying, before replying.

'The most obvious answer is that, together with the man who employs you, he founded this community.'

'And the less obvious answer?'

'That he's the only person I know who has one foot in this world and one foot in the other.'

Miss Prim started.

'You mean, he's dying?'

'Dying?' said Virginia, with another of her tinkling laughs. 'No, I hope not! Why would you think that?'

'Let's see if we can explain it without shocking you, Prudencia,' interjected Horacio. 'What Virginia means is that in this old Benedictine monk, Plato's allegory of the cave has been realized. He's the prisoner freed from the cave who returns here to the bleak world of shadows with the rest of us, after having seen the real world.'

San Ireneo's bookseller added quietly, looking at Miss Prim: 'Horacio phrases everything in his own poetic way, Prudencia, but it's really quite simple: our dear Father is a man who sees things the rest of us cannot.'

Hearing these words, Prudencia felt a wave of weary indignation wash over her. He could see things the others could not? It couldn't escape one's notice that there were more eccentrics in this village than seemed possible. On principle she mistrusted people who claimed to see the invisible. In the world she knew – a safe, clean, comfortable world – invisible things were invisible. If they couldn't be seen, they didn't exist. Of course, she had nothing against people seeking some kind of crutch to make life more bearable – spiritual beliefs, philosophies, children's stories, emotions, feelings, sensations – as long as it was clear that such things were unreal or, if they were real, they existed only in the mind or heart of whoever experienced them. In the real world, as she conceived it, everything could be captured or recorded in some way. Whether through poetry or art, literature or music, everything had to be capable of being translated into the visible world. Invisible things, she repeated to herself, only existed in the imagination. And then the image of dark, mysterious mirrors suddenly flashed through her mind.

'So you mean he's a mystic?' she asked coldly.

'If he is, he's too humble to admit it,' said Horacio,

signalling to the bookseller that she should pour him another cup of tea from the samovar. 'But I have to say that if *something* exists, and I speak as a sceptic, he's on strangely familiar terms with *it*, whatever *it* is.'

Miss Prim smiled smugly.

'And how do you deduce that? Is it something in his eyes? Does he have an aura around him?'

'It's not what one sees in his eyes,' said Virginia gently, 'as much as what he sees in the eyes of others.'

'You mean he can read your thoughts?' asked the librarian with a wry expression.

'We mean that he knows what you *are*.'

Miss Prim suddenly felt uneasy. She found the idea deeply troubling: an old man going around knowing what other people were. Not only troubling, but inappropriate. At best, it was a subtle, mysterious way of invading the privacy of others; at worst, it was gross deception. One way or another, there was something improper about it; improper and unpleasantly morbid. Miss Prim flatly refused to have someone know her essence. She refused both in principle and in practice.

'And I thought you were a man of science,' she said sadly.

'Ah, am I not?' her friend replied in mock surprise.

'You can't be, and at the same time believe that this man divines things.'

'Of course I can't. But that's not what I said. What I said was that "this man", as you call him, *knows* things.'

Virginia quietly began clearing the table.

'But isn't that one and the same?' insisted Miss Prim.

'Definitely not. I challenge you to go and talk to him some time.'

'I don't think I will, thank you.'

'Why not? Are you afraid?'

Prudencia looked peeved.

'Afraid? Of a poor, elderly monk?'

Horacio glanced at Virginia before replying.

'Tell me, Prudencia. Is there a black hole in that young life of yours? Something you have to live with but would like to be rid of? A stain on your conscience? A fear not dealt with? A rumble of despair?'

'And what if there is?' answered the librarian with her chin held high. 'We all have not just one, but many of those.'

'You're right, we all do. But what I'm trying to say is that he knows what they are. He knows what's in people's minds – he can read them like a book.'

'That's impossible.'

'Just go and see him. He may not say anything revelatory – he doesn't always. But whatever he says, it will hit the mark, I assure you.'

After paying for the book and thanking the bookseller for the tea and conversation, they left the shop and emerged onto the streets of San Ireneo, which were cold but aglow with Christmas lights.

'I still maintain that I'm surprised to hear all this from a man who isn't exactly gullible,' said Miss Prim.

Laden down with yet another parcel – Abbé Fleury's cat-echism – Horacio smiled affably.

'That's just it, Prudencia. My scepticism isn't of the Pyrrhonist sort, but scientific. I accept any premise that has empirical evidence to support it.'

'Really?' said the librarian. 'So is there empirical evidence for this faculty you've mentioned that lets the old monk know what one is?'

Her companion stopped and looked straight into her eyes.

'Is there empirical evidence? Of course there is.'

'And what is it, may I ask?'

Miss Prim guessed what Horacio was going to say a split second before he said it.

'The black holes in my own life, of course.'

6

News of Mr Mott's disappearance shattered the peace of San Ireneo with the abrupt violence of a punch in the solar plexus. Miss Prim heard about it at the butcher's. She was buying an enormous turkey which she intended to roast for Christmas dinner – behind the cook's back, though she wasn't quite sure yet how she would accomplish this.

'I never liked him,' declared the butcher. 'I said as much when I saw the way he served his customers. He always seemed to be looking past you, like a caged lion dying to escape. Poor Miss Mott, men like that never change.'

The librarian dashed out of the shop and ran to the schoolhouse. Reaching the front door, she stopped short, out of breath, not daring to ring the bell. She just stood, in silence, the huge turkey in her arms. Movements behind the net curtains, slow and furtive, raised her hopes that someone had seen she was there. A few minutes later the door opened and the Man in the Wingchair, looking grave, asked if she would like to come in.

'So he's gone?' she said, still breathless from running with the heavy turkey.

The classroom was deserted. There were no children, no overalls, or pencil boxes, or chalk at the blackboard, or maps, or wooden models for geometry. A shiver ran down the librarian's spine. Who had left? Mr or Mrs Mott?

'They've both gone,' said the Man in the Wingchair slowly as the two of them each sank into a diminutive classroom chair, 'but not together, I'm afraid. Maybe my mother was right, after all. I'm so sorry for Eugenia. She didn't deserve this.'

Miss Prim felt pity for the schoolteacher, though she still didn't understand what had gone on.

'Where has Miss Mott gone? What's happened?'

'Mr Mott has done it again. He didn't come home last night. He left her a note saying that he'd tried, but he felt trapped. She's packed her bags and gone to her sister's. I don't think she'll come back.'

The librarian looked at her employer sympathetically. She slid out of her seat and went to sit beside him.

'I think you're too intelligent to feel guilty.'

He looked up at her and smiled absently.

'I don't feel guilty, I feel responsible. Eugenia is a very

romantic, fragile woman. She's so sensitive. I should have been more cautious and given her better advice.'

On hearing the word 'sensitive', Miss Prim flinched.

'What's wrong with sensitivity?'

'Absolutely nothing. It's a wonderful quality, but it's not ideal for thinking.'

'Do you mean that we sensitive people don't know how to think?'

The Man in the Wingchair looked at her again, this time with curiosity.

'Ah, so we're talking about you, are we?'

Prudencia reddened and began to rise from her chair, but he stopped her.

'Of course we're not talking about me,' she said, head held high, 'it's just that I don't understand what sensitivity's got to do with imprudence, naivety or lack of judgement, which is what I think you mean when speaking about poor Miss Mott.'

'Sensitivity is a gift, Prudencia, I'm perfectly well aware of that. But it's not a suitable tool for guiding thought, when it can be disastrous. It's the same with ears and food. A wonderful organ, the ear. A miracle of design, intended down to its last cell to facilitate hearing, but try using it to eat with and see how you get on.'

She laughed, causing her companion to give a genuine smile for the first time.

'So you think that Eugenia Mott was trying to eat with her

ears and you weren't strong, or skilful, or responsible enough to tell her so? Is that it?'

'It doesn't sound very flattering, but I suppose that is it.'

After a few moments' reflection, Miss Prim suddenly rose and turned to face her employer.

'Well, let me tell you, you're incredibly arrogant.'

He looked up, shocked by this outburst and the triumphant grin on her face.

'Are you trying to start an argument?' he asked in disbelief. 'Because if you are, I have to warn you, this is the wrong day for it.'

'Not at all,' she replied. 'I'm just trying to help. You should know that the world doesn't run on your advice. It might seem strange, but that's the way it is. Yes, you may impress some and dazzle others with your learning and those good manners, even when you're being self-important, but don't delude yourself. The people around you listen but that doesn't mean they always do what you say.'

The Man in the Wingchair now looked confused. Taking advantage of this, she went on.

'There's no point denying it. This morning you got up convinced that Eugenia Mott's unhappiness was entirely down to you and your supposed irresponsibility. This not only places a huge, unwarranted burden on your shoulders but also shows an excessive regard for your own opinion, if you don't mind my saying so.'

'Would it make any difference if I did mind?'

Miss Prim paused, apparently pleased with the effect of her words. She realized she'd managed to change his mood. Miss Mott's plight was very sad and Miss Prim felt profoundly sorry. But she was sure that he had acted loyally and properly in advising the teacher as he had, and Miss Prim wasn't prepared to let him berate himself. Now he was slightly angry with her, but at least he no longer appeared dejected and his voice had recovered the beat of war drums that had so alarmed her when they'd first met. But this wasn't enough. She had to continue the attack. And she knew exactly how to do it.

'Why have you kept Louisa May Alcott out of Teseris' and Eksi's lives?' she demanded out of the blue.

'What?' His tone was quite different. 'Prudencia, what is the matter with you? Did you have enough breakfast?'

'Quite enough, thank you. So tell me, why?'

He stared at her for a moment in silence.

'If I weren't a gentleman, I'd take your temperature right now. What on earth are you talking about?'

'I'm talking about *Little Women*, of course.'

'*Little Women*? What the hell has *Little Women* got to do with it?'

The librarian cleared her throat, to buy herself some time.

'It's got nothing to do with it directly.'

He stared at her in growing disbelief.

'I'm waiting for you to explain.'

'Let me see,' Miss Prim summoned all her powers of improvisation and looked gravely at the Man in the Wingchair. 'In a way, we are what we read.'

'I'm sorry?'

'I'm saying that in a way we are the product of our reading.'

'Really? That's very interesting, and it gives me some ideas about you.'

She drew herself up, determined not to be browbeaten.

'We're not talking about me, we're talking about Miss Mott.'

'I was under the impression we were talking about Louisa May Alcott.'

'You don't see any connection between what's happened to Eugenia and what she's read, is that right?'

'That's right, I don't.' The Man in the Wingchair looked at the floor, a grin playing across his lips. 'Prudencia, if you're trying to distract me with a deliberately preposterous argument so that I stop regretting my part in Eugenia's misfortune, believe me I'm grateful. But don't try to make me accept this nonsense about our being what we read. It's not worthy of you.'

She began pacing around the classroom in an agitated fashion.

'I don't think it's nonsense. I can't speak for you, but for myself I can say that my personality has been moulded to a large extent by the books I've read. That's why,' she said, wringing her hands, 'it concerns me to find gaps in the girls' literary education. I'm not saying they're deliberate gaps – maybe I was too hasty – but they are gaps none the less. And they're no doubt due to the fact that, hard as you might try, you are not a woman.'

'Hard as I might try?'

Miss Prim made a face.

'What I mean is . . .'

'I know perfectly well what you mean. My dear Prudencia,' the Man in the Wingchair laughed as he noticed the turkey for the first time, 'if anyone's concerned about the role of literature in the children's lives, it's me. I've carefully chosen not only which books, but when and how they become part of my nieces' and nephews' existence.'

The librarian was about to speak, but he stopped her with a decisive glance.

'Despite the chaos you see in my library and in my house in general – the mess that bothers you so greatly – there's not so much as a single improvised comma in the children's education. Every book that passes through their hands has passed through mine first. It's no coincidence that they read Lewis Carroll before Dickens, and Dickens before Homer. There was nothing fortuitous in the fact that they learnt to rhyme with Robert Louis Stevenson before getting to Tennyson, and that they were introduced to Tennyson before Virgil. They met Snow White, Peter Rabbit and the Lost Boys before Oliver Twist, Gulliver and Robinson Crusoe, and those before Ulysses, Don Quixote, Faust and King Lear. They read things in that order because that's what I wanted. They're being brought up with good books so that later they can absorb great books. And, by the way, before you start expounding your annoying, cerebral educational theories, I know perfectly well that every child is different. That's why they set the pace, not me. But the rungs on the ladder they're climbing have been put there by me, using the experience accumulated over centuries by others before me. Others to whom I'm profoundly grateful.'

Miss Prim, who'd listened carefully, cleared her throat gently before speaking.

'And *Little Women*? Where does it fit into this plan? I'm sure it doesn't count as a great book, but I hope there's room for it in the good books category.'

'No, I have to admit that there isn't.'

'Oh, but why not?' cried the librarian. 'Can't you see that erudition is one thing and delicacy quite another? You know a great deal about literature, but you know nothing about femininity.'

'However hard I might try.'

'Don't take this as a joke, it's important. And, for your information, Herminia agrees with me. No one's claiming that Louisa May Alcott is Jane Austen, but then Robert Louis Stevenson isn't Dante.'

The Man in the Wingchair looked at her with interest.

'You know what surprises me about all this, Prudencia? I

look at you – a highly qualified, determined, modern woman – and I can't picture you reading *Little Women*.'

Miss Prim put her turned-up nose in the air with even more emphasis than usual.

'And why not, may I ask?'

'Because it's a prissy, syrupy book, and if there's one thing I hate it's cloying sentimentality. I'm delighted that you and Herminia recognize that Louisa May Alcott isn't Jane Austen, because she most definitely is not.'

'Have you read it?' she said. '*Little Women*, I mean.'

'No, I haven't read it,' he replied, unfazed.

'Then for once in your life, stop pontificating and read it before giving an opinion.'

He burst out laughing and looked at her with renewed interest.

'Are you telling me to read *Little Women*? Me?'

'Yes, you. The least you could do before condemning a book is read it, don't you think?'

'But what about Miss Mott? Have we already forgotten Miss Mott?'

The librarian pulled on her coat and gloves, picked up the turkey and, heading to the door, muttered: 'Of course we haven't forgotten Miss Mott. I bet you she hasn't read *Little Women*, either.'

The Christmas Eve dinner was a success, despite the unpleasant argument that preceded it involving reproaches, accusations and the threat of tears from the cook. Miss Prim managed to assert her authority with skill and courage. After all, she explained to the dragon who so jealously guarded the kitchen, Christmas was a congenial, family occasion, a time for sharing and celebration. And what better way to share and celebrate than to cook together? Thrown off course by Miss Prim's eloquence, the cook had given in at last, but not without pointing out that Christmas was far more than this. That was what she'd learnt, what her mother had taught her, and her mother before her; and that was what the old Father at the abbey had explained, and the master himself said the same. No, this was only a small part of Christmas, the least important, if she didn't mind her saying so.

'Of course I don't mind, Mrs Rouan, because it's the truth. And truth never changes, as you well know.' Drawn by the delicious smell of roasting turkey, the Man in the Wingchair had come sauntering into the kitchen, but at the sight of Miss Prim's dismayed expression he stopped in his tracks.

'I don't think this is a good evening for an argument,' he said, sensing the tension between the two women. Then, approaching the cook, he whispered in her ear: 'Let her do her cooking, Mrs Rouan, that turkey won't be a patch on your delicious roast beef, no doubt about it.'

Puffed up with pride, the cook didn't say another word, and instead applied herself to her soufflé while keeping an eye on the three types of cake baking in the old oven. An hour and a half later, the meal was ready. The children were rushing around in excitement at the prospect of bedtime being so much later than usual, the ancient family dinner service was laid on a spotless linen tablecloth and the guests – Horacio Delàs and Judge Bassett, who had come for dinner on that day for years – were settled comfortably in the sitting room. While Miss Prim was changing she could hear the commotion of everyone embracing, laughing, singing and exchanging Christmas greetings.

Half an hour later, seated at the immense dining-room table, as she let the lively conversation wash over her and smiled from time to time at the Man in the Wingchair, Miss Prim felt nostalgic, though she could not say exactly why. Along with the others, she listened in silence to the youngest child read from the Gospel according to St Luke. After dinner, she walked with them as, wrapped in coats and scarves and furnished with candles, they processed merrily through the freezing night air to Midnight Mass at the old abbey. But she left them there, at the doors to the ancient monastery, whose illuminated windows shone like a lighthouse out of the darkness.

'Are you sure you won't come in?' asked Horacio. 'You know I'm not a believer, but I attend out of respect and appreciation. Believe me, at least on an evening like this, it's worth it. The ancient Roman liturgy is incomparably beautiful.'

'Thank you, Horacio, but I'm very tired,' Prudencia replied politely, as she watched all the residents of San Ireneo arrive in groups, large and small, including numerous children muffled up to their eyebrows against the bone-chilling cold.

The stars were shining brightly in the sky as Miss Prim turned and headed back to the house. At a fork in the road, she stopped and looked at her watch. After a few moments' hesitation, she took the path that led to the village. The cheerful shop lights had been extinguished but the windows of the houses were softly lit, as if waiting for their occupants to return from the service, and they lent the streets a warm, welcoming air. She reached the main square and, with resolute steps, made her way to the old tearoom, which was still open. A wave of warmth greeted her as she opened the door. Inside, the tables and counter were deserted. It took her a moment to notice the woman sitting at the window, bent over a cup of tea with a book in her hand.

'I thought you were at the abbey with the others,' said Miss Prim.

The mother of the Man in the Wingchair looked up and gestured for the librarian to sit down.

'I never stay for the service. I find it too emotional. I walk all the way there with them but when we arrive, I tell the children that Grandmama would rather sit at the back. I've done it ever since they've been old enough to know what's what, but you know something?'

'This year it didn't work,' replied Miss Prim with a mischievous smile, removing her scarf and gloves and ordering a cup of hot chocolate.

The old lady looked at her, impressed.

'That's very perceptive.'

Miss Prim laughed and said that her perceptiveness was merely the fruit of a little experience.

'You can fool children for a time, but we adults mostly don't realize when the period of grace has expired.'

Her companion nodded thoughtfully.

'This evening I went with them as usual. I waited for them to settle in the family pew, but when I told them that Grandmama was going to sit at the back as she always did, they said something they've never said before.'

'Let me guess.'

'I don't think you'll be able to. "Wrap up well when you leave, Grandmama," they said. I've never been so astonished in my life. I didn't know how to respond, and just mumbled something quite incoherent. And then what could I do? I rushed out.'

Miss Prim smiled kindly. She knew it was the old lady's last evening at the house, just as she had known – or at least guessed – that she might find her at the tearoom. Following Eugenia Mott's marital disaster, the librarian and the mother of the Man in the Wingchair had barely spoken. Miss Prim's days had been busy with presents, Christmas cards, small errands and accumulating a backlog of work. She took a bite of lemon cake, observing her companion in silence. She'd come to appreciate the old lady, to appreciate and respect her. But since the day of their conversation beneath Eugenia Mott's camellia, the fragile trust they had established seemed to have evaporated. Miss Prim wondered whether the exchange of confidences had been a dream. Would she see the old lady again after this evening? She shivered. They would probably – or rather, definitely – never meet again.

'Do you remember telling me that it was the children who were responsible for your son's following the path you so disapprove of?'

'Of course I remember.'

Miss Prim paused to spread butter and jam onto a thick slice of toasted farmhouse bread.

'How did it happen?' she asked.

The mother of the Man in the Wingchair did not reply, busy buttering her own piece of toast.

'What I mean is,' continued the librarian, 'how was it possible? How could such young children bring about such an enormous and profound change?'

The old lady stopped eating and looked up.

'It was Teseris.'

'Teseris?'

'It was those amazing intuitions of hers. Has she told you about the Redemption being a *real* fairy tale? An exceptional insight for a little girl of ten, though she's not the first to come up with it. Others – Tolkien, for instance – did so before her. Have you ever spoken at length with my granddaughter?'

'Yes, of course,' replied Miss Prim.

'She's a strange child, isn't she?'

'Yes, she is. She's not like any child I've ever met. Sometimes it seems as if she's keeping some secret.'

Prudencia bit her lip. Despite her natural aversion to discussions of a metaphysical nature, she had to admit that the child gave the impression of inhabiting depths that were beyond anyone else's reach.

'My granddaughter has always been different.'

The old lady concentrated on stirring a lump of sugar into her tea.

'She's startlingly at ease with the supernatural. She has been since she was tiny. And what's most interesting is that for a long time she couldn't understand that the rest of us didn't feel the same.'

'Do you mean ...' Miss Prim swallowed. 'Do you mean that Teseris is some sort of child mystic? Surely not.'

With careful deliberation, the Man in the Wingchair's mother cut a second sliver of cake and placed it on Prudencia's plate, before helping herself.

'No, Prudencia, I'm not saying she's a mystic. I don't know what mystics are like but I'm sure they're nothing like her. But the fact is, I never suspected to what extent the supernatural touches the natural until I saw it reflected in her.'

Miss Prim, cake forgotten, was now staring fixedly at the old lady and remembering the day she arrived at the house.

'The first time I met Teseris she mentioned a mirror. I thought she must be talking about Alice and the looking glass.'

The old lady smiled gently.

'Teseris is well beyond Alice. *Videmus nunc per speculum in aenigmate*. Do you know any Latin? "For now we see through a glass, darkly, but then face to face. Later we'll see everything as it is, we'll know even as also we are known."'

Miss Prim quietly cleared her throat. Outside, snow was falling again.

'But if you believe in all of this, why didn't you stay with your family at the abbey this evening? Why keep that distance?'

She picked up her cup in both fine-boned hands and finished her tea. Then, with a severe look at the librarian, she said quietly, almost in a whisper: 'Because I can't. I'm not ready yet. I don't feel ready.'

'Not ready for what?'

The old lady smiled wryly. 'Not ready to lay down arms, my dear. To bow this proud old head and lay down arms.'

Part 3

Unravelling Skeins

1

he departure of the Man in the Wingchair's mother left an odd void in the house. Outside, the bitterly cold weather continued, with snow piling up on window ledges, blocking doors, freezing on tree branches. Inside, Miss Prim's work was progressing despite frequent interruptions from the children, who burned off their inexhaustible energy playing, running and hiding in the rooms, corridors and staircases of the house. The librarian spent her afternoons cataloguing heavy, dusty volumes, some with no more value than the fact of having been in the house for many lonely years; others were true survivors, brought long ago to San Ireneo by the family's forebears. Miss Prim liked these books. It moved her to think of them there, on those old shelves, bearing witness to the stealthy arrival of night and the dawning of each new day.

'I'm amazed that I've never once heard you sneeze, Prudencia. There's more dust on those books than any human could possibly endure.' The Man in the Wingchair came huffing and puffing into the library, bundled up in a scarf that nearly covered his face, a hat, thick coat and heavy snow boots.

'Is that really you under there?' asked the librarian jokingly.

'Laugh all you like, but it's fiendishly cold outside. You can't stay out in the garden for more than half an hour,' he replied, removing his scarf, hat, gloves and coat.

'You should take off those boots and put something warm on. Shall I ask for tea to be brought in?'

'Yes, if you would, I'd be really grateful. Damn, my hands are so cold I can't untie my laces,' he complained.

Miss Prim went over silently. She bent down, taking care not to kneel, and began undoing his bootlaces.

'That's very kind. Believe me, I appreciate the significance of the gesture,' he said with a smile.

'What do you mean by that?' she asked sharply, struggling to keep her balance and untie his right boot still without kneeling.

'That I think I can guess the symbolic resonance certain attitudes and gestures have for you.'

'If that were so, I wouldn't be doing this, would I?'

'Of course you would. Your Prussian sense of duty always triumphs.'

She pursed her lips and continued with her task.

'I think it's done.'

'Thanks,' he said gently.

Miss Prim went to fetch the tray that the cook had left on the hall table. Since their recent falling-out, the two women had tacitly agreed to avoid each other insofar as was possible. They greeted each other as they passed in the hall or came across each other in the kitchen or garden but, beyond this minimum of politeness, relations between them were as icy as the weather. The librarian was quite happy with this arrangement; after all, she was not part of the domestic staff. If she needed anything, she asked one of the three girls from the village who worked at the house as cleaners, maids of all work and ad hoc nannies. She didn't need to speak to the dragon at the stove; not at all.

And yet, she reflected as she set out the tea things on the table in front of the fire, she had to admit that Mrs Rouan was good at her job. Her cream puffs, wonderfully light cheesecake, delicious carrot cake and dainty sandwiches, arranged in four stacks of triangles, each with a different filling, were beyond compare. Her tea trays always featured China tea, creamy milk and slices of toasted home-baked bread, thickly spread with butter and honey. Miss Prim was compelled to concede that this was all very much to the cook's credit.

The Man in the Wingchair rubbed his hands together and observed in silence as Miss Prim performed the ritual of serving the tea. The house was unusually quiet as the children were in the greenhouse, watching the gardener take cuttings and lovingly tend the seedlings that would be planted out next year.

'The variety of books that has accumulated in this room is fascinating,' remarked the librarian. 'I've been playing a game, guessing which belonged to men and which to women.'

The Man in the Wingchair smiled, slowly stirring his tea.

'Not very difficult. I think it's pretty easy to identify what's aimed at women: just check the sex of the author. It's strange that men mostly write for both sexes, but women write for women. With a few honourable exceptions, of course.'

Miss Prim helped herself to a foie-gras sandwich and took a deep breath before turning to him.

'Women haven't always written for other women,' she retorted. 'It's a fairly recent sociological phenomenon. Until around a hundred years ago, it was as common for men to read female authors as male.'

'If less pleasurable,' said the Man in the Wingchair with a laugh.

The librarian put the sandwich down on her plate.

'Would you mind telling me what you're laughing at?' she asked frostily.

He looked at her with calm delight.

'At you, of course. Isn't that what I'm always doing?'

'And what's funny about me at this moment, may I ask?'

'The fact that you always have a psychosociological explanation for everything. You should learn to see the world as it is, Prudencia, not as you'd like it to be. You don't have to be very perceptive to see that a small boy will hugely enjoy reading *Treasure Island* but feel quite sick at the thought of—'

'*Little Women*, for instance?'

He nodded, smiling. 'Indeed, *Little Women*.'

'Incidentally,' Miss Prim raised her nose self-importantly, 'have you read it, finally? Or did you suddenly feel too sick to go through with it?'

The man drew his feet away from the fire, sat up straight in his chair and moved it closer to the table, leaning forward as if about to play chess. She in turn reclined into her armchair and folded her arms across her chest, awaiting an explanation.

'I have read it.'

Miss Prim's eyes widened, but she composed herself instantly, resuming her appearance of defiance.

'And?'

'I have to admit, it has a certain charm.'

'Well, well.'

'Yes, and I don't mind the girls reading it, but it's of no interest to me.'

'What do you mean by that?'

'I mean, it's a minor novel, cloying and sentimental.'

The librarian sat up, glowering.

'Which is the greatest sin a human being can commit, isn't it?' she said cuttingly. 'You think sentimentality is a sort of crime, even a perversion, don't you? Ice-cold, intelligent people don't go in for sentiment. That's for the common people and uneducated women.'

The Man in the Wingchair stretched out his legs and leant back again.

'I wouldn't say that,' he said. 'You'd be amazed at what good taste in literature the common man has shown at various times in history.'

'Times that are past, never to return, I presume.'

'I'm not sure "never" is the right word, though I suspect it may be. But now you mention it, I have to say that what you said about uneducated women and sentimentality is accurate. Of course nowadays the problem affects highly educated women as well.'

'As in my case, of course.'

'Indeed, as in your case.'

Miss Prim clenched her jaw so tightly that her teeth ground together. Losing her temper now would be the worst thing she could do when she was being accused of sentimentality. Instead, she must prove that sentiment did not hamper proper reasoning. She struggled for a few seconds that seemed to last for ever.

'Tell me,' she said with forced sweetness, 'how do you manage to be so cold?'

He looked up in amazement.

'Cold? Me? You think I'm cold?'

'You detest sentimentality, you just said so.'

'That's true, I do, but it doesn't make me a cold person. Sentimentality is one thing, sentiment is another, Prudencia. Sentimentality is a pathology of the mind, or of the emotions, if you like, which swell up, outgrow their proper place, go crazy, obscure judgement. Not being sentimental doesn't mean that one lacks feelings, but simply that one knows how to channel them. The ideal – and I'm sure you agree – is to possess a cool head and a tender heart.'

The librarian remained silent for a few moments while she released her jaw. As usual, this discussion with him had given her a headache. She didn't understand the logic of the conversation. How had they reached this point? When had they gone from women's literature to the pathology of the emotions?

'Dickens used to read Mrs Gaskell. Your hero, Cardinal Newman, read Jane Austen. And Henry James read Edith Wharton,' she said determinedly.

'Three good writers. Three intelligent and unsentimental women.'

'The question is not whether they're good or bad writers, or whether they're sentimental. The question is whether there was a time when men – great men – read novels written by women.'

'True,' said the Man in the Wingchair, pushing his seat

even further away from the fireplace. 'But in my opinion this is for two good reasons. One, a woman publishing a novel still had an allure of audacity; and two, women provided a reasonable but different view of the world. Nowadays women's writing has lost its capacity to make us change our gaze, look at things in a different way. When I read a novel by a woman I get the impression that the author is doing nothing more than looking at herself.'

Miss Prim stared fixedly at her employer. She was shocked by how easily he maintained all sorts of outrageous opinions. Most people would feel ashamed of thinking, let alone saying, such things. He said them calmly, almost cheerfully.

'Maybe women look at themselves now because they've spent too long looking at others,' she muttered.

'Come on, Prudencia, that's much too simplistic for you.'

'You're wrong,' she said, leaping to her feet and going back to the shelf she'd been working on. 'Nothing is too simplistic for me. I'm a woman ruled by sentiment, remember?'

The Man in the Wingchair stood and, gathering up his hat, coat and scarf, headed to the library door.

'I'd say you're a woman who looks at herself far too much.'

'Really?' she heard herself say in a trembling voice, her back to him. 'And what about you? Do you look at yourself?'

He turned his head and said with a half-smile from the

door: 'I have to confess that I find it much more interesting to look at you.'

As soon as he left the room, Miss Prim's trembling turned into a stream of fat tears that poured silently down her face. She felt she had been insulted, ill-treated and mocked. She was tired of the dialectical game where she was the mouse and he the cat. But one thing annoyed and hurt her more than anything else: the conviction that he was quite unaware of his ill-treatment of her and never had the slightest intention of playing any game; the awareness that the person who had caused her anguish was quite oblivious of her drama – her petty, silly drama; and the fact that, much to her regret, that person had become important to her. He was the question mark on Hortensia and Emma's list of potential husbands; that was the truth, and it was useless to try to hide it from herself any longer. She knew the symptoms. She knew them all too well.

What did he really think of her? Miss Prim freely confessed her ignorance on the matter. At times he seemed attracted to her, no point denying it; but then at others he plainly saw in her all of humanity's deformities and character flaws, making her believe that the attraction existed only in her mind. A deeply sentimental and somewhat impulsive mind, as he made sure to remind her regularly. It was also possible that his attitude was due to his interest in becoming some sort of Pygmalion and turning her into the perfect example of her sex. Miss Prim shuddered at the possibility of having to play the part of Galatea or, even worse, Eliza Doolittle, in that particular drama. But that wasn't all: there was a third, even more terrible hypothesis, so terrible that she shivered at the thought. Maybe he spent his spare time engaging in these wide-ranging debates with her because, purely and simply, he had nothing better to do.

At this point, the librarian's distress overflowed. She had to do something to settle her doubts. She must do something.

After discreetly blowing her nose, she gazed out of the French windows that opened onto the garden. Snow was still falling in large, heavy flakes. Walking to the village in such weather was unthinkable, but she needed to get there urgently. The time had come to have a frank conversation with the ladies of San Ireneo; to lay her cards on the table in the ridiculous detective game of searching for a husband, consult their opinion on the situation with her employer and ask them what she should do. As she gloomily watched the snow, sure the conversation would have to wait until the weather improved, she caught sight of the gardener emerging from the greenhouse and heading to the garage. Lightning-quick, she jumped to her feet, grabbed a warm coat, scarf and wellington boots and rushed out to ask for a lift to the village.

The journey was slow and tedious, partly because driving in the snow required extreme caution, partly because the gardener kept his mouth resolutely shut out of loyalty to the cook, with whom he had been friends for many years. At last they reached the village, and he dropped Miss Prim at Hortensia Oeillet's house. The florist was surprised and delighted to see her.

'My dear Prudencia, what an unexpected pleasure on such a dreadful afternoon! Come in, take off your coat and sit down while I make tea,' she cried.

'Please, don't trouble yourself, I've just had tea. But a cup of hot chocolate would do me good. And would you mind preparing a litre of coffee?'

Hortensia Oeillet looked at her guest in dismay.

'A litre of coffee? My goodness, this must be serious.'

'No, it's not serious but it is important. I've come because I need advice, from you and your friends, all of you eminently sensible ladies. What I mean is, I need you to convene a sort of . . .'

'Extraordinary conclave?'

Miss Prim sighed with relief.

'Is that what you call it?'

'It is indeed. Do sit down, dear. I'll call Emma, Virginia and Herminia. I think that'll be enough. We don't want all of San Ireneo finding out, do we?' The florist smiled affectionately and went to the kitchen.

Miss Prim sank into the sofa in front of the fire. Hortensia Oeillet's sitting room was small and pretty. Old photographs, vases of camellias, children's drawings of plants – the librarian recalled that her hostess was San Ireneo's botany teacher – pressed flowers in collages and books, lots of books, made it a very pleasant place to be.

'What a lovely room, Hortensia!' exclaimed the librarian as the florist returned with a jug of hot chocolate, a plate of butter buns, lemon biscuits and a large custard tart on a tray, which she set down on the table by the fire.

'Do you like it? It is a bit old-fashioned, but here in San Ireneo we enjoy that. We live with one foot in the past, as you know, my dear.'

Miss Prim assured her that she did know and had started to appreciate it herself.

'Oh, I'm so pleased! I was afraid you'd never adjust – it's so different. After all, we do live slightly on the fringe of things here.'

'Or even *contra mundum*,' laughed Prudencia, accepting a cup of hot chocolate.

'That's true. What was I going to say? Ah, yes! Our guests are on their way, they'll be here in five minutes and coffee will be ready in three. I've also invited Lulu Thiberville. I hope you don't mind.'

'Lulu Thiberville?'

'She's the oldest and most respected woman in the village. She's almost ninety-five. I asked her because she's very wise and because . . .' Hortensia hesitated and glanced sideways at Miss Prim '. . . she's outlived three husbands. You didn't say exactly why you needed advice, but something in your face told me it might be a problem of a romantic nature, shall we say, so I thought of her.'

The librarian blushed crimson.

'You did the right thing. I look forward to meeting Lulu Thiberville,' she said with a smile.

Mrs Thiberville turned out to be a wizened little woman with a rasping, imperious voice and the gift of making herself the absolute centre of attention. She was wearing an old astrakhan coat that smelt of mothballs and a small grey hat adorned with a feather.

'So it's you,' she said as she entered, followed by the other guests. They settled her by the fire, propping her feet on a small footstool and hovering like worker bees around their queen.

'Well?' asked the old lady. 'To what do I owe the honour?'

Hortensia introduced the librarian and briefly set out what she knew of the situation: Miss Prim had arrived unexpectedly, anxious and upset and in need of help; she'd requested an extraordinary conclave, an unscheduled meeting of the ladies of San Ireneo to discuss an urgent matter.

'My dear Prudencia, would you be so kind as to tell us about your problem?'

Encouraged by Herminia Treaumont's smile, Miss Prim began. In deference to Lulu Thiberville, she started by explaining the eccentric method of searching for a husband that she had agreed to, and how, that afternoon, she had concluded that the question mark on the list denoted her employer. Then she described her strange, tense relationship with him, the lively conversations and confidences, the smiles and courtesies and the sudden reprimands. Endeavouring to appear calm, she confessed reluctantly that she was attracted to him. She couldn't understand why, as he was an odd man with extreme religious beliefs, utterly insensitive and intolerably domineering. Like all independent women, Miss Prim was opposed to domination of any kind. In her opinion, the marital relationship should be based upon the most exquisite and refined sort of equality.

'You're starting out all wrong,' the queen bee pronounced from her armchair.

'Why?' asked the librarian, stunned.

Shifting uneasily, Herminia opened her mouth to intervene, but a magisterial gesture from the old lady stayed her.

'All this talk of equality is complete nonsense,' declared Lulu starkly.

'But why?' Miss Prim asked again.

'My dear Prudencia,' began Hortensia, 'what Lulu means—'

'Be quiet, Hortensia,' snapped the old lady. 'I don't need anyone to explain what I mean. I'm sure you and Emma are partly responsible for this poor girl's distress, always going on about ridiculous Eastern theories on harmony, the whole and the parts. They've been on about harmony and the whole and the parts, haven't they?'

With an apologetic glance at her hostess, she replied that

she had indeed been instructed in the theory of harmony and the whole and the parts.

'You can forget about all that. More nonsense.'

'Lulu, please, I'd like to . . .' began Hortensia gently but firmly.

'Hortensia,' said the old lady wearily, 'I assume you invited me, at my great age, to an extraordinary conclave in order to hear my opinion. Isn't that so?'

'Of course, my dear.'

'Absolutely, Lulu,' concurred Herminia cautiously. 'It's just that there can be so many ways of approaching a situation like this. I'm sure Hortensia and Emma had the best of intentions when . . .'

'Of course they did, Herminia. Don't be silly. Nobody's questioning that.' The tiny old lady straightened and fixed the librarian with a beady stare. 'Pay attention, Miss Prim: you have before you a woman who's buried three husbands. In my view, this gives me authority to speak on the matter, and from that standpoint I have to tell you that equality has nothing to do with marriage. The basis of a good marriage, a reasonably happy marriage – don't delude yourself, there is no such thing as an entirely happy marriage – is, precisely, inequality. It's essential if two people are to feel mutual admiration. Listen carefully to what I'm about to tell you. You must not aspire to finding a husband who's your equal, but one who's absolutely and completely better than you.'

Miss Prim was about to object, but the steely glint in the

old lady's eyes gave her pause. From her seat by the fire, Virginia Pille suppressed a smirk.

'Does that only apply to women,' asked Miss Prim, 'or must men also marry women they admire?'

'Of course they must. They must seek women who, from one or several points of view, are better than them. If you look back over history you'll see that most great men, the truly great ones, have always chosen admirable women.'

'But in that case admiration does not exclude equality, Mrs Thiberville. If I admire my husband and my husband admires me, then we're equal,' she retorted, elevating her nose a couple of degrees.

The old lady turned her head with difficulty and looked at Virginia, who smirked again.

'My dear Miss Prim, if you reflected a little more deeply you'd realize that you can only admire that which you do not possess. You do not admire in another a quality you have yourself, you admire what you don't have and which you see shining in another in all its splendour. Do you follow me?'

'We follow you, Lulu,' said Herminia, and the other ladies nodded.

'Well, good. And this isn't wisdom, it's basic logic. If two people admire each other, they're not equals. If they were, they wouldn't admire each other. They're different, as each admires in the other what they don't find in themselves. It's difference, not similarity, that fosters admiration between two people. Similarity has no place in a good marriage. Difference does. Claiming otherwise is pure foolishness, which is so prevalent nowadays and typical of people who haven't been taught to reason.'

Miss Prim lowered her head, meekly accepting the scolding.

'In any case, Lulu,' Virginia's adamantine voice filled the sitting room, 'what Miss Prim wants is our view of her present situation with her employer and her attraction to him.'

'Do you admire him, child?' asked the old lady, suddenly less severe.

'In many ways I suppose I do, but in others I detest him deeply.'

'Ah, that's no impediment, not in the least. I detested all my husbands intensely and it didn't stop me loving all three very much.'

Herminia cleared her throat discreetly, and Miss Prim turned to her. Meanwhile Lulu leant back in her armchair and closed her eyes.

'Prudencia,' said Herminia, 'I'd like to say something. I've observed you more than once with your employer and I think it's more than possible that the attraction is mutual. I truly believe it.'

Miss Prim slowly picked up a lemon biscuit and leant forward as if the better to hear.

'Do you mean it?' she asked. 'I know you and he are close friends.'

Lulu opened her eyes and coughed loudly. At this, her hostess rose quickly and fetched her a glass of water from the kitchen.

'We are, now. But years ago we were considerably more than friends,' said Herminia.

Miss Prim tensed, gritting her teeth.

'Oh!'

'It was a long time ago, of course. It's all over now.'

'Oh!' she said again. And, making a huge effort to control her uneasiness, she asked: 'What happened?'

Herminia drew her chair up to the fire and, after a pause, as if weighing each word, she began.

'I won't go into the details of our relationship because it's not relevant, but I think you should know why we parted. We spent a wonderful time together, but then the man I was in love with turned into the man you know now, and everything changed.'

'You left him?'

'He left me.'

Miss Prim gave an almost imperceptible sigh of relief.

'You shouldn't feel relieved,' declared the queen bee, who did not miss a thing. 'If you had a little more sense you'd ask Herminia why he left her.'

'Why did he leave you?' she asked obediently.

Just then, the door opened with a creak and they turned their heads towards the noise, all except Lulu whose arthritis obliged her to maintain a rigid posture. An enormous long-haired grey cat sauntered in, approached the table and leapt onto its mistress's lap. Hortensia smiled fondly and began stroking the animal. Herminia went on, her voice seeming to Miss Prim to come from a great distance, as if in a dream.

'Because I didn't believe what he started to believe.'

For a few moments nobody spoke. All that could be heard in the room was the measured ticking of the clock unhurriedly marking the progress of the afternoon's events in Hortensia Oeillet's sitting room. Outside, the snow was falling more lightly now. The flakes were smaller, and they seemed to flutter erratically in the icy February wind.

'But I can't believe that was the reason,' stammered Prudencia at last. 'Do you mean he left the woman he loved just because of that?'

'I mean that when that door opened, the ties that bound us were broken. It changed his life, and I could not, or maybe would not, share in it. Oh, of course, we tried, Prudencia, I can assure you. But it was obvious that he was living in one world and I in another, that he was speaking one language and I another, that he could see—'

'Oh, please,' interrupted Miss Prim, irritably. 'Don't give me all that business about him seeing things that others can't.'

'Not in the physical sense, definitely not,' said Herminia cautiously. 'What I'm simply trying to say is that we reached a point where if he hadn't left me, I would probably have left him.'

Prudencia stood up and leant over to stoke the fire. As she did so she felt the other women staring at her back. Only Lulu Thiberville, reclining in her armchair with eyes closed, seemed indifferent to the conversation.

'So what you're telling me is, the fact that I don't believe what he believes will prevent me from truly falling in love with him?'

Herminia reached out and stroked the cat gently before replying.

'No, my dear, no. What I'm telling you is the fact that you don't believe what he believes means he will never, ever consent truly to fall in love with you.'

2

It can't be, murmured Miss Prim under her breath as she hurried away from Hortensia Oeillet's house. The afternoon had ended unpleasantly. It was obvious that all the women, except old Lulu Thiberville, pitied her. It was also obvious that they believed Herminia's story implicitly. But she herself did not. She refused to accept that an intelligent, erudite man could permit his ideas to drive him away from the woman he loved. But as she trudged through the snow, it dawned on her that she had a more pressing problem. How was she going to get back to the house in this weather? Her hostess had entreated her to call someone to pick her up, but Miss Prim had expressed her determination not to. Now she saw that she'd been foolish. She should have waited for Lulu Thiberville's gardener, who was due to collect the old lady at eight.

She felt humiliated by Herminia's revelation. It had been an unexpected confidence and in unaccountably poor taste. Miss Prim firmly believed that certain things in life should never be revealed. But in the event that it was necessary, wasn't a private chat the best way? Wouldn't her visit to the newspaper office have been a more appropriate time and place for the disclosure? Miss Prim had no doubts on the matter, or on the part her hostess should have played. Shouldn't Hortensia have warned her, suggested she talk with Herminia in private? Miss Prim was convinced this would have been the proper course of action.

The whole business was ridiculous, she reflected as she struggled across the road. She couldn't believe that her employer had ever behaved so despicably. He had never shown her any hostility over differences in belief. He had never given the slightest hint that this might be a problem. Though officially their relationship remained that of employer and employee, unofficially it had gone much further. The discussions and conversations, confidences and debates, all went beyond the boundaries of a contract of employment. And in all this time she'd never had any sense that he despised her or looked down on her because she didn't share his religious beliefs.

Perhaps Herminia had been deceiving herself, she thought as she tried to shield herself from an icy gust of wind. Herminia was a refined, intelligent, sensitive woman but that was no defence against self-deception. Miss Prim had a theory about self-deception: the female sex seemed particularly and cruelly vulnerable to it. It wasn't that men didn't fall prey to this psychological mechanism, but in them its workings were much more superficial and considerably less elaborate. Self-deception in women, she mused as she tried not to slip on the sloping path, was a weapon of immense power and subtlety. Like a sea monster with enormous tentacles that stretched out over the years, poisoning not only its victim but many of those close to her. Miss Prim herself could testify to it; she had experienced the process at firsthand. She'd seen the monster emerge from the depths of her mother's mind and watched it wrap itself like a giant squid around her father's life.

'Isn't this an odd day to go rambling, my imprudent Prudencia?'

The librarian valued Horacio Delàs' friendship, but she'd never realized quite how much until that evening.

'Horacio, you have no idea how glad I am to see you!'

Her friend laughed loudly and offered her his arm.

'I don't usually take a stroll on evenings like this but Hortensia called me. She was worried you might be lying in a ditch by now.'

Miss Prim smiled with relief.

'It was very stupid of me.'

'And from what I hear, this isn't the first time it's happened.'

'No,' she replied, lowering her head.

'Come now, cheer up, my dear. I can offer you a good fire and a hot meal. You know I don't drive, so I can't include a lift home afterwards, but we can call the house and they can send the gardener to pick you up after dinner. For now you need to get warm, rest and eat.'

Obediently, she let her friend guide her down the street to his house. He opened the gate to his large garden full of camellias, and steered his guest up the path to the stone house. Like the rest of San Ireneo, its windows were all lit up, as if inviting passers-by to stop and visit. After tidying herself up, changing out of her boots into a pair of old slippers several sizes too big for her and eating an excellent dinner accompanied by a very good wine, Miss Prim was offered an armchair by the fire and a cup of tea.

'This is heaven, Horacio. I'm so comfortable, I could stay all night.'

Savouring a glass of whisky, her host beamed with pleasure.

'You'd be very welcome, but I don't think your employer would be too happy. He's sending someone for you in an hour.'

'No, I don't think he would be,' she replied, laughing. 'How is it that everyone here is such a good host – always coming up with delicious sweets, cakes and roast meats, a warm fire and good company?'

'Civilized pleasures from an earlier era, Prudencia.'

'I suppose so,' she sighed, slipping off the enormous

slippers and moving her bare feet closer to the fire. Its crackling was the only sound in the room.

Outside the windows snow was still falling, muffling the few sounds that came from the village at that late hour. Miss Prim stared into the flames. She was starting to gauge the true significance of all she had thought, said and heard during the day. And the conclusion did not please her.

'I think I did something very silly today,' she said, almost to herself.

'You mean trying to walk back? It all turned out all right in the end. It's not worth worrying about.'

'I mean, confessing publicly that I'm attracted to the man I work for, when I'm not sure if it's true.'

The librarian thought her host hadn't heard, but then realized he had.

'I've been foolish, haven't I?'

Horacio poured himself another couple of fingers of whisky before replying.

'Naturally, I wouldn't say foolish. A little rash, maybe.'

His guest smiled, eyes fixed on the fire.

'You're so unlike him! He wouldn't have shown me any mercy.'

'Of course he would, Prudencia, don't be so hard on him. I know him – he'd never hurt you deliberately.'

'Is that a warning?' she asked stiffly.

'Not at all. Of course not. I don't know what his feelings are, my dear; I can't tell you whether he feels anything more for you than friendship or interest. But didn't you just say yourself that you're no longer sure if you feel the attraction you've mentioned?'

She averted her gaze.

'I see,' said her friend. 'In that case, I'm afraid you'll have to find out if your feelings are reciprocated.'

'Or whether any obstacle stands in the way of their being reciprocated.'

'Now I don't follow you,' he said, looking at her with curiosity.

Briefly, Miss Prim recounted the events of the extraordinary conclave.

'Could it be true? And if it were, wouldn't it be bigoted and fanatical? Could it be possible? You know him.'

'I do, but not so well as that, my dear. I'm afraid the only way of finding out is to ask him.'

'Ask him? Oh no, it would be the same as admitting my feelings. It's out of the question.'

'Not so fast, Prudencia. Didn't you say this was the reason he split up with Herminia?'

She nodded.

'Well, it's Herminia you must mention, not yourself. It's his relationship with her you've got to talk about. That's the first step, and I think you should talk to him as soon as possible. You know I wish you all the luck in the world.'

Miss Prim remained lost in thought for a few moments before drawing her feet away from the fire and pulling her long socks and boots back on. She looked at her host solemnly.

'You have a wonderfully feminine mind, Horacio. No, don't object, please. I know you don't consider it a compliment. But I do. I consider it a great compliment.'

Before her friend could say anything, the doorbell rang. The gardener had arrived and the evening was at an end.

Miss Prim slept badly that night. How could she have been so impulsive? Confessing at last that she cared for her employer had brought no relief. Instead she felt terribly agitated. Putting her feelings into words seemed to have magnified them excessively. The women of San Ireneo de Arnois, though well intentioned, had interpreted them as a declaration of love, almost a marriage proposal. Why else would an old lady like Lulu Thiberville have explained the principles of a successful union? Prudencia was worried that the ladies of San Ireneo would now start working on marrying her off to the Man in the Wingchair. Had nobody ever told them that not all attractions between men and women led to a relationship? Did they not know by now that not all relationships ended in marriage? Miss Prim's views on marital union had grown more moderate with time, but that didn't mean she was a wholehearted supporter of it. And there were other factors to consider. What if her employer found out about the conclave at Hortensia's? What if she was simply wrong and he had not the slightest interest in her?

Overwhelmed by these worries, she jumped out of bed, put on a coat over her dressing gown and crept quietly out of her room. The house was completely still. She crossed the landing, tiptoeing past the children's bedrooms, and went downstairs to the large hall on the ground floor. The front door was unlocked, as was the custom in San Ireneo. Locked doors were considered a snub to one's neighbours.

As she entered the garden an icy blast of wind took her breath away. Shivering, she reckoned she could stay outside for about five minutes. It was something she'd done since she was a child. When she couldn't sleep she got up in the middle of the night and went outside, remaining there until wind, rain or heat made her miss the comfort of her bedroom. Then she'd go back in and sleep peacefully till morning.

'Prudencia, you have an odd habit of braving the cold in flimsy footwear. If I were you, I'd put on snow boots.'

Miss Prim turned with a start on hearing the voice of the Man in the Wingchair.

'Did I wake you?' she asked. 'I'm so sorry, I tried to be as quiet as possible.'

He smiled gently, drew his coat tightly around him and blew on his hands to warm them.

'You didn't; I'm always awake at this hour.'

'A real night owl,' said the librarian with a teasing grin.

'More like a sheepdog. Eksi has nightmares sometimes and wakes up crying at around two or three. She's the most fragile lamb in my flock.'

'Really? I've never heard her.'

'She cries very quietly. You have to be awake to hear her.'

Miss Prim nodded thoughtfully before vigorously rubbing her hands.

'Why don't we go back inside and have a hot drink? You're frozen, Prudencia.'

'When you say a hot drink, do you mean a hot toddy?' she asked mischievously.

'I mean cocoa, chocolate or hot milk with a dash of rum. Nothing that could go to your head.'

She laughed, and they went back into the house. The Man in the Wingchair opened the door to the library, switched on a small lamp and crouched in front of the fireplace to light a fire.

'There's no need. It's quite warm enough in here.'

'I know, but I just can't conceive of a room in winter with an empty hearth. A fire is much more than heating, it's the heart of a home.'

'I'm not going to argue,' she said with laughter in her voice. 'Not at this time of night, and not if you're offering to light it. Shall I make some cocoa?'

'That would be great,' he answered as he stoked the fire.

In the old kitchen, Miss Prim prepared the drinks. This was her chance to do as Horacio advised and ask her employer about his romantic history. As she slowly stirred the cocoa with a wooden spoon, she realized how very difficult this would be. How could she ask him about a relationship when, officially, she didn't know about it? Of course, she reflected, there was really nothing out of the ordinary about her knowing. Not in a small place where everybody knew everybody else's story.

When she returned to the library, a fire was blazing. She put the tray down on the tea table and settled herself in one of the armchairs, as did her employer. Then she poured two cups of cocoa, took a slice of cake, removed her slippers and stretched her legs towards the fire.

'You've never told me that you and Herminia used to be a couple,' she said with studied nonchalance, not daring to look up from her cup.

He stirred his cocoa and took a sip before answering.

'There are lots of things about my life I haven't told you. I didn't realize I had to, but if it's important to you I'm quite happy to start now.'

Miss Prim reddened, drew her feet away from the fire and curled them beneath her on the armchair.

'Of course you don't have to. But we've talked about Herminia so often that I'm amazed you've never mentioned it, that's all.'

'That's all,' he echoed in a low voice.

They both sat staring into the fire for a few minutes. From the depths of the house came the distant, familiar sound of a clock chiming three times.

'Everyone knows that sentimental women are also nosy

and malicious,' the librarian said suddenly. 'So tell me, why did you and she part?'

The Man in the Wingchair looked at her with amusement.

'If there's one thing I'm sure of, Prudencia, it's that you're not a nosy person.'

Miss Prim smiled and got up to remove her coat.

'No, I'm not, but I'm keen on sociology, remember? I'm interested in human nature.'

'Sociologists aren't interested in human nature. They just study human behaviour in social groups, which is more limited and much less interesting.'

The librarian regarded her employer calmly. She was determined not to be provoked. It wouldn't be easy, of course – nothing with him ever was – and she would be naive to expect otherwise.

'Did you leave her?'

'No.'

'That's gallant of you, but it's not true.'

'If you know it's not true then why are you asking me? You don't know me at all if you think I'm going to brag about leaving a woman,' he said sharply.

Miss Prim bit her lip and shifted position. This was going to be hard, very hard, extraordinarily hard.

'I'm sure you would have had a compelling reason. I know I have no right to ask about it.'

'You're right. You don't.'

Under normal circumstances she would have left it there.

Deeply embarrassed, she would have mumbled an apology and fled upstairs. But these were definitely not normal circumstances. This evening Miss Prim felt possessed by a feverish urge to question him, to press beyond the bounds of courtesy, prudence, even common sense. She wanted to know the truth, she needed to know it and she wouldn't back down.

'Was it because of your ideas? Because you're deeply religious and she isn't?'

He stared thoughtfully at the cup his employee was resting on her knees. Then he gave a gentle shake of the head and smiled.

'Ideas, Prudencia? You think faith is an idea? An ideology? Like market economics, or communism, or animal rights?' Now his tone was slightly mocking.

'In a way, yes,' she replied stiffly. 'It's a way of seeing the world, a view on how existence should be, as well as a big help in easing life's problems.'

'Is that really what you think?'

'Of course. And partly because of you. Why else would a sensible, intelligent, rational person try to convert?'

With a half-smile, he leant his head in his hands.

'Try? You are absolutely priceless, Miss Prim.'

'That's not intended as a compliment, is it?' she murmured sadly.

The Man in the Wingchair rose and went to the fireplace. He picked up the poker, stirred the fire and stared into the flames.

'Nobody *tries* to convert, Prudencia. I told you once, but you clearly didn't understand. Have you ever seen an adult playing with a child, running away and pretending to be caught? The child thinks he's caught the adult, but anyone watching knows perfectly well what's really happened.'

'*Console-toi, tu ne me chercherais pas si tu ne m'avais trouvé*, isn't that so?' she said softly. '"You would not seek me if you had not found me"?'

'Exactly. You've read Pascal. Nobody begins the search unless they've already found what they're looking for. And no one finds what they're looking for – the One they're looking for – if that One doesn't take the initiative and allow Himself to be found. It's a game in which one player holds all the cards.'

'You make it sound as if belief was impossible to resist, but that's not true. You can say no. The child can say to the adult: "I'm not playing, leave me alone."'

The Man in the Wingchair drained his cup. Then, adjusting his position, he stared directly at his employee.

'Of course you can say no. And in many ways that makes life much simpler. It's common even for someone who says yes to look back and realize that he's said no many times during his life.'

She raised her eyebrows.

'Life is much simpler when you say "no"? Life is much simpler and easier to bear if you believe it *doesn't* end in a coffin underground. You can't deny it, it's common sense.'

He got up and tended the fire again.

'As a theoretical belief it can serve as a wild card for a time, undoubtedly. But theoretical beliefs don't save anyone. Faith isn't theoretical, Prudencia. Conversion is about as theoretical as a shot to the head.'

Miss Prim again bit her lip. The conversation was not going as she'd hoped. This was all proving very revealing, but she didn't want to talk about conversion, she didn't want to talk about religion at all. The only thing she wanted to know was why the 'shot to the head' had caused his relationship with Herminia Treaumont to end.

'So was that the reason?' she asked stubbornly. 'Was that why you left her?'

He looked at her in silence for a few seconds, as if trying to guess what lay behind the question.

'Would you think it ridiculous if it were?'

'I'd think you didn't really love her.'

'No, that's where you're wrong,' he said firmly. 'I did love her. I loved her very much. But the day came, or maybe the moment, I don't know, when I realized that she was asleep, whereas I was fully, absolutely and totally awake. I'd climbed like a cat up onto a roof and I could see a beautiful, terrible, mysterious landscape stretching out before me. Did I really love her? Of course I did. Perhaps if I'd loved her less, cared for her less, I wouldn't have had to leave her.'

236

Miss Prim, who had begun to feel a familiar pain in her stomach, cleared her throat before replying.

'I thought the religious were closer to other people than anyone else.'

'I can't speak for anyone else, Prudencia. I only know what it's meant to me and I don't claim to speak for others. It's been my touchstone, the line that's split my life in two and given it absolute meaning. But I'd be lying if I said it's been easy. It's not easy, and anyone who says it is is fooling themselves. It was catharsis, a shocking trauma, open-heart surgery, like a tree torn from the ground and replanted elsewhere. Like what one imagines a child experiences during the beautiful, awesome process of birth.'

The Man in the Wingchair paused.

'And there's something else,' he continued, 'something to do with looking beyond the moment, with the need to scan the horizon, to scrutinize it as keenly as a sailor studies his charts. Don't be surprised, Prudencia. My story is as old as the world. I'm not the first and I won't be the last. I know what you're thinking. Would I turn back if I could? No, of course not. Would a newly awoken man willingly go back to the sleepwalking life?'

Miss Prim pulled her dressing gown tightly around her and stared at her hands, toasted pink by the heat of the fire. So in the end, it was all true. How naive she'd been to think that it was only a part of his personality. How dim of her not to sense that whatever it was that had changed him, it was something powerful, something profound and troubling. Herminia was right. She had never seen that look blazing in his eyes before. The force, the conviction, the strange, savage joy.

'Then there's no hope,' she whispered with regret. 'Is there?'

He gave her a long, pensive look before replying.

'Hope, Prudencia? Of course there's hope. I have hope. My whole life is pure hope.'

She rose and picked up the tray.

'It's very late. If you don't mind, I'm going back to bed. I'm tired and, unlike you, I do lack hope tonight.'

Before the Man in the Wingchair could reply, Miss Prim had closed the library door quietly behind her.

3

*P*rudencia Prim folded her jade-green kimono neatly and laid it in her suitcase. The reality was, she thought sadly as she slipped a pair of shoes into a cotton shoe bag, her work no longer detained her. Her employer's library was now perfectly catalogued and organized. The history books stood on the history shelves, the tomes on philosophy were lined up where they should be and all the volumes of prose and poetry were in their proper sections; science and mathematics were now in their rightful places to the millimetre; and the section on theology – the great passion in that house, the absolute ruler of the library – shone imposingly, neat and perfect. Glimpsing her red-rimmed eyes in the mirror from time to time, she recalled her first conversation, months earlier, with the Man in the Wingchair.

Do you know what this is, Miss Prim?

No, sir.

De Trinitate.

St Augustine?

Smiling wistfully, Miss Prim kept on with her packing. She wasn't going to go away immediately. She intended to leave enough clothes in the wardrobe for a few days, just enough time to say her goodbyes and calmly decide what to do next. She couldn't stay. Not now that she knew what she felt; not now that she also knew her feelings would never, could never, be reciprocated. But where would she go? And, above all, how would she explain her departure? Slowly she went to her bedroom window, pulled back the curtains and looked out. It was a cold morning and the snow shone like polished marble in the sunlight. She'd woken late. After all, after the previous night's conversation there wasn't much left to do other than face her employer and tell him she was leaving.

Despite the overwhelming sadness and disappointment, she also felt relief. The last few days had been too turbulent for a woman like her, accustomed to order, balance and neatness. She'd brooded too much, worried too much, gone over the words again and again, assessed the gestures, registered smiles, analysed glances. Romance, she reflected wisely, could be an unbelievably heavy burden for the female psyche. What she needed now was somewhere pleasant and remote where she could rest, a refuge where she could write, an Eden where she could surround herself with beauty and admire emerald-green lawns and wisteria in flower.

Of course, she was also in pain: she didn't want to – couldn't – deny it. It had been a long time since she had experienced such anguish, had such difficulty organizing her thoughts, felt so acutely the impossibility of scanning the horizon and seeing any glint of light in the darkness ahead. But it would all pass. Miss Prim was sure of it. She knew herself well enough to estimate how long the sadness would last. By the spring, or the beginning of summer at most, the sun would come out again.

Tentatively, the librarian opened the door to the study. 'Could I have a quick word?'

Bent over a document, the Man in the Wingchair indicated that she should enter and sit down. She obeyed. For a few minutes, just long enough to rehearse in her mind how she would inform him of her departure, the only sound in the room was the crackling of the fire in the hearth.

'Look at this, Prudencia,' he said, holding out what appeared to be a facsimile of two small papyrus fragments.

With a sigh Miss Prim peered at the Man in the Wingchair's face. There was no sign of tension or anxiety, no hint that their conversation in the early hours had affected him in any way.

'Are you all right?' he asked, noticing how pale his employee was. 'You look tired.'

The librarian assured him that she was fine and that her pallor was due to lack of sleep.

'We did talk till quite late last night, that's true. Look at this,' he said, indicating the manuscript. 'What do you think? Have you ever seen anything like it?'

Miss Prim examined it closely.

'What is it?'

'A facsimile of P52, commonly known as the Rylands Papyrus.'

'Let me guess . . . A little piece of the Book of Wisdom? Or the Book of Daniel?'

'No luck, it's neither. They're verses from the Gospel of John. Look closely, they're written in koine Greek. See these lines?'

ΡΗΣΩ ΤΗ ΑΛΗΘΕΙΑ ΠΑΣ Ο ΩΝ ΕΚ ΤΗΣ ΑΛΗΘΕΙ
ΑΣ ΑΚΟΥΕΙ ΜΟΥ ΤΗΣ ΦΩΝΗΣ ΛΕΓΕΙ ΑΥΤΩ Ο
*ΠΙΛΑΤΟΣ ΤΙ ΕΣΤΙΝ ΑΛΗΘΕΙΑ ΚΑΙ ΤΟΥΤΟ**

'I'm sure even a distinguished Jacobin like yourself has heard this before. Would you like me to translate it for you?'

---

* 'Every one that is of the truth heareth my voice. Pilate saith unto him, What is truth?' John 18: 37–8, KJV

Not deigning to reply, she continued to study the two tiny yellowed fragments.

'Is it very ancient?'

'The oldest found so far. It's been dated to around AD 120. It was found in the desert in Egypt by Bernard Grenfell, a British Egyptologist. The consensus is that it's from around thirty years later than the original written by John in Ephesus. Does that seem a bit much? Come over here, I'll show you something.'

He opened an enormous filing cabinet at the other end of his study, and began taking out what Miss Prim could see were facsimiles of papyri, parchments and codices.

'Do you know what this is?' he asked, pointing to one of them.

She shook her head.

'It's one of the Oxyrhynchus Papyri. Have you ever heard of them?'

Miss Prim again shook her head.

'We owe them to Grenfell too. He and Arthur Hunt, another British archaeologist, found them at the end of the nineteenth century in a rubbish dump near Oxyrhynchus in Egypt. They excavated many fragments from great works of antiquity. I think you'll be delighted with the one you're holding now. It's an extract from Plato's *Republic*.'

'Really?' she said, impressed.

'Really. Do you know how many years separate Plato from the first fragments we have of his works?'

'I have no idea.'

'I'll tell you: approximately one thousand two hundred. The texts we have of Plato's thought and, through them, of Socrates' – the works we've all read and studied – are copies made over ten centuries after the originals were written.'

He extracted a thick manuscript from the filing cabinet.

'And this? Any idea what it might be?'

The librarian, who now seemed to have forgotten the reason for her visit, scrutinized the manuscript.

'Let's see,' she said with a smile. 'I can decipher this. It's Latin, at least. Tacitus?'

The Man in the Wingchair shook his head.

'Julius Caesar. *De Bello Civili – The Civil War*. This is the *Laurentianus Ashburnhamensis*, the oldest remaining manuscript of this work. Do you know when it dates from? No, of course you don't. It's from the tenth century, a little over a thousand years after Julius Caesar wrote the original. The oldest copy we have of the *Commentaries on the Gallic War* is from around nine hundred and fifty years after it was originally written.'

'This is all so interesting!' she murmured.

Her employer took up the copy of the Rylands Papyrus again.

'Interesting doesn't come close, Prudencia. It's absolutely fascinating. Now do you understand what the Rylands Papyrus is? Do you know how many copies just in koine

Greek we have of the Four Evangelists' writings? Around five thousand six hundred. Do you know how many we have of the *Commentaries on the Gallic War*, for instance? Ten copies. Only ten. And now, look closely,' he said, glancing over another facsimile. 'How do you get on with Homer?'

Miss Prim assured him that if she were ever condemned to life in prison she'd want to take Homer with her. While the Man in the Wingchair continued talking animatedly of papyri, parchments and copies, she remembered with sadness why she was there. She would miss him, that was obvious; and not just him, but everything to do with him – the chats, the reading, the debates, the children, the books and San Ireneo itself.

'Now that you've finished work on the library,' her employer was saying at that moment, 'maybe you could help me catalogue all of this. I'm giving a lecture in London next month on the Bodmer Papyri.'

'I'm afraid that won't be possible,' replied Miss Prim, heroically resisting the urge to ask what a Bodmer Papyrus was.

He looked at her, dumbfounded.

'Why not?'

She crossed her legs with a deliberate movement and took a deep breath before answering.

'Because I think my work here is finished. I came to tell you, I've decided to leave. I've completed the job, so I can't see any reason to stay.'

Without a word, the Man in the Wingchair gathered up

the documents and returned them to the filing cabinet. Then he went over to the fireplace, freed an armchair from its heap of books and gestured for his employee to sit.

'Has something happened that I should know about, Prudencia?' he asked.

'Not at all.'

'Has somebody in this house offended or upset you?'

'I've always been treated wonderfully well here.'

'Maybe it's me. Have I said something that's bothered you? An instance of the insensitivity you continually accuse me of?'

Miss Prim bowed her head so as to hide her face.

'It has nothing to do with you,' she whispered.

'Look at me, please,' he said.

The librarian raised her head, and at that moment it occurred to her that she would have to come up with an excuse or explanation immediately if she didn't want him to find out or at least guess why she was leaving.

'I have to go to Italy,' she said suddenly.

'To Italy? Why?'

Quivering with nerves, Miss Prim played with her amethyst ring.

'It's to do with my qualifications. No woman's education is complete without living in Italy for a time.'

'Surely you don't need any more qualifications? What would be the purpose?' he asked in consternation. 'Are you trying to beat some record?'

Seeing his expression of bewilderment, she smiled faintly.

'You obviously don't listen to your mother,' she said, her eyes glistening. 'She has a fine theory that living in Italy has a beneficial influence on the conversation and manners of members of the female sex.'

'Are you serious?'

'Absolutely.'

'Well, it's a completely stupid theory. You know that, don't you?'

'May I remind you this is your mother you're talking about,' she said in mock reproach. 'I very much doubt she's said a stupid thing in her life.'

'Well, in this instance I'm afraid she has.'

'At any rate, I'm leaving. I need to travel. I've been here too long.'

'But I thought you liked it here,' he muttered.

Sensing she wouldn't be able to keep her emotions in check much longer, Miss Prim stood up resolutely.

'Please, don't get sentimental,' she said with apparent nonchalance as she made for the door.

'I'll miss you, Prudencia,' said the Man in the Wingchair, raising his head.

'That's very gallant of you, but it's not really true and you know it.'

'Is that honestly what you think?' he said hoarsely, just before the librarian opened the door and left the room.

*

Miss Prim pulled the study door shut behind her and scurried along the corridor to the first-floor landing, then up a flight of stairs until at last she reached her bedroom. She closed the door quietly, took off her shoes, lay down on the bed and, after staring at the coffered ceiling for a few moments, burst into disconsolate tears. Why was she always crying these days? She'd never been an emotional woman. If she was honest with herself, and just then it wasn't hard to be, what she felt for the man couldn't be called love. It had been an attraction forged practically against the odds. Perhaps it had been the challenge. Perhaps even an infatuation; but it wasn't love. So was she crying out of pique? That must be it, she sighed, wiping away tears. For some reason, no doubt her conceited vanity, over the last few days she'd convinced herself that he felt something for her. And though he might have been attracted to her – she couldn't rule it out – it was nothing like love.

Lost in thought, she heard a floorboard creak outside her room. Somebody had stopped in the corridor but did not want to make their presence known. She got up from the bed and stole towards the door. Her heart thumping, she didn't hesitate another second – she grabbed the handle and flung open the door.

'What are you doing there?' she asked in surprise.

Septimus' blond, dishevelled head retreated.

'I wasn't listening,' he said with absolute conviction.

Miss Prim's expression softened and she gestured with her head for him to come in.

'You're leaving, aren't you?' he said, glancing at the half-packed suitcase on the bed.

'Who told you?'

'The gardener. He hears everything through the study window. Why are you crying? Has someone smacked you?'

The librarian, who had picked up a silk-jersey blouse and delicately begun to fold it, was startled.

'Smacked? No, of course not. Do you cry only when you get smacked?'

The child pondered for a few moments.

'I never cry,' he said firmly. 'Not even when somebody smacks me.'

'That's good,' Miss Prim heard herself say. 'I mean, sometimes you need to have a cry, but it's good not to cry over just anything.'

'Maybe I could cry in a war,' reflected the child. 'In a war I could probably do it. It's probably justified then.'

'Completely justified,' she assured him.

'Hey,' said Septimus, seeing the tears sliding silently down her cheeks. 'I'd rather you didn't cry so much.'

'I'm sorry I can't oblige. Unlike you, I cry in peacetime as well.'

The boy observed her flushed face closely and then ran his eye over all the cosmetics bottles on the mantelpiece.

'What can I do to make you stop crying?'

'Nothing, I'm afraid,' replied Miss Prim, touched. 'This advice won't be any use to you now, Septimus, but when you grow up and see a woman crying, remember that the best thing you can do is absolutely nothing.'

'That's really easy.'

She burst out laughing and started to dry her tears.

'Easy? Wait till you're older. There's nothing harder.'

'Going to war is probably harder, and also hunting a whale with a harpoon,' the boy remarked, his attention now drawn by something outside the window.

'Maybe hunting a whale with a harpoon is,' she conceded.

'You know what?' said the child, his gaze now fixed on the floor. 'I think we're going to miss you.'

'And I'm going to miss you,' she murmured. 'Come here. Will you give me a kiss?'

The boy recoiled.

'No,' he said firmly, 'no kisses. I never give kisses. I hate them.'

'I think you'll get over that too when you're grown up,' she said, smiling.

'Don't bet on it,' replied the boy before rushing out.

'So you're leaving,' sighed Mrs Rouan, offering Miss Prim a chair at the old marble table in the kitchen.

The librarian sat down and accepted the mug of duck consommé that the cook kindly served her.

'That's right, Mrs Rouan, I am.'

A fire was burning cheerfully in the hearth and a stew was simmering on the wood-fired range. Outside, the sun seemed to have hidden itself away and leaden clouds promised a night of snow.

'We're going to miss you,' mumbled the cook. 'I know things haven't always been easy between us.'

'No, they haven't,' said the librarian softly.

'I don't like change, I never have. And to tell you the truth,' the cook glanced furtively into the stewpot, 'I don't like new women in the house. They all have their own ways of doing things, and God knows, as you get older it's hard to change.'

Miss Prim smiled sweetly.

'I quite understand, Mrs Rouan. And I'd like to apologize for the times I might have upset you or been insensitive.'

The cook smiled back and patted Miss Prim's hand with one of her own plump, time-worn hands.

'Oh, we've both been rather pig-headed, miss. I'm not an easy woman, I never have been. I'm used to things running my way. Take the master's mother – we had our ups and downs at first, too.'

'Really?' said the librarian, trying unsuccessfully to picture her employer's mother brooking any argument from the cook.

'Of course she's an older lady, and she's used to domestic staff. She realizes that the cook is the heart of a house and that it's best to get on with her. But she is definitely not an easy woman.' And, lowering her voice to a whisper, she added: 'Did you know she's half German?'

'Austrian.'

'Same thing. The first time I met her she asked me to make a strudel. I said very good, no problem. I'd always made it for the children. Ah, but it wasn't a *normal* strudel she wanted. She wanted a *Topfenstrudel*. Do you by any chance know what that is?'

Miss Prim assured her she'd never heard of such a thing.

'That's what I said. Madam was very considerate, of course, and she wrote out the recipe. But no one likes having a lady come into her kitchen on the very first day and ask for a *Topfenstrudel* and, to cap it all, give you the recipe. Do you know what I mean?'

She nodded sympathetically.

'So what is a *Topfenstrudel*?'

'It's just a strudel with a cream-cheese filling,' grumbled the cook. '*They* call cream cheese *Topfen*. Well, anyway, it's not difficult to make, not at all. So I took the recipe and I made it, of course. What else could I do?'

'And did she like it?'

Mrs Rouan got up and returned to the range. She lifted the lid of the stewpot, leant her old head over to inhale the smell, picked up a wooden spoon and tasted the contents with an air of satisfaction.

'That was the problem,' she explained, sitting down at the table again. 'I spent all morning on the wretched thing. I bought the best cheese I could find and I followed the recipe to the letter. And when it was ready and we took it to the table on a lovely Meissen platter decorated with leaves from the garden, do you know what she said?'

Miss Prim declared that she couldn't imagine.

'"Mrs Rouan," she said to me, "Mrs Rouan, you haven't brought the *Vanillesoße*. Where's the *Vanillesoße*, Mrs Rouan?"'

The librarian hid her smile in her consommé cup.

'"I don't know anything about a *Vanillesoße*, madam," I said to her in all seriousness. "In my entire life as a cook, and let me tell you I've worked in a lot of houses, I've never heard of *Vanillesoße*."'

'And what is it?' asked Miss Prim.

'Vanilla custard, no more, no less. How was I to know? And how was I to know that *Topfenstrudel* was served with it?'

Prudencia hastened to confirm that no one could have guessed such a thing.

'But I have to say, she is a lady,' continued the cook. 'Of course she didn't back down at the time. But the next day she turned up in the kitchen and she said to me: "Mrs Rouan, the *Topfenstrudel* was delicious yesterday. But I can see that the children are used to your strudel. So, if you wouldn't mind, from now on we'll give up on the *Topfenstrudel* and *Vanillesoße*, and go back to your strudel."'

'And it all ended there,' sighed Miss Prim with a smile.

Mrs Rouan got to her feet once more and lowered the heat under her stew.

'Now this has to be left to rest for two hours,' she muttered. 'What were you saying?'

'I said it all ended there.'

The cook looked at her, eyes wide.

'End? Quite the opposite. It didn't end there, miss. That's really where it all started.'

Miss Prim nodded pensively and gazed out of the window. Thick flakes of snow had begun to fall on the garden.

'Mrs Rouan, do you remember the tart I baked on my birthday?'

The woman smiled good-humouredly.

'I do. The master and the children loved it. It was very kind of you to have some sent in to us here in the kitchen, we all liked it very much. It's an old family recipe, isn't it? They're the best.'

From beyond the garden, the path and the fields came the distant, solemn sound of the abbey bells.

'They're ringing for Vespers,' said the cook.

'I know,' Miss Prim whispered, eyes fixed on the landscape. 'Mrs Rouan, would you like the recipe for my tart?'

The cook was amazed.

'But, miss, I thought the recipe . . .'

'I thought so too,' grinned Miss Prim. 'Would you like to have it?'

Eyes shining with emotion, the cook extended her rough hand and laid it on top of the librarian's.

'I'd be honoured, miss, I really would.'

4

*M*iss Prim worked her way diligently through the list of people she had to visit before she left. She knew that news of her departure would spread quickly around the village, and she didn't want her friends to find out from anyone but her. As she walked through San Ireneo to Horacio Delàs' house, she recalled the day of her arrival. She'd hurried through these streets, annoyed that she couldn't find a taxi, and hardly noticed the austere beauty of the stone houses or the charm of the cheerful, neat shops. She'd been completely oblivious – she of all people, who so loved beauty – of the beating heart behind these walls.

A week had passed since she'd discovered her mistake about her employer's feelings, and the pain had been replaced by a serene inner sadness. It was more than disappointment in love – Miss Prim rebelled inwardly at the thought of succumbing to such a sickness of the soul – it was the prospect of having to leave this delightful place, its quirky people, the way of life. She didn't want to go, she admitted to herself as she crossed the village, she really didn't. But what was the alternative?

'I remember when you arrived, so young and inexperienced and knowing nothing about the place.'

Having offered his guest a seat, Horacio settled himself in the old armchair from which he cast his kindly, measured, intellectual gaze upon the world and shot her a searching look.

Miss Prim cleared her throat before replying.

'It was only six months ago, Horacio. I hope I'm still almost as young.'

Smiling, her friend poured her a glass of wine and cut her some cheese with an enormous knife.

'But now you know so much more about us.'

She nodded, raising the wine glass to her lips.

'And yet you're leaving us,' he continued. 'Was that conversation really so difficult? Could you not turn the page and stay?'

Miss Prim looked at him sorrowfully. She had asked herself the same question every day since the night she had spoken to the Man in the Wingchair. Couldn't she carry on as before? Ignore it all, pretend it had never happened, simply continue with her job?

'I can't,' she said.

'Are you really so much in love with him?'

She hopped up and went to straighten one of the pictures that lined the sitting-room walls.

'I don't know,' she said, resuming her seat. 'I mean, it probably isn't love, it may just be infatuation. But it isn't really that. As least, not only that.'

'So,' he asked, 'what else is it?'

'I'm afraid I wouldn't know how to explain. It isn't always easy to know what one feels, Horacio. There are submerged currents colliding, then combining and merging.'

'Skeins,' murmured her friend.

'Skeins?'

'Yes, that's right. Like we used to help our mothers or grandmothers unravel as children. Of course it's not easy to know what one feels, Prudencia, especially when the feelings are intense, if not contradictory. Human nature is complex.'

Prudencia accepted another piece of cheese.

'In a way,' she confessed, 'I think I'm angry with him.'

'That's quite normal,' replied her friend. 'Pride is one of the big tangles in the skein.'

'I'm not proud,' she protested, discomfited at being compared to a tangle of wool.

'Of course you're not, my dear. But what about self-esteem?'

She weighed the question.

'Possibly,' she admitted.

Horacio smiled to himself and started paring the rind from the cheese.

'Let's call it self-esteem, then. You felt rejected and, quite understandably, it was painful. Though, unless I'm much mistaken, you weren't actually rejected, were you?'

'That's true,' she said, momentarily encouraged.

'But, even so, you're sure he doesn't have feelings for you, are you?'

Again, she reflected before replying. Outside, through the windows, a low grey sky hung over the village.

'I can't say with absolute certainty,' she sighed. 'But I can say that even if those feelings exist, he'd never allow them to become anything deeper. I've found out that there's a much more powerful reason for it than I could have imagined. A reason so powerful that it's not just something that is related to him, but is a part of his very being. Do you see? He may feel attracted to me, Horacio, or he may not. But even if he did, he wouldn't let it go any further. And he'd probably be right, because it might not work.'

'Reason and will,' murmured her friend. 'You can't understand that, can you? You're all emotion.'

Miss Prim shifted in her armchair. She didn't want to talk about reason and emotion, she didn't wish to be accused of sentimentality again and she definitely didn't intend to embark on another long and tedious discussion of the matter.

As if he'd guessed what she was thinking, Horacio asked:

'Have you ever wondered what would have happened if things had turned out as you'd hoped? If he had fallen in love with you?'

She admitted that she hadn't given it much thought.

'You'd probably have embarked on a relationship that would have ended in marriage much sooner than you expected.'

Miss Prim half-closed her eyes, determined to picture such a scene.

'And ...?' she asked, seemingly pleased with what she'd glimpsed.

'And? My dear Prudencia, marrying a man like him would mean being *radically* married.'

'What do you mean?'

'I mean being *truly* married, married *till death do you part.* Divorce would not be an option, my dear, that's what I mean.'

Absently, she took another sip of wine. She'd always found the thought of being loved until death rather moving, but also deeply troubling and, to be honest, it made her feel a little dizzy.

'Fine,' she said guardedly, 'divorce would be out of the question, for him. But if it didn't go well, nothing would prevent my divorcing him, would it?'

'True,' said her friend. 'It wouldn't. But you're an honest person. Would you think it right to enter into such a marriage knowing that you weren't as fully and utterly committed to it as he was? Wouldn't you feel bad knowing that there was this difference between you? Would you be able to look him in the eye knowing that if the marriage hit the rocks, you'd jump ship while he would stay on deck?'

Miss Prim, who'd never contemplated such a possibility, had to admit that she would indeed feel bad.

'And another thing, Prudencia. Could you live with the knowledge that, despite your divorce, there was someone who would, his whole life, until his very last breath, consider himself married to you?'

At the same time attracted and frightened by the awesome beauty of this image, she accepted that such a point of view was valid.

'In any case,' she said wistfully, 'it would never have come to that. I know him well enough to be sure that he wouldn't have consented to a civil wedding, so really I wouldn't even have had the option. I could leave him, of course, but would that change anything? I'd always feel tied to him, because I'd know that he'd always consider himself joined to me.'

Horacio smiled as he took a cigar from his breast pocket.

'Do you mind if I smoke, my dear?'

Calling upon her unwavering sense of what was polite, Miss Prim assured him that she didn't mind in the least.

'I've never understood why people enjoy cigars,' she said pleasantly. 'They have such a strong smell. Why don't you smoke a pipe? It's very dashing, and smells so much better.'

Her host lit the cigar and drew on it deeply, peering at his guest through the smoke.

'Because a pipe requires commitment, Prudencia. A pipe requires perseverance, loyalty and commitment. In a way, and to make it quite clear, the cigar is to romance what the pipe is to marriage.'

The librarian laughed, regarding him with affection.

'And now what?' he asked suddenly. 'Where will you go?'

'To Italy, I've told you.'

'So you're going through with it? I thought you were just saying that. Surely you don't believe all that nonsense about needing to live in Italy to round off your education?'

A little queasy from the cigar smoke but determined not to let it show, Miss Prim seemed for a moment to be lost in thought.

'No, I don't believe it,' she said at last. 'I'm not going there for my education, Horacio. I'm looking for fulfilment. I'm looking for beauty and perfection.'

'I see. And you think you'll find that in Italy?'

She stood up again and went to the window. The garden was covered in a thick blanket of snow. The branches of the ancient trees stood out against it like hard, dark charcoal strokes.

'I don't know,' she sighed. 'I realize that what I'm looking for may not exist, that I may never find it. But, having said that, is there anywhere in the world as full of beauty as Italy?'

Suddenly aware of his guest's growing pallor, Horacio extinguished his cigar and looked at her fondly.

'I want you to know how much I've come to value your friendship, my dear. I'll miss you with all my heart.'

Touched, Miss Prim went to her friend and, perching on the arm of his chair, took his hand in hers.

'I'd never have fitted in here if it hadn't been for you. I wouldn't have understood the little I've understood without your help, your gentlemanliness and your company. I'm more grateful than I could ever express, Horacio.'

'Nonsense,' he replied, trying to conceal his emotion by tightly squeezing her hand.

And, after a long silence, he added tenderly: 'Will you ever come back?'

She too was quiet for a moment before answering.

'I wish I knew, Horacio. I wish it was possible to know.'

Hortensia Oeillet was making up a colourful bouquet of peonies and roses when she glimpsed Miss Prim through her shop window. Delighted, she smiled to herself, quickly hid the flowers behind the counter and rushed out to the back to put the kettle on. She was just bringing out a carrot cake from the pantry when she heard the tinkling of the bell above the door.

'I saw you cross the street,' she said, embracing the librarian. 'Virginia, Emma and Herminia are on their way. I'll put the closed sign up so that absolutely no one disturbs us. So you're leaving in a week? You don't know how sorry I am.'

Miss Prim followed the florist out to the back room. A cheerful fire was lit in the fireplace and the small tea table, on which Hortensia also did her accounts, was covered with a blue damask tablecloth and laden with food. The librarian smiled and breathed in the fragrance of the tea as it brewed.

'Oh, I'm going to miss San Ireneo's old-fashioned, civilized ways so much!' she said, winking at her hostess.

'It's only a small farewell tea,' said Hortensia with a smile. 'Each one of us has contributed something. Emma baked a lemon sponge and the cheesecake whose recipe she refuses to give anyone. Herminia made the foie-gras and apple sandwiches and the roast-beef canapés. Virginia brought her Krasnodar tea; and the carrot cake and toast, butter and honey are my contributions. It's a shame we don't have one of your wonderful birthday tarts.'

'It's Mrs Rouan's tart now, too,' said Miss Prim as she sat down by the fire. 'It's a shared secret.'

'Really? Mrs Rouan is a good woman, if a little stubborn,' said her hostess, placing the teapot on the table.

'As am I.'

As they chatted, the other guests began arriving at the flower shop: first, Emma Giovanacci, out of breath; then, Virginia Pille, so well wrapped up in her thick camel coat that she was almost unrecognizable; and last, Herminia Treaumont, as delicate and exquisite as a flower.

'Any second thoughts, Prudencia?' asked the editor of San Ireneo's newspaper a few minutes later as the five women were enjoying the food and merry conversation around the fire.

They all looked expectantly at the librarian as she swallowed her mouthful of roast-beef canapé before answering.

'You were right, Herminia, as always. Now that I'm sure of it, I can't stay.'

'I wish I hadn't been,' replied Herminia, with a pained expression. 'I know I wasn't very tactful that evening. I've thought it over a lot since then, and I realize I should have taken you aside and told you sooner. I'd like to apologize now, in front of everyone, and I hope you believe me when I say I never wanted to hurt you.'

Miss Prim smiled and, moving nearer to the table, tenderly laid her hand on her friend's.

'I never thought you did. Now that we're being open, I have to confess that I would have preferred to have been told in private, but I never doubted you meant well. Of course,' she said with a wink, 'I have felt very jealous of you.'

'Really? There was absolutely no reason to, I can assure you. He's very fond of me, but not in any way that might trouble you.'

Hortensia rose from the table and went to refill the pot. The aroma of Krasnodar tea again pervaded the room.

'Well, now that that's all over,' said Emma cheerfully, 'and just in case anyone hasn't noticed, we've clearly got a real heartbreaker here in San Ireneo de Arnois. And the most interesting thing is that he has no idea he's doing it.'

They all laughed and refilled their cups.

'Oh, I'm sure he knows,' said Virginia. 'How could he not? I'm not saying he does it on purpose – he's an absolute gentleman in the sense we *still* give the word here – but how could you be unaware of something like that?'

Prudencia seemed to ponder the question as she dithered over whether to have a slice of carrot cake or a piece of buttered toast with honey.

'All I can say,' she said, opting for the cake, 'is that he's never consciously toyed with my feelings or tried to take advantage of the situation. He's always behaved with perfect courtesy.'

'Of course, Prudencia. Of course he has. But that's the *point*, isn't it?' said Hortensia.

'What do you mean?'

'The attraction of courtesy, of course. Is anything more powerful?'

'Do you think so?' asked Miss Prim, interested. 'I had the impression it was the other way round, that women were supposed to be attracted to cads.'

The florist and the other guests shook their heads vehemently.

'That's not true, Prudencia, at least not if we're talking about adult, emotionally balanced women,' said Virginia, swallowing a mouthful of lemon cake. 'Of course, we know what you mean. All young girls experience the kind of obscure attraction you refer to, but things change when they grow up.'

'I'm not sure that's right, Virginia,' said Miss Prim. 'It would speak well of our intelligence and good sense, but I fear it's not so. The world is full of grown women who are in dreadful relationships with deeply dishonest men.'

'It's not a matter of chronological maturity, Prudencia. And those women aren't the majority, in any case,' insisted the bookseller.

Herminia topped up her teacup before settling back in her chair.

'I expect it seems a little obsessive, always returning to the same source, but what about the duel between Mr Darcy and Mr Wickham? Or the confrontation between Mr Knightley and Frank Churchill? I'm convinced Jane Austen is the touchstone here. I don't think you'd find a single woman who, on reading *Pride and Prejudice*, would choose Mr Wickham rather than Mr Darcy, or after *Emma* would pine for Frank Churchill and despise Mr Knightley. Do you remember I once said to you that men hate Mr Darcy because they feel dull by comparison? And women adore him because, once he's repented of his pride, he's the ideal man – strong, sincere and honest.'

'And rich, you're forgetting that. Ten thousand pounds a year would make anyone attractive,' Emma pointed out wickedly.

'This is all true,' said the librarian, eyes shining. 'But unfortunately the modern world thinks otherwise. Very few women nowadays read nineteenth-century English novels.'

Emma sighed.

'We've strayed off the subject, ladies. The question was: is our man aware of what he's doing, as Virginia claims, or is it rather a case of what one might call collateral damage?'

'I've always thought he was very like his father,' said Hortensia. 'He was perfectly well aware of his effect on women.'

Miss Prim stopped eating, intrigued.

'You knew his father?'

'Of course,' replied the florist. 'I'm one of the few residents of San Ireneo who lived here before the community was created.'

'What was he like?'

'A real swine, but an attractive swine, and he had class – attractive until you realized he was a swine.'

The librarian was curious.

'When you say he was a swine, what do you mean, exactly?'

'He was in the habit of abandoning his family. There was always another woman, but it never lasted long. That's typical of men like that. I've known lots, and they never change. I suppose he loved his wife. She was a great beauty, and is still a handsome woman today. But that didn't stop him going off with a different woman as soon as her back was turned. It was very painful for her. Very painful.'

'What about the children?'

'They suffered in a different way, because he was a very loving father. They suffered when their mother, who had had enough, decided not to take him back.'

Miss Prim recalled sitting beneath a camellia one icy evening as the old lady spoke bitterly of choosing between two paths.

'So that was it,' she whispered.

'It's very difficult to judge in such situations. Many women would have done exactly the same; but the children adored their father and suffered hugely when they separated. She never relented, never let him back into her life, and she also made it difficult for him to see the children. He died alone and far away from all of them.'

Herminia stood up to put more logs on the fire.

'So, what do we conclude?' asked Virginia with a deep sigh. 'Is our Man in the Wingchair aware of his appeal, or is he entirely oblivious of the havoc he wreaks?'

They all stared expectantly at Prudencia, who smiled and then drained her third cup of tea.

'I'd say he has no idea,' she said softly. 'And that, precisely, is his charm.'

5

Miss Prim had not expected to find it so difficult to say goodbye to the children. If anyone had predicted as much upon her arrival in San Ireneo, she'd have given a dismissive smile and a look that said *on your way*. She'd never been especially inclined to glow with maternal tenderness at the sight of children. It wasn't that she disliked them, but their charm would not be fully revealed until she was a parent herself and, even then, she would remain gratifyingly confined to her own offspring. Miss Prim was not one of those women who stop in the street to coo over babies, or strike up conversations with toddlers swinging from their parents' hands in a cinema queue, or joyfully improvise ballgames with lively throngs of schoolchildren. So she was shocked by how emotional she felt at the thought of leaving the four children she'd lived with for the past few months.

'Will we never see you again?' little Eksi asked after she had told them the news.

The four children were gathered round Miss Prim in the library, as solemn as a council of war.

She paused at length before replying.

'"Never" is rather a strong word. Who knows what might happen? Maybe we'll see one another again sooner than you think. Maybe you'll go to Italy to study Bernini and Giotto and we'll meet there.'

The children looked doubtful, so she went on.

'Imagine you're going to visit the Basilica of St Francis, for instance. Do you know where that is?'

'In Assisi,' replied Teseris from the aged ottoman.

'That's right,' said the librarian brightly, 'it is in Assisi. Imagine you're there to see Giotto's frescoes. You walk through the Upper Basilica, overawed by the beauty of the walls and ceilings decorated with scenes from the life of Il Poverello, and as you're engrossed in admiring the paintings, you hear a familiar voice behind you say . . .'

'"Don't even think about touching them!"' exclaimed Deka with an impish grin.

Miss Prim winked at the little boy as she opened a tin of apple biscuits. Then Septimus spoke from the depths of his uncle's wingchair.

'I don't think we'll be able to visit you in Assisi. We already *know* it. We went there when we were *small*.'

The librarian suppressed a smile and began handing out biscuits.

'I don't think we will ever see you again,' said Eksi sadly

from the rug. 'You'll go to Italy and have adventures and never want to come back, like Robert Browning's wife.'

Miss Prim laughed.

'I wouldn't be so sure. My trip is nothing like hers. She was called Elizabeth Barrett, by the way. She was in love, and she left for love, remember?'

'You too,' said the little girl with conviction.

'Me?' said the librarian, taken aback. 'For love? That's ridiculous! I'm doing no such thing. What gave you that idea?'

'It's not my idea, it's the gardener's,' the child replied.

'He hears *everything* through the library window,' her older brother confirmed. 'He can probably hear us now.'

Miss Prim shot a furtive glance at the window to make sure it was firmly closed.

'The gardener couldn't have heard something that isn't true. Do you really think if I were going to Italy for love I'd tell anyone? Anyway, you shouldn't snoop or spread gossip, it's not a nice habit. I'm sure the gardener got it wrong. He wasn't talking about me.'

'He was talking about you,' said Deka, adamant.

The librarian handed round the biscuits a second time while trying to think how to get out of this fix.

'How do you know? Did he mention my name?'

The children exchanged eloquent looks.

'If we tell you, will you be cross with him?' asked Septimus warily.

'Of course not.'

After a moment, during which he seemed to be weighing whether she meant what she'd said, the boy continued.

'What he said was: "*She*'s going to Italy to look for a husband." *She* means you. That's what he calls you,' he explained.

Miss Prim took a deep breath but said nothing. A grave silence reigned in the room for a few minutes. Then a sound at the door made them all turn: the two enormous dogs came in, brushing against the librarian's knees and flopping down on the rug.

'*She*,' muttered the librarian.

Then she addressed the children.

'Will you miss me when I go?'

'Of course, though we won't know for sure until after you've left,' replied Septimus philosophically.

'We weren't sorry when the others left,' added Teseris in an undertone. 'But they weren't like you.'

Miss Prim stared into the fire. Her eyes stung with a pleasant, watery sting. She felt comforted by the children's honesty, the simplicity with which they spoke of what they disliked and what they loved, the lack of duplicity in their opinions, the absence of the tangled skeins that so often complicated adult relationships.

'*He* likes you too. He's sad you're leaving,' declared Eksi, stroking the shaggy fur of one of the dogs.

Prudencia blushed and averted her eyes, staring into the fire once more.

'I'm sure he liked the previous librarian too. What he likes is for the work to be done well, that's all.'

'He didn't like the one before that because he kicked the dogs.'

'Really?' said Miss Prim, horrified.

The children nodded.

'I'd like to go to Italy with you,' said Eksi. 'We could *study* things and you could look for that *husband*.'

For a moment Miss Prim pictured herself walking around Florence, wandering in a blissful haze into the Accademia, then standing enraptured before Michelangelo's *David*. She imagined a figure who appeared at her side and whispered mockingly into her ear: 'Are you ready to take out your ruler and compasses?'

'I have no intention of looking for a husband, Eksi, really I haven't,' she said sternly, unsettled by her vision.

'Miss Prim,' Teseris' voice had a dreamlike quality, 'I think we will see you again.'

Prudencia stroked the hair of the three children sprawled on the rug and directed an affectionate look at the little girl lying on the ottoman.

'Do you really think so?' she asked with a smile.

The child nodded.

'Then I'm sure you're right. Absolutely sure.'

Lulu Thiberville's note came as a surprise to Miss Prim. The news that the old lady wanted to say goodbye to her made her feel deeply anxious. She was an imposing personality – the librarian had been very conscious of it the afternoon they met – and Miss Prim believed that imposing personalities, like forces of nature, were dangerous and unpredictable. As she walked through the village to the Thiberville house, she scattered greetings and salutations among shopkeepers and residents. All responded warmly. A wave for the butcher, who had told her how to cook the Christmas turkey. A smile for the cobbler, who had taken such good care of her shoes over the past few months. A few words with the owner of the stationery shop, who reserved a pack of her handmade notepaper for Miss Prim every month since she had adopted the local custom of writing letters. She went into the doctor's surgery, to thank him for the cough syrup he'd prescribed for the children a couple of weeks earlier. And she said goodbye to the owners of the haberdashery where she bought her underwear, since she now knew it to be of equal or superior quality to any in the city.

The hall of the large old house where Lulu Thiberville lived had a smell of birdseed and medicine, but also of cake batter baking and bread toasting in the kitchen in preparation for the librarian's visit. Miss Prim found the old lady reclining on a sofa by the window. A heavy silver tea service was set out on a pedestal table beside her. Miss Prim approached and seated herself on a little padded footstool.

'For the love of God, child, sit on a chair!' cried the old lady in her cracked voice. 'You'll put your back out on that thing.'

Prudencia assured her that she was quite comfortable on the stool. She never hunched; she'd been taught not to as a child.

'Yes, I've noticed you always sit properly, on the edge of your chair with a very straight back. It's a comfort to think that there are still some women who know how to sit correctly. I can't stand to see all those young things slouching along the streets with sunken chests and rounded shoulders. I blame modern schools. Tell me, Miss Prim, did you learn to sit as you do in a modern school?'

She explained that her excellent posture was not a product of her schooling but was thanks to an old aunt of her mother's who had trained her from an early age to walk with books balanced on her head and to sit with the elegant rigidity of an Egyptian queen.

'They used to teach it in schools. Of course in those days they were still places where children learnt something. Now they're factories of indiscipline, hatcheries for rude, ignorant little monsters.'

Miss Prim looked uneasily at the old lady.

'I wouldn't put it quite so strongly,' she murmured.

'Of course you wouldn't, but I just have. You have no idea what schools used to be like, have you?'

She confessed meekly that she hadn't.

'Then you're in no position to compare. You simply have well-meaning opinions. And people of an optimistic outlook, as you seem to be, not only don't improve things but contribute to their decline. They convey the false impression that everything is going well when in fact – don't deceive yourself – it is going hopelessly badly. But please explain,' she said, motioning to the cook to place two serving dishes on a side table near her, 'why you're leaving us? Is it because of that business we discussed at Hortensia's house?'

Miss Prim nodded. She'd wanted to avoid this. In the past week she felt as if she'd done nothing but take her leave of people who wanted to delve over and over into the matter.

As if guessing how she felt, the old lady went on: 'Don't worry, I'm not going to get you to tell me the whole story. This is a small place. I assume you realize I don't have to enquire directly to find out what's going on?'

Prudencia, pouring the tea, shuddered.

'I had hoped that my private affairs wouldn't be spread around the village. Maybe I was being naive.'

The old lady smiled wryly, accepting a cup of tea.

'No, not naive, just young.'

'Isn't that the same thing?'

'It used to be, and it should be. But nowadays, who knows?'

Miss Prim looked gravely into the old lady's face.

'What do you mean?'

'Well, that the young should be as naive as human nature permits, child. Young people still walk in a certain innocence, still view the world with wonder and hope. Later on, as time passes, they find things aren't as they'd imagined and they begin to change, to lose that luminosity, that innocence. Their gaze clouds over and darkens. In one sense it's very sad, but in another it's inevitable, because it's precisely these sorrows that lead to maturity.'

Prudencia took a piece of buttered toast.

'And you think this has changed?'

'Of course it has. You'd have to be a fool or a lunatic not to see it. Young people today extend childhood well beyond the chronologically allotted time. They're immature and irresponsible at an age when they should no longer be so. But at the same time they lose their simplicity, their innocence and freshness early. Strange as it sounds, they grow old early.'

'Grow old? What an extraordinary idea!'

Lulu sipped her tea and gestured to her guest to cut her a piece of cake.

'Scepticism has always been considered an affliction of maturity, Prudencia, but now that is no longer the case. Those children have grown up unfamiliar with the great ideals that have shaped people for generations and made them strong. They've been taught to view them with contempt and, in their place, to substitute something cloying and sentimental that even they quickly find unsatisfying and even repellent. They lose the most valuable thing – I'd say the only truly valuable thing – that youth possesses and maturity does not. It's terrible to have to say such things, don't think I don't know.'

Miss Prim wondered how a woman of ninety-five who spent most of her time lying on an ancient sofa could have developed such acerbic views on the education system and the failings of young people. Before she could say anything, the old lady leant forward with a shrewd grin on her face.

'You think I'm too old to know the modern world and its problems.'

'Of course not,' she lied.

'Don't fib, child. You're partly right, but you must bear one thing in mind. Many different kinds of people pass through here. They like coming to the village. They visit our community as if it were a museum. And I'm very observant, my dear. At my age, there's not much else to do.'

Miss Prim made as if to protest but the old lady took no notice.

'That's not enough, though. You can't rely just on your own experience. The experience of a single human lifetime constitutes a narrow field of study, even a lifetime as long as mine. It's easy to fool oneself, God knows.'

Lulu paused as if for breath before continuing.

'Because, fundamentally, nothing changes, you know. The

huge old mistakes emerge time and again from the depths, like cunning monsters stalking prey. If you could sit at the window and watch human history unfold, do you know what you'd see?'

A little apprehensively, Miss Prim said she did not.

'I'll tell you. You'd see an immense chain of mistakes repeated over the centuries, that's what. You'd watch them, arrayed in different garb, hidden behind various masks, concealed beneath a multitude of disguises, but they'd remain the same. No, it's not easy to become aware of it, of course not. You have to stay alert and keep your eyes open to detect those evil old threats, recurring endlessly. Do you think I'm raving? No, my dear. You can't see it – most people no longer can – but it's growing dark, and I sense night falling. Those poor children, what do you think they get in schools?'

She blinked, trying to make sense of the old lady's speech.

'Knowledge, I suppose.'

Lulu sat up, unexpectedly spry.

'You're wrong. What they're getting is sophism – foul, rotten sophism. Sophists have taken over schools and are working hard for their cause.'

'Aren't you being rather pessimistic?' Miss Prim asked tentatively, glancing surreptitiously at the clock.

Lulu stared at her in silence.

'Pessimistic? Not at all, my dear. What is a gatekeeper to do if not to warn of what she's seen? Gatekeepers aren't optimistic or pessimistic, Prudencia. They're either awake or asleep.'

Prudencia sighed. She couldn't grasp the full scope of Lulu Thiberville's ideas. It would take more than an afternoon to plumb the depths of the old lady's mind. It was as dark and opaque as a cup of hot chocolate, too rich for afternoon tea and cake.

'So you're bound for Italy,' Lulu abruptly changed the subject as she poured more tea. 'What part are you going to?'

Miss Prim confessed that, though this was an obvious question, as yet she had no complete answer. Of course she knew where she would go first: she'd decided to start with Florence, where else? She'd spend part of the winter there, making the city her base, while travelling deeper into the country, getting to know its hidden corners, exploring its palazzos, towns and churches, reading lazily beneath its sun and sky, soaking in the beauty she so craved. She also thought she knew where she'd end her trip: Rome. But in between? Miss Prim wasn't sure. And despite this, or perhaps precisely because of it, she felt extraordinarily happy.

Lulu listened patiently to all these explanations, then closed her eyes, leant back on the sofa and said: 'You must go to Nursia.'

Miss Prim crossed her legs and looked out of the window in resignation. Since she announced her plan, the entire village had been intent on telling her where she must go and what she must not miss out.

'Nursia,' echoed Miss Prim.

'The birthplace of Benedict,' said the old lady, as if the saint were a friend of hers. And she went on: 'I'm very fond of the monks who live there.'

Miss Prim remained resolutely silent. She felt intensely annoyed at the thought that Lulu Thiberville might ask her to run some errand that would force her to go to a place she hadn't intended to visit. She'd always thought it inconsiderate to use one's age as leverage to make others do one's bidding. After all, she had her own plans, her own duties and obligations. She had no intention of going to visit monks of whom Lulu Thiberville had decided to be fond. Absolutely not.

'Don't rush to conclusions,' said Lulu with the imperious air that had created such an impression on the librarian at their first meeting. 'I'm not about to get you to run an errand in deepest Italy. Would you be so kind as to bring me that green book from the shelves? And that red one on top of the piano?'

Miss Prim went to get the books, which turned out to be two enormous photograph albums. Her hostess took them in her thin hands and started turning the pages. After about five minutes, which felt more like fifteen, she found what she was looking for.

'Here we are,' she said.

She indicated a group of photographs and her guest studied them closely.

'It looks like a beautiful place,' murmured Miss Prim, 'and a beautiful monastery.'

'San Benedetto,' said the old lady, adopting a light Italian accent.

'San Benedetto?'

'That's right. Doesn't it sound like music?'

'Actually, it does,' she replied, examining the photographs. 'But the monks . . . it's strange, I thought they'd all be very old.'

'You know little of life,' muttered Lulu with delight. 'Tradition is ageless, child. It's modernity that ages. Before I forget, you must go down to the crypt.'

'Why?' asked Miss Prim, far from overjoyed at the prospect of descending into any kind of crypt.

The old lady eyed her sternly, like a teacher faced with a child who stubbornly refuses to understand and whom she's beginning to suspect may not be worth teaching.

'Look at this,' she said, turning another few pages of the album. 'Isn't it beautiful?'

Miss Prim looked at the photos and nodded. Nursia had an austere piazza dominated by a statue of St Benedict. At one end stood a basilica of the same name with a rose window set into its white facade. 'Probably thirteenth century,' registered Miss Prim's methodical mind. Another photograph showed a vast, deserted meadow between mountains, where thousands of poppies, primroses, violets and other wild flowers formed a resplendent carpet.

'How wonderful,' she exclaimed admiringly. 'It looks like a high plateau.'

'An apt comparison, since it is a high plateau. There's an excellent hotel in the village, run by a delightful family. It's perfect for you. The best thing to do there is rest, watch the world go by and mix with the locals. You can't imagine how inspiring it is to walk through the village to the market, saying hello to people, and then watch the monks tilling their land and listen to them singing Gregorian chant in the crypt. They're restoring a second monastery. They may need help.'

'Nursia,' repeated Miss Prim in a murmur. 'Who knows?'

Lulu peered at her with renewed attention.

'I think it'll do you a lot of good, Prudencia. It'll temper your modern hardness.'

She laughed, stirring her usual two lumps of sugar into her tea.

'Modern hardness? What do you mean?'

Lulu sat up so as to observe her guest more closely.

'Look at me, child, and tell me what you see. A sweet little old lady, perhaps?'

Miss Prim shook her head, smiling.

'I wouldn't say that, exactly.'

'And you'd do well not to. I'm a hard woman. And do you

know why? Because I'm old. Now look at yourself. What do you see?'

The smile slowly faded from the librarian's lips.

'I don't know, it's difficult to judge oneself.'

'I'll tell you: a hard young woman.'

'I'm not sure what you mean,' said Miss Prim, who had never considered herself a hard woman.

'Don't take offence, child. Maybe I wasn't being clear. I'm not saying that you, specifically, are a hard woman. What I mean is that modern women like you are all, to a greater or lesser extent, hard.'

The librarian fiddled nervously with the zip to her bag. According to this last explanation, maybe she hadn't been insulted personally, only generically, but she still felt she had to object out of a sense of honour. Lulu listened with a slight smile before responding.

'So you're wondering how I justify what I said, is that right?'

Miss Prim declared that this was indeed what she was wondering.

'It's the yearning. Plainly and simply, it's the yearning.'

'Yearning? For what?'

The old lady hesitated almost imperceptibly before continuing and, when she did, it seemed as if she would never fall silent again.

'The yearning you all display to prove your worth, to show that you know this and that, to ensure that you can have it all. The yearning to succeed and, even more, the

286

yearning not to fail; the yearning not to be seen as inferior, but instead even as superior, simply for being exactly what you believe you are, or rather what you've been made to believe you are. The inexplicable yearning for the world to give you credit simply for being women. Ah, you're getting angry with me, aren't you?'

Prudencia, lips clenched and knuckles almost white, did not reply.

'Of course you are. Yet you only have to listen to yourself talk about the man you work for to realize that some of what I say is true. Why do you seem so angry? Why do you compare and register everything as if life were designed to be measured with a ruler? Why are you so afraid of losing your ranking, of being left behind? Why, my dear, are you so defensive?'

Miss Prim stared at the old lady, lost for words. She tried to calm herself as she wondered how to respond to what she was hearing. Meanwhile, Lulu went on, her voice rasping and weary.

'You say you're looking for beauty, but this isn't the way to achieve it, my dear friend. You won't find it while you look to yourself, as if everything revolved around you. Don't you see? It's exactly the other way round, precisely the other way round. You mustn't be careful, you must get hurt. What I'm trying to explain, child, is that unless you allow the beauty you seek to hurt you, to break you and knock you down, you'll never find it.'

Miss Prim stood up, roughly shaking the cake crumbs from her tweed skirt. She glanced coldly at the old lady on the sofa, who nodded in silent farewell, and then she walked out of Lulu Thiberville's sitting room and life, firmly resolved never to return.

6

During her last few days in San Ireneo de Arnois, Miss Prim tried to avoid the Man in the Wingchair. She wasn't sure if it was her imagination, but during that time of suitcases, packages and farewells, she had the feeling that he was avoiding her just as assiduously. The weather had turned particularly cold, as it always did in late February, and the frozen fields beyond gave the house and garden the aspect of a lifeless landscape painting. On the morning of her departure she was in her room checking her packing one last time. Everything was there – the few books she had brought with her, her clothes and shoes, one or two personal objects and the countless presents received in the past few hours from friends and neighbours all over the village. Miss Prim contemplated the pile of luggage with a sad smile. After inspecting the chest of drawers and bedside tables to make sure she hadn't forgotten anything, she straightened up and let her melancholy gaze rest on the view outside the window. At that moment, she was startled by a snowball striking the glass with a dull thud. She opened the door onto the balcony and looked down. There in the garden, bundled up to his eyes, stood the Man in the Wingchair.

'Will you come down?' he called out.

'Come down? It's several degrees below zero – not a good day for a stroll in the garden.'

He smiled, or so she deduced from the crinkling of his eyes, the only part of his face that was visible.

'I think it's a perfect day. For the garden and for you there won't be a better one. I won't have the pleasure of seeing you both together after today.'

'That's true,' murmured Miss Prim.

'What did you say?' he shouted.

'I said that's true,' she repeated more loudly. 'But the gardener's picking me up in half an hour. I haven't got time to chat.'

He came and stood right beneath the window.

'Come on, Prudencia, surely you've got time to say goodbye?'

Elbows resting on the parapet, she thought for a moment.

'You're right. Let me get my coat and I'll be straight down.'

Hurrying downstairs, the librarian realized she had been

invaded by a familiar anxiety which she hated to admit she hadn't mastered – despite the sleepless nights, all the conversations and confidences, the tears spilt; despite the rebukes and well-meaning advice she'd received on the absurdity of her sudden access of love – despite it all, she hadn't mastered the anxiety. She hadn't overcome that upset, that violent disturbance which had plunged her perfectly and carefully cultivated equilibrium to the bottom of the ocean.

'You should take more exercise, you're very flushed.'

'Oh!' she said, wondering for the umpteenth time why he seemed unable to appreciate the distinction between honesty and tactlessness.

It was cold – intensely, bleakly cold – as they headed to the south side of the garden where an old wooden summerhouse stood, full of gardening tools, empty pots, useless junk of all shapes and sizes, a white-painted table and four decrepit garden chairs that had been around for more years than anyone could remember.

'Why don't you fix this place up?' asked Miss Prim, sitting down on one of the chairs.

'Because I like it like this.'

'Why?' Somewhere inside her the librarian could hear a clashing of swords.

He regarded her in silence, as if gauging whether her question had been innocent or more of a provocation.

'Why what?'

'Why do you only like old things?'

'That's not quite true. I like some new things.'

'Really?' she asked. 'Name one.'

He smiled in a way she now understood.

'You, for instance.'

She sighed in feigned dismay.

'I don't know whether to take that as a compliment. I'm glad you don't think of me as old, but I'm not sure it's flattering to be considered a thing.'

He laughed and she felt her eyes fill with tears. She lowered her head and, when she looked up, her eyes met his.

'I'm sorry,' she said. 'The thought of leaving makes me sad.'

'Really?'

Miss Prim looked at him with a mixture of surprise and reproach.

'Of course,' she said, eyes glistening.

'I'm glad to hear it,' he said, 'because I'm sorry you're leaving too. You've been a marvellous opponent, as well as great company. I'll miss our arguments.'

She dropped her gaze, a mischievous smile playing on her lips.

'Don't lie. You know perfectly well that I've never been any sort of opponent for you. You've won all the arguments, you've twisted my words and you've always done me the favour of infuriating me.'

'That's a favour?' he said wryly.

'Yes,' she said, unbowed. 'When I arrived I was reluctant

to entertain any viewpoint other than my own. In that respect I'm afraid I'm rather like you.'

'Well, I have to admit that your attacks have helped me understand certain things.'

Resisting the urge to say she had never attacked anyone, Miss Prim straightened slightly in her chair and leant forward.

'Such as?' she asked.

'Such as what you call delicacy, I suppose.'

'That surprises me,' she said, pleased. 'I thought you despised it.'

'That's not true.'

'I thought you considered it – how shall I put it? – a soft quality.'

'I consider it a feminine attribute.' Prudencia grimaced. 'But that doesn't mean I don't think it can, or even should, be present in a man's character.'

'But it's not in yours.'

'No. That's why knowing you has been so enriching.'

They were quiet for a few minutes, watching the falling snow through the summerhouse windows.

Then Miss Prim said: 'I'd like to thank you.'

'For what?'

'For nothing, and for everything. I just think I should. I'll probably realize at some stage that I should have thanked you and, when that happens, I don't want to feel that I missed my chance. Do you see?'

'Not at all,' he said baldly.

She stared at him, crestfallen, wondering how such brilliance and such exasperating, blunt, pig-headed insensitivity could coexist within the same person. She felt she'd been perfectly clear. Half of humanity, if not all, had at some time experienced the intuition, the conviction that they should thank someone for something. But many had let the words die on their lips, and Miss Prim didn't want to be one of them.

'You are a strange person. You absolutely lack empathy,' she said.

'And yet you are fond of me,' he said.

'Vanity is another of your great faults,' she continued, unperturbed. 'I'd say I respect you. With that, I think I've said enough.'

The Man in the Wingchair smiled.

'But we're friends, even so,' he said, looking into her eyes.

'We are,' she replied in a whisper. Then, in one of the emotional outbursts that seized her occasionally and made her say things abruptly and almost breathlessly, she added: 'Do you really believe that love between two very different people is impossible?'

He stood up and pulled the door of the old summerhouse half closed so the snow didn't blow in.

'I've never said that,' he replied, returning to his seat. 'No, I don't think it's impossible. I'd say it's very common.'

'But you . . .' stammered Miss Prim, astonished by the

strange recklessness that had impelled her to say such a thing, 'you and Herminia . . .'

'We separated because we were very different?' The Man in the Wingchair shook his head. 'You haven't understood, Prudencia. You haven't understood at all what I tried to explain the other day.'

'Perhaps you didn't explain it well,' she replied coolly, annoyed by the idea of being classified as a person who understood nothing. 'Perhaps you were too cryptic.'

'Right, well, I'll make it easy then.'

Miss Prim wondered if, in defence of her own dignity, she shouldn't object to this didactic condescension but, as so often with her employer, curiosity overcame pride.

'I'm listening.'

'Imagine for a moment that you and I – two very different people – decided to go to St Petersburg together. Are you following me?'

'Perfectly.'

'You'll agree that we would probably argue for the entire trip.'

'Very probably.'

'I'd want to stay in monasteries and converse with old *starets*, whereas you would insist on booking luxurious, spotlessly clean hotels. I'd want to meander through small, insignificant villages and hamlets on our way; you'd no doubt have our route strictly planned and would find it annoying to stop off at places with little historic or cultural interest. But eventually, despite all these difficulties, you and I would arrive in St Petersburg.'

'And what then?' asked the librarian, resting her elbows on the table.

'Let me continue, I'm doing my best not to be cryptic. Now imagine that we decided to go on another journey. But this time you wanted to go to St Petersburg and I wanted to go to Tahiti. What do you think would happen?'

Miss Prim smiled sadly.

'Sooner or later we'd go our separate ways,' she said.

'I see you understand now.'

'Unless,' said the librarian softly after a long pause, 'unless I convinced you to go to St Petersburg instead of Tahiti.'

He took off his gloves and regarded her with interest.

'But that's part of the problem, Prudencia. I don't want anyone convincing me to go to St Petersburg, and if I thought there was any chance of anyone succeeding, I wouldn't take the risk.'

'But also, the thing is,' Miss Prim searched for the words, 'the thing is, you might convince me to go to Tahiti.'

The Man in the Wingchair was silent for a moment that seemed to the librarian to last an eternity.

'I'd go to the ends of the earth to convince you to come to Tahiti,' he said with a strange intensity to his voice. 'I'd do anything in my power, absolutely anything. But I think the journey would be a failure – a terrible failure – unless you were sure at the outset you wanted to know Tahiti.'

'You've never tried to convince me to go to Tahiti,' she said quietly.

'How do you know?'

'How do I know what?'

'How do you know I haven't tried?'

'Because you've never forced or pressured me into anything. You've never done anything to try to convince me. That's probably why we're friends; you've always respected my opinions.'

He leant back in the battered metal summerhouse chair.

'That's true. I've never forced or pressured you. But if I haven't, it's only because I thought it would be counterproductive. Don't attribute virtues to me – since you consider it a virtue – that I don't possess.'

'Whatever the reason,' said the librarian, 'you haven't gone to the ends of the earth to persuade me to join you in Tahiti.'

'You don't think so?' he asked with a smile. 'Perhaps one day you'll realize that one can go to the ends of the earth without leaving one's room, Prudencia.'

'Now you're being cryptic again,' she said, then went on in a jesting tone: 'Tell me something. If I'd wanted to go to Tahiti, if I'd never thought of going to St Petersburg, would you have dared invite me on that journey with you?'

The Man in the Wingchair bowed his head with a smile.

Then, looking into her eyes, he asked softly: 'And what about you? Would you have come?'

She was about to reply when the gardener's wrinkled, sullen face appeared at the door.

'It's time, miss.'

Flushed, Miss Prim got to her feet. Rising at the same time, her employer held out his hand and said: 'It's very cold in St Petersburg, Prudencia. I know, I've been there. But maybe some day . . . ' He broke off.

She crept to the door without a word. On the threshold, she turned and looked at the Man in the Wingchair one last time.

'I don't think so,' she whispered.

Miss Prim did not turn to take a last look at the house and garden. In accordance with her wishes, which had been expressed as firmly as a military order, neither the children, nor the cook, nor the girls from the village, nor even the Man in the Wingchair were at the door to see her off. Miss Prim disliked farewells. Despite all the unfounded accusations of sentimentality, she was very conscious that she wasn't comfortable with emotional scenes: she didn't know how to handle them or how to strike the right tone. This couldn't be said of him, she reflected as she huddled in the back of the car and glanced out of the corner of her eye at the gardener's solemn face. The Man in the Wingchair always, or almost always, knew how to behave; was capable at all times of finding the appropriate look, the happy or serious expression. Miss Prim believed it came down to manners. Not the kind that could be acquired from magazines, or books on etiquette, or even the kind displayed by people who boasted of having good manners. What he had, and she appreciated it, was quite different, perhaps because it couldn't be studied or emulated. It couldn't be taught or learnt. It was simply breathed in. It seemed so natural, so simple, so intrinsic to the person that it took you some time – a few weeks, even months – to realize how serenely harmonious such behaviour was. Magazine columns, books on etiquette and correspondence courses couldn't compete with a code instilled from the cradle, perfected over the centuries since the forgotten dawn of chivalry and courtly love.

As she mused, the car rounded a bend in the road and the huge, solid structure of the abbey of San Ireneo came into view. The librarian contemplated its ancient stone walls, admired its symmetrical beauty and then glanced at her watch. She had plenty of time to get to the station. She had allowed almost two hours for a journey that took half an hour by car; Miss Prim was a staunch advocate not only of punctuality but also, and above all, of precaution. Out of respect for precaution she had decided to set out two hours early and by that glorious virtue, at that precise moment, without knowing why or even how, she felt a strong urge to meet the venerable monk who lived within those walls, the elderly man whom she had so assiduously avoided throughout that long cold winter in San Ireneo de Arnois.

'Could we stop at the monastery for a moment?' she asked the gardener.

'Of course, miss. Do you want to buy some of their honey?'

'No,' she replied, meeting his gaze in the rear-view mirror. 'Actually, I'd like to have a quick word with the padre.'

'With the padre?' asked the gardener, flabbergasted. 'Are you sure?'

'Quite sure,' she said, lifting her chin resolutely. 'Could you help me?'

'Of course,' said the gardener, taking the turn that skirted the fields and led straight to the abbey.

After speaking to the monk at the gatehouse, Miss Prim entered the monastery and was ushered to the reception rooms, where she was told to wait. She stared at the bare walls until a young monk, wearing an apron over his habit, greeted her warmly and asked her to follow him to the vegetable garden.

'He's getting some fresh air,' said the monk by way of explanation, apparently seeing nothing unusual in this on a morning when the temperature was several degrees below zero.

She was led down a corridor, through a hushed, austere cloister and eventually to a corner of a small kitchen garden where a very elderly man was sitting on a bench.

'Miss Prim has come to see you,' said the young monk, before indicating to the librarian that she should approach.

The old man sat up, dismissing the younger man with a tender smile, and invited his visitor to sit beside him.

'Please, take a seat,' he said in a low tone. 'I've been expecting you.'

'Have you?' she asked, worried he had mistaken her for someone else. 'I'm not sure if you know who I am, Father. My name's Prudencia Prim and I've been working as a librarian for the past few months at—'

'I know exactly who you are,' interrupted the monk gently. 'I've been waiting for you. You've taken a long time.'

Miss Prim observed the old man's wrinkled face and thin, frail body and wondered if he was of sound mind.

'They've often talked about you,' he said, and she thought she glimpsed delight in his eyes.

'They? Do you mean the man I work for?'

'I mean all the people who know you and are fond of you.'

She blushed with pleasure. It had never occurred to her that anyone might visit the ancient monk and mention her. She'd never dreamed that her presence could have penetrated those rigid walls, filtering into the Benedictine's routine of silent contemplation.

Before she could say anything, the monk continued: 'You're going to Italy.'

Miss Prim replied that yes, indeed, she was.

'Why?'

'Why?'

'Yes.'

She frowned a little. She was reluctant to explain herself. The circumstances and reasoning behind her departure were private and she had no desire to share her private life with the old man. And more to the point, she thought suddenly, did she herself really know why she was leaving?

'I suppose I'm not entirely sure. If you asked people who know me you'd get different answers. Some would say I'm going because I've been disappointed in love, others because I need to shed my modern hardness and yet others would claim I'm leaving to look for a husband.'

The monk smiled suddenly and his open, serene expression immediately set his guest at ease.

'And you,' he said, 'why do you think you're leaving?'

'I don't know,' she replied simply.

'People who leave a place without reason are either running away, or seeking something. Which is it for you?'

She contemplated her answer for a long time. When she spoke, she saw that the old man had closed his eyes.

'Both, I think,' she said quietly, afraid that he might be asleep. 'Perhaps that's what I need to find out.'

He gradually opened his eyes and stared at the snow-covered vegetable garden.

'Can I ask you something?' he said, as if he hadn't heard his visitor's last words. 'How do you close doors? Do you leave them ajar, pull them to gently, or slam them shut?'

Miss Prim's eyes widened in surprise, but seconds later she

recovered her composure. Now she was sure: the old man was senile.

'I think I leave them ajar, or close them gently. I definitely never slam them.'

'As novices, Carthusians are taught to turn round and close doors without pushing them or letting them swing shut. Do you know why?'

Miss Prim replied that she had no idea.

'So that they learn not to rush, to do one thing after another. So as to train them in restraint, patience, silence and mindfulness in every gesture.' He paused. 'You must be wondering why I'm telling you this. It's because this is the spirit in which to set out on a journey – any journey. If you travel in a hurry, without pausing or resting, you'll return without having found what you're looking for.'

'The problem is,' she replied, having pondered his words, 'I'm not sure what I'm looking for.'

He looked at her with compassion.

'Then perhaps the journey will enable you to find out.'

Miss Prim sighed. She'd been afraid that the old monk would try to discern the black holes in her life, that his eyes would bore into her and see her darkest secrets. But he wasn't the intimidating visionary with a foot in each world whom she'd so feared meeting. He was just a kindly, tired little old man.

'I was told you could read minds. I was warned you'd tell me things that would surprise and upset me,' she blurted.

He shivered in his worn habit before responding very gently.

'Many years ago, when I was a young man, I had a teacher. He taught that a priest, any priest, must always be a gentleman.'

She blinked, confused.

'You came here worried that I would tell you something that would frighten, disturb or trouble you. What kind of courtesy would I have shown if I'd behaved like that the first time you came to see me, without your even having asked for guidance? Don't be afraid of me, Miss Prim. I'll be here. I'll be here waiting for you to find what you're looking for and to return to tell me all about it. And you can be sure that I'll be with you, without leaving my cell, even as you search.'

'You can go to the ends of the earth without leaving your room,' whispered the librarian.

'I've been told that you value delicacy and yearn for beauty,' the old man went on. 'So seek beauty, Miss Prim. Seek it in silence, in tranquillity; seek it in the middle of the night and at dawn. Pause to close doors while you seek it, and don't be surprised if it doesn't reside in museums or in palaces. Don't be surprised if, in the end, you find beauty to be not Something but Someone.'

She looked into the venerable Benedictine's eyes and wondered what he could have taught her if she'd agreed to come to him sooner, as her friend Horacio had suggested.

Then the intense chill made her glance at her watch. It was getting late and she had a train to catch.

'I'm afraid I have to go,' she said. 'Thank you for your thoughts, but it's getting late and I have to get to the station.'

'Go,' he said, 'don't miss your train. That would be no way to start a journey as important as this.'

Miss Prim rose, taking her leave warmly and politely, and started walking back towards the abbey. But before she had quite crossed the kitchen garden, she stopped and retraced her steps to where the old man was still sitting on the bench.

'Father, I'd like to ask you something. These past few months I've heard people say many things about love and marriage. They've given me plenty of advice, and expounded many theories. I'd like to know what you think is the secret of a happy marriage.'

His eyes widened as if this was the first time anyone had ever asked him such a question. Smiling, he struggled to his feet and slowly approached.

'As you'll appreciate, I don't know much about it. No man could who has devoted himself to God from his earliest youth, as I have. No doubt the people who gave you advice have experience of marriage and therefore can say much more on the subject than I can. And yet . . .'

'Yes?' she said, painfully aware of the fast-moving minute-hand of her watch.

'And yet, I think I can say what constitutes the spiritual core of marriage, without which it can never be much more than a house of cards that stays up more or less by chance.'

'And that is?' she pressed, seized by a feverish desire not to leave doors ajar, but to slam them shut.

'And that is, my dear child, that marriage involves not two, but three.'

Astonished, Miss Prim was about to reply when she remembered the time. She held out her hand to the old monk, turned and hurried away from the abbey of San Ireneo to catch her train.

Nursia

*P*rudencia Prim climbed the last few steps up from the crypt of the Basilica of St Benedict and, unhooking the crimson rope that cordoned off the entrance from the rest of the building, went outside. She felt the cool morning air on her face as she descended the steps into the main square in Nursia. The market was mostly still closed but some of the stalls were coming to life, ready to sell local handicrafts to early passers-by. In the *norcinerie*, which sold impressive arrays of sausages, prosciutto, mortadella and salami as well as lentils, rice, pasta of all shapes and colours and the most delicious truffles, shopkeepers were raising shutters, opening doors and arranging baskets and attractive displays of goods outside their premises. The town hall, adorned with the Italian flag that flapped in the wind, and, opposite, the severe edifice that housed the Castellina

Museum, were delightfully familiar to her. Yet she'd only been living there for sixteen weeks.

It was a Friday and, as she always did, Miss Prim turned the corner at the church and walked down the street to the small terrace of the Bar Venezia. Looking forward to a large breakfast, she sat at a table, picked up the menu and ran her eyes down the list of cured hams and brawn on offer. When the waiter came to take her order with his usual friendly smile, she sighed happily.

'Buongiorno, signorina.'

'Buongiorno, Giovanni.'

'Cappuccino?'

'Cappuccino,' she said. 'And some of your excellent prosciutto.'

He looked at her dubiously.

'Prosciutto? I don't think so. You must be mistaken.'

Miss Prim shot him a look of surprise. She opened her mouth as if to say something but merely grinned in embarrassment.

'Of course, what was I thinking?'

'How about some toast with cream cheese and jam?'

'That'll be lovely, thank you.'

She settled herself in her chair and half-closed her eyes. She'd arrived in early May, just in time to enjoy spring in all its finery, the spring that filled the Piano Grande of the Monti Sibillini – a vast plain surrounded by mountains that stretched like a lake only a few miles from Nursia – with flowers. On the advice of the hotel owner, one morning she had walked up to the plateau and admired the incredible sight: an endless carpet of poppies, daisies, clover and violets, dandelions, yellow, pink and red ranunculus, blue gentians, bellflowers and many other wild species. That morning Miss Prim had stepped onto the carpet of flowers, wandered among them, sat and even – who would have thought it? – lain down. With dazzled eyes she could make out the tiny, isolated village of Castelluccio, a lost kingdom in a fairy tale, rising like an island from the sea.

And yet it wasn't the abundance of nature that had kept her there. It wasn't the ancient Sybilline Mountains, the vibrant red poppies or the slender cypresses edging the wheat fields. Nor was it the serene faces of the monks or the austere radiance of their chant. It was all these and much more that had made her stay.

She'd criss-crossed Italy, from north to south and from east to west. She had absorbed the grandeur of the cities and the beauty of the landscapes. She had given herself up to the dazzling coasts of Liguria and Amalfi, strolled along the shores of Lombardy, surrendered to the harmony of Florence, the beauty of Venice, the spirit of Rome. She'd been captivated by the bustle of Naples and lost all sense of time along the coasts of the Cinque Terre; she'd admired the luminosity of Bari and wandered the sober streets of Milan. For two long months she wandered down narrow streets and around harbours, palaces, fields and gardens. She'd sauntered through the villages of Tuscany and lands of Piedmont. But only in Umbria, that corner of Umbria, had she come to a stop at last and unpacked her bags.

'What a small thing happiness is, yet what a big thing,' she said to herself as she munched her toast and sipped her cappuccino.

She had to plan her day. She had thought of spending the morning answering letters – Miss Prim was one of the few guests at the hotel, if not the only one, who sent and received letters – and the afternoon visiting Spoleto. What a pleasing prospect to be able to spend hours on a café terrace, observing the people around her, occasionally reading some poetry – since she'd been in Italy she'd only been able to read poetry – and breathing in the gentle warmth of the summer air. She bit into a second slice of toast and motioned to the waiter, who was lingering benignly in the café doorway, watching the morning unfold.

'Cappuccino, signorina?'

'Cappuccino, Giovanni.'

'The postman left a registered letter for you yesterday,' said Giovanni a few moments later, placing a steaming, fragrant cup of coffee, more toast and a tray with three envelopes on the table.

'Thank you.'

'Prego.'

Miss Prim opened the first letter, read it and put it down. She drank some coffee, opened the second letter, read it and put it down. She took a bite of toast, opened the third letter, read it and put down the toast. For a few minutes she simply reread the sheet of paper she had taken from the envelope. Then she unfolded a newspaper cutting that had come with the letter, smoothed it out on the table and examined it closely. It was a page of small ads from the *San Ireneo Gazette*. At the bottom of the third column an item was circled in red.

Wanted: a heterodox teacher for an unorthodox school, able to teach the trivium – Greek and Latin grammar, rhetoric and logic – to children aged six to eleven. Preferably with no work experience. Graduates or post-graduates need not apply.

As her eyes alighted on the last two sentences, Miss Prim's heart began to beat faster. She took a few deep breaths and her pulse slowed. At last, there it was: the moment had arrived. During her months of travelling she'd corresponded regularly with some of her friends in San Ireneo. None of them had mentioned it, nor had she. But in a way, they had all been waiting for the moment to arrive. So many letters sent and received, so many anecdotes recalled, so many small events recorded on sheets of paper shuttling back and forth, north to south, linking the librarian to the place she had found so difficult to leave and to which she so feared returning.

So much had changed during those months. Sometimes she was quite shocked when she remembered how indignant she'd been when leaving San Ireneo that frozen February. How angry she was as she stormed out of Lulu Thiberville's house – dear Lulu Thiberville, with whom she'd exchanged so many letters over the past month. How could she not write to Lulu after her seventh visit to the crypt? How could she not write to her after walking, kneeling – who would have thought it – and lying down on the carpet of a thousand colours overlooked by the Sybilline Mountains? How could she not explain that she'd learnt to look, scan the horizon, close her eyes and travel back to the past, to identify monsters and avoid icebergs, to understand and appreciate the arduous labour of the gatekeeper?

She also wrote often to her dear, much admired Horacio. How could she not write when one day she succeeded at last in admiring Giotto without trying to dissect him? How could she not tell him that in some local villages children still played football in church courtyards, just as all the children in all the villages of Europe had played before Europe forgot games and courtyards? How could she not tell Horacio about the silence of afternoons in Spoleto, the beauty of the narrow streets of Gubbio, the tranquillity of the gardens around the monastery of San Damiano? She missed her friend, she missed his severe, gentlemanly kindness, she felt its loss keenly. But she knew that she missed more than that, and more than him.

'Cappuccino, signorina?'

'No, thank you, Giovanni. Could I have the bill, please?'

Miss Prim paid, gathered up the letters and left the terrace of the Bar Venezia just as on any other day. She crossed the main square and paused to chat with the *carabiniere*, asking after his wife and mother just as on any other day. She stopped briefly at the shop of the Monastery of St Benedict, bought a few things and left with a smile on her face just as on any other day. Then she returned to her hotel, located a stone's throw from the square. She walked up to the reception desk and waited patiently while the receptionist dealt with a young Japanese couple who, with much gesturing and giggling, were asking how to get to Assisi. Miss Prim looked at them warmly.

Tutti li miei penser parlan d'Amore

Dante: *Every one of my thoughts speaks of love*. Since setting out on her travels, she kept remembering poetry. It flooded her mind with the vigour of the wild flowers blooming on the Piano Grande. It wasn't her own – Miss Prim had always had sufficient respect for poetry not to write any herself. But since the morning when she had gazed out to sea in Santa Margherita Ligure and, astonished and bewildered, whispered: *E temo e spero; ed ardo e son un ghiaccio – I fear and hope; I burn and freeze like ice* – she'd felt overwhelmed by poems long forgotten, poems studied, poems learnt, dissected and analysed. In Santa Margherita Ligure it was Petrarch, in Naples it was Boccaccio. In Florence it was

Virgil, in Venice it was Juvenal's turn. And the strange thing was that never during these lyrical invasions had Miss Prim felt any urge to study, dissect or analyse. Poetry seemed to have taken possession of her and done so with no hint of study, dissection or analysis. It was not her enjoying the poems, it was the poems enjoying themselves in her. They alighted in her mind – or was it her soul? – at dawn, as she rose to watch the sun rise. They startled her at midday, as she watched the Benedictines out in the fields put down their hoes to go and recite the Angelus. They lulled her in the evening as she sat at a café terrace reading until the diminishing light and evening chill roused her from her reverie.

In this feverish poetic ecstasy, Miss Prim had looked to her favourite authors. But all that came to her lips were odd lines of Ronsard or triplets from Dante or stanzas from Spenser. At first she'd been put out by her inability to recite exactly what she wanted, but soon she realized that the ancient verses were soothing to her soul. Who could remain tense or anxious when Queen Gloriana and her knights echoed in their mind? How could you fail to feel uplifted when a voice was telling you at every step that the year, month, day, season, place, even that very moment were blessed? She couldn't fight it and she had absolutely no desire to. The images that had always so moved her with their terrible, desperate humanity no longer lodged in her mind, no longer took control of her but fled to be lost in the brilliance of the day. Then beauty returned and harmony was restored; and Miss Prim surrendered. And with her surrender, Dante, Virgil and Petrarch also returned.

'You need to take this road,' the receptionist was saying to the Japanese couple. Becoming aware that another guest was waiting, she gestured in apology.

Miss Prim sighed benevolently and found a chair to sit on.

She'd learnt how to close doors. She'd learnt to open them gently and close them carefully. And when you learnt to close doors, she reflected as she watched the pair of lovers, in a way you learnt to open and close everything else correctly. Time seemed to stretch out indefinitely when you did things properly. It froze, halted, stopped suddenly, like a clock that has wound down. Then the small things, the necessary things, even the ordinary, everyday things, especially those one performed with one's hands – how mysterious that man could do such beautiful things with his hands – were revealed as works of art.

She'd given up trying to achieve perfect virtue on her own. She'd realized how exhausting, how inhuman and wrong it was to live enslaved by this goal. Now that she was aware of her overwhelming imperfection, her fragility and contingency, she no longer bore the burden of the hammer and the chisel on her back. It wasn't that she'd accepted imperfection, or grown accustomed to it, but she no longer carried the load alone, she no longer shouldered the yoke with only her own strength, she was no longer shocked when she struck a bad

317

patch. She also knew that none of this would last, that after the joy there would be dips, caverns, tunnels and ravines. But for now, everything was a gift that she was learning to accept.

'No, signore, not that turning. Here, I'll give you the map. It shows it clearly.'

The previous week she'd had a call from her old employer, Augusto Oliver. He needed her urgently, he missed her, he wanted her to come back to work for him. Naturally she would no longer be a mere administrative assistant – a woman like her should never have been employed in such a capacity – she was too talented, too capable for administrative tasks. Miss Prim had laughed inwardly. For forty long seconds she hadn't been able to say a word because she had been silently laughing. Then she'd said no and hung up.

She didn't want to go back. She couldn't bear the thought of burying herself again in that dark, narrow place, shutting herself up in the dull grey cell where she'd spent so much of her life. She wouldn't return to the trivial chit-chat, wouldn't listen or take part. And she definitely had no intention of going back to the sordid game of dodging her boss's advances.

There was also the matter of air. Miss Prim now *needed* air. She needed to feel it on her face as she walked, to smell it, to breathe it. Sometimes she found herself wondering how she'd lived so long without the need for air. On winter mornings in the city she left home wrapped up to her ears, scurried to the underground, descended the steps with dozens of other people and shoved and jostled her way onto a train. She emerged with the crowds and rushed to her office, where she spent a long day. Meanwhile, where was the air? At what point in her life had she forgotten about the existence of air? Walking without having to rush, a pleasure as simple as taking a stroll, wandering, ambling, even idling – when had something so ordinary, so humble, become a luxury?

No, she wouldn't, couldn't go back.

'That's right, signori, have a good day.'

The Japanese couple left, all smiles. The receptionist turned to the waiting guest and signalled apologetically that she was now free. But the guest did not move.

'Can I help you, signorina?'

Miss Prim, staring absently at the piano that dominated the hotel lobby, did not reply.

'Signorina?' said the receptionist. 'Can I help you?'

'Something unexpected has happened,' Miss Prim said at last, advancing towards the desk. 'I'm afraid I have to leave in an hour. I apologize for any inconvenience. Could you prepare my bill, please?'

'Of course,' replied the receptionist, dismayed. 'I hope it's not bad news.'

'Bad news? Oh no, definitely not,' beamed the librarian, her mind busy in a hall of mirrors.

The receptionist smiled back.

'Actually,' said Miss Prim, eyes shining, picturing a door

being closed with infinite patience, 'it's good news. Extraordinary news, I'd say.' She sighed euphorically. 'It's strange and wonderful news.'

'*L'amor che move il sole e l'altre stelle*,' love that moves the sun and the other stars, murmured the receptionist half an hour later, as she watched the beautiful, graceful woman walk out of the hotel towards the waiting taxi with her chin held high and a gentle smile on her lips.